WINTER FALLS

A JIMMY BLUE NOVEL

IAN W. SAINSBURY

For Ash Robin

CHAPTER ONE

THE HOT, bright evening sun made the shadowed corners darker, and it was in the dusty gloom under the scaffolding that Tom saw him. Tom hadn't thought about Jimmy Blue for a while. Not much, anyway. He'd dreamed of him, but Tom's dreams were confusing, and often hard to remember.

How long had it been? Was it while Tom was working here, on the housing site in North London? Or at the last job in Manchester? If Manchester was the last job. It might have been Cambridge. Cambridge had been the site near a river. Tom tried to think back. When he concentrated, the images that drifted through his mind didn't help. There weren't enough of them, and he couldn't sort them into the right order. He gave up. It might be weeks, or months, since Jimmy Blue last came for him.

The figure in the shadows nodded; wraithlike in the dust, insubstantial. Two men were laying an exterior wall in the shade of the planks. Neither of them had noticed they weren't alone. Tom knew he mustn't acknowledge Blue. He looked away, ducked under the wooden planks, squatted, and tipped the hod to slide its load next to Kev and Craig. They didn't pause, caught up in the rhythm of bricklaying, their movements out of time with the thin beat from a dust-caked, paint-splattered radio hanging on a ledge. Craig spoke without looking up.

"Two more of 'em, Tiny."

The men on the building sites used more than one nickname for Tom. On a good day, when they accepted his mostly silent presence, they called him Tiny. *Tiny* seemed strange until Tom's latest landlady, Myra, explained that sometimes people used the wrong word deliberately.

"You know, dear, like Little John. Robin Hood's friend. He was a big fella like you. They call you Tiny because you're huge." It made no sense.

The nickname Tom didn't like was Mad Tom, but he didn't react when they said it behind his back, and when they said it to his face, he blinked and ignored them.

"Mad Tom! What are you mumbling about?"

He looked up. He was still standing by the pile of bricks. Craig had stopped to roll a cigarette and now waved a hand in front of Tom's face.

"C'mon, pal. Shake a leg. Two more trips. Off you pop."

Tom picked up the hod and walked back the way he'd come. He couldn't see anything in the shadows, but he knew Jimmy Blue was there.

Tom Brown was thirty-two years old, maybe thirty-three; he wasn't sure. His real surname was Lewis, he knew, but he had to pretend it was Brown. The police lady, Debbie, had told him that. She had tried lots of other surnames for him, but Brown was the only one he could remember.

His childhood had been a happy one, he thought. Sometimes, when about to fall asleep, or during the confusion of waking, he would remember his mother's voice, or the roughness of his father's beard.

Trying to remember more didn't work. It was like picking up wriggling wet fish. Thinking about the future was equally pointless. Tom existed where he was, and when he was. Jimmy Blue took care of the rest.

Physical labour suited Tom best. Cash in hand, a few days here, a week or two there. This building site had kept him busy for more than a month without the usual restlessness.

In the building trade, few hod carriers were as strong and as tireless as Tom. The hod, a three-sided box on the end of a rod, carried bricks from the pallets by the office to whoever needed them on site. Tom braced the wooden handle alternately against his shoulders. Brick hods usually held twelve bricks. Tom carried eighteen without a problem, and the first foreman to realise this built him a bigger hod.

Carrying more bricks than anyone else didn't make Tom any more popular with those who worked alongside him. He was a good, strong, reliable worker, but he was tolerated, rather than liked. The other men—and they were usually men—didn't like his silence; they were suspicious of his solitude. He didn't laugh at their jokes and turned away when they made fun of him. Tom frowned when they called him the Odd Carrier. Being odd meant not fitting in. The bricks he hefted hour after hour onto his shoulder slotted into the hod, each individual block nestling perfectly against its fellows. If Tom had been a brick, he would have been rejected before reaching the building site. He didn't fit with the others. Too big, roughly cut, unfinished, wrong.

It was Friday, so Tom joined the back of the queue leading to Mrs Hartnell's office. The creature in the shadows had gone, but Tom's hand went up to the hard, raised scarring on his skull. Jimmy Blue was calling him.

The men talked louder and laughed more easily at six on a Friday. A hard day's graft at the conclusion of a long week meant the brown envelope they picked up from Mrs H would travel less than half a mile before being ripped open and its contents depleted at the bar of the Coach and Horses.

Tom kept his head down and shuffled behind the rest. It had been Ken's birthday last week, and Tom hadn't been able to avoid being added to the invitation to meet for drinks. His lemonade tasted funny, and when the lads told him it was his turn to buy a round, it had cost eighty pounds. When Tom tried to protest, they all pretended not to understand.

He smoothed the black bandana over his shaved head. Kev had pulled it off when he'd left the pub last week, and everyone had laughed. When Tom asked for it back, and they all saw the front of his head, they stopped laughing. Steve had even said sorry when he threw the bandana back to him, but, once outside, Tom heard their voices through the open window.

"Car accident, d'ya think?"

"Brain damage, I reckon."

"Explains why he's such a numpty, though, dunnit?"

Inside the office, Mrs Hartnell, a skinny middle-aged woman with a Jack Russell always at her feet, kept the wage slips and cash in a plastic box on top of her desk. Everyone signed for their pay, so Tom preferred to be last in line.

Mrs H pushed the paper across to him. Her husband, Les, faded blue tattoos on his muscled forearms, stood behind her. He glared at Tom. The only time Les Hartnell didn't glare was when asleep. The brickies described him as 'hard but fair', but Tom had never known Hartnell to be fair. He paid as little as possible, and he paid Tom less than anyone else, because Tom couldn't argue his case, and no one was there to argue it for him.

Bobby, the Jack Russell, darted out from under the desk, sniffed Tom's trousers, then lay on his feet, tail wagging. The small dog was infamous on the site for hating everyone apart from his owner, and for confirming his opinions with a bite or two. But, like most animals, he loved Tom, much to the disgust of Mr Hartnell, who muttered, "Get off him, you stupid little bastard." Bobby huffed happily and ignored him.

Tom made his mark on the paper. He drew something that looked like *Tom* and added a squiggle. The squiggle changed from week to week, but if he looked at the letters for long, his head ached. Les added a smirk to his glare.

"There you go, love." Mrs H handed him the envelope. It felt even thinner than normal. He opened it. Four of the pinky purple notes.

There should be many more. He looked back at the thin, brittle-haired woman.

"It's a government thing, Tom." She'd never used his name before. "It's your last week, I'm afraid. No more work. We've deducted your National Insurance, your contractor's insurance, and your union dues."

"Mm, mm." Tom couldn't remember if the last time he'd spoken was today or yesterday. It took a while to get the first words out.

"But mm, but—"

"But nothing." Les Hartnell took a step forward. He stood a few inches shorter than Tom's hunched six feet, but his glare, his knotted muscles, and an old murder conviction he made sure everyone knew about, meant he wasn't shy about picking a fight.

"You're lucky I gave ya a job at all."

"Mm. Work hard." Tom pushed the words through his tight lips.

Hartnell seemed momentarily stunned at the interruption. He leaned across the desk and put a dusty, cracked and blackened fingernail on Tom's sternum. "You're a hoddie, pal. You carry bricks. I could train a monkey to do it, and it would be less of a bloody liability than you. What if there was an accident, an emergency? You couldn't find your own arse with both hands. What use are you if the scaffold collapses, or there's a fire?"

Les Hartnell talked too fast, and Tom struggled to keep up.

"Mm. Mm."

"Yeah, yeah, mm all you like. Mrs H's sister's boy gets out on Monday, so you're surplus to requirements. We don't need you anymore. That's your pay up to date. Now piss off out of it. On yer bike."

Tom rested his fingers on the scar under his bandana. "No bike," he whispered.

Les Hartnell's neck turned purple. Mrs H put a warning hand on his arm.

"He doesn't understand, Les. Look, I'll make it easy for you. Job is finished. You go home. Don't come back."

Tom looked blankly at her. She pointed at the door.

"Fuck off, love."

Tom looked at the few notes in the envelope one more time, then up at the hard-set faces of his former employers. Before leaving, he took a last look around the cramped office and bent down to stroke Bobby's head.

The bus stop was a hundred yards out of the site to the right, but Tom turned left and headed downstairs to the underground, boarding the first tube south. He wouldn't be going back to Myra's bed and breakfast tonight, or ever again.

Jimmy Blue was waiting.

CHAPTER TWO

SOHO WAS PACKED. Tourists from every nation jostled ad agency designers and office staff on their way to the pub. Actors, restaurant staff, and sex workers hurried to another paid performance. Motorcycle couriers darted through the traffic shoals, helmets flashing like silver minnows. Taxis inched forward, sweaty arms hanging out of their windows, leaning on their horns.

Tom moved through it all with his head down, shoulders hunched, following the sinuous progress of the masses, allowing the crowd to guide his route.

As he passed an alleyway, its entrance half-blocked with black and green bin bags, Tom joined a human tributary hugging the shopfronts. He left the flow, diverting into a passage just wide enough to accommodate a vehicle. A white Transit van meant Tom had to turn sideways, folding its wing mirror to squeeze past. The van's owner, bearded and belligerent, registered his displeasure as he came out of the door at the end of the alley.

"Oi! What are you playing at? Hands off, unless you—"

Tom straightened, pressing his back against the wall to ease his bulk through. The bearded man looked him up and down, registering his size. "Nah, don't worry, no harm done, mate. You coming in? I'll get the door for ya. Nice one."

Tom's gaze dropped back to the floor. The door slammed shut behind him. In the outer room, a middle-aged woman flicked through a magazine behind a counter. Shelves full of packing materials filled the walls; boxes, sticky tape, bubble wrap, polystyrene pellets, all marked with a bright orange sticker stating Sam's Soho Storage.

The woman didn't look up. Tom entered a five-digit number into the keypad on the door. Tom remembered the pattern his fingers needed to make, and the door beeped. He pushed it open.

Inside, the bright orange theme continued on the roller shutters of every unit. The height of the ceiling suggested the building's Victorian provenance, and the birds in the rafters were far from the first generation to nest there.

Tom could count to ten, and he only needed to get to seven to find his unit. It was on the left side, the same as the scar on his head. He unlocked the metal grille, sending it clattering upwards. Inside, he yanked it halfway down again before clicking on the light. Then he pulled the grille shut and slid the bolt.

The unit was half the size of a standard garage. Big enough to accommodate a double cupboard, suitcases, cardboard boxes and a clothes rail. Chests of drawers of various sizes partially obscured one wall. Against the other, the most notable item was an old-fashioned writing desk with a red leather swivel chair.

Tom was, as always, drawn to the writing desk first; antique walnut, with three drawers on one side. He sat on the swivel chair, which creaked under his weight. His thighs, even with the chair lowered as far as possible, pressed against the underside of the desk. He slid out the felt-topped guide rods and lowered the writing lid on top of them. The writing surface was topped with the same red leather as the chair. It was a beautiful piece of furniture, marred only by the side blackened and scarred by fire.

Tom placed his hands on the stretched red leather surface, closed his eyes, and breathed in, leaning right to avoid the charred wood.

The mixed scent of old leather and skin cream brought him a sense of peace, of *home*. There were no accompanying images, no comforting memories, but he knew this desk had been his mother's.

The sense of peace didn't last. Jimmy Blue was waiting.

Blue didn't frighten Tom - but he could no more refuse his call than a starving baby could refuse the breast that kept it alive.

He shut the desk and opened an empty wheeled suitcase, propping the lid against the wall. He took running shoes, underwear, and a razor from a drawer, a black motorcycle helmet from one of the boxes. The clothes rail yielded designer jeans and two shirts. All of it went into the suitcase with a roll of bin liners, a MacBook, and a charger.

Tom's last stop was the cupboard. Each shelf held four mannequin heads. The hairpieces on the heads were blonde, dark, ginger, and many shades between. Half of the staring faces also sported facial hair, from sideburns, through moustaches and goatees, to a full beard.

Tom picked up a bag containing glue, double-sided scalp tape, and various bottles and tubes. He removed a shoulder-length black wig, putting it into a net. He couldn't have explained why he chose the items he did, only that they were *right*.

With the suitcase zipped up, Tom took one last look around the storage unit. Jimmy Blue had acquired this eclectic collection of odds and ends. Tom didn't know how long it had taken. His concept of time periods longer than a week or two was hazy.

Tom smiled. This unheated aluminium box, lit by a single fluorescent tube, comforted him.

He put his thumb on the bolt to slide it open. Something was different this time. Jimmy Blue's call had been stronger than ever. Tom thought back to the earlier glimpse, Blue's insubstantial form twisting through the shadows, watching him. His head throbbed with the effort of assembling his scattered and amorphous thoughts. Something had changed. Something.

A rare sliver of memory: his father coming into his bedroom late one night, putting an object on the bedside table.

Tom, half-asleep, lifting this object, holding it up so the light from the street illuminated his prize. A book. A new story. He reached down the side of his bed, found the torch and—once he'd tucked the duvet back around him—clicked it on to read. It didn't seem strange that he could read. He accepted it. It was the way the book made him feel that was important. Tom was almost feverish with excitement. He'd been waiting for this a long time. It was the final story in a series. He was dry-mouthed with anticipation as he turned the first page.

The memory faded, but the excitement remained. Jimmy Blue's call was stronger because he was excited. This was the beginning of a story.

Or, perhaps, the end of one.

Tom flicked the light switch and the desk, shelves, boxes, and cupboard disappeared into the blackness.

Only the faintest scent of skin cream and burned wood remained.

CHAPTER THREE

THE HOTEL WAS one of an increasing number of establishments trying to dispense with the need for human contact. Rooms were booked online, and the check-in process involved scanning a QR code to release each room's keycard.

Tom watched the lobby from the opposite side of the street. Only one member of staff on duty, but her role as hotel receptionist—besides answering the phone and greeting guests—also included running a bar and kitchen. Despite this, she still tried to help new arrivals with the check-in machines.

It was ten minutes before an opportunity presented itself. A group of Chinese students, led by a tired teacher, dragged their enormous suitcases into the hotel lobby.

Tom crossed the road, squeezing in behind the last student. The teacher stepped up to the first screen; the students flocked round her like needy ducklings, and the receptionist came over to help. As soon as she turned to the machine, Tom took his phone from his pocket, scanned his code, and was through the door to the rooms before the first student received their key card. The burst of concentration made his head ache.

Room 18 was small but contained everything he needed. A bed, a bathroom, and a decent Wi-Fi connection.

Tom took off his bandana and stripped, stuffing his work clothes into one of the bin liners. He showered. Brick dust and dirt swirled around the drain. After drying off, he shaved his face and head.

Muted sounds from the neighbouring rooms provided a confused soundtrack: snatches of conversation, indecipherable dialogue from a television, the dull thump of dance music. Tom sat naked on the edge of the bed, slumped, his eyes on the brown and black carpet under the rough soles of his feet.

He waited for the first signs to appear. It didn't take more than a few minutes. The surrounding objects lost their names. The television at the foot of the bed was a shape with no purpose. The motorcycle helmet on the desk became neither familiar nor exotic, merely a reflective sphere. The bed underneath him was softer than the wooden desk. The light diffused by the thin curtains was different to that provided by the yellow glare of the lamp. But Tom forgot what made light different from darkness.

There was no panic. The opposite was true. The sense of peace fleetingly experienced in the storage unit flowed into the gaps left as identification and meaning dwindled. Tom looked back at his feet, his legs, his hands resting on his knees, but did not recognise them as his own.

His identity, and any awareness of being distinct from the television, the desk, or the last of the sunlight, followed the rest into obscurity. No thoughts. No body. Nobody.

Time may have passed, but as there was no Tom to mark it, there was no way of knowing. A human being sat on a bed in a compact hotel room near Leicester Square.

The very last thing to dissolve was the sense of waiting. The room itself seemed to collude with the anticipation, the stale air like a held breath. Then that too was gone.

When only emptiness remained, Jimmy Blue arrived.

CHAPTER FOUR

IN ANY NORMAL sense of the word, nothing *changed*. But, if anyone had witnessed what happened to the man in room 18, they would have seen a transformation.

It started with the bald man's eyes. For a while, unfocused, gaze fixed downwards, they saw nothing. Now the pupils moved from left to right, from the door to the darkening curtains. The big head moved next as the man's posture altered, chest expanding, shoulders relaxing.

The body language of the man now sitting on the hotel bed was so altered, it was hard to believe it was the same person. There was confidence in the squaring of those shoulders, a latent energy in the previously indolent frame.

The man stood up and stretched, pulling one hand behind his head and holding it, then swapping to the other arm. He worked through a sequence of gentle yoga-like exercises, then stretched every muscle group.

He took the MacBook out of the suitcase, booted it up, and connected to the hotel Wi-Fi. A series of passwords opened hidden folders, and he accessed a program he had coded months before. He picked up his phone and tapped the screen, opening an app. Now the phone showed the same view as the laptop: Lo-Fi security camera footage of an end-of-terrace house, a Peugeot van parked on the drive.

The naked man got dressed, pulling the clothes out of the open suitcase on the floor. Jeans, shirt, running shoes.

In the bathroom, he cut six pieces of scalp tape into strips. He shook the black wig out of the net, sticking two pieces of tape onto it. He stuck the rest onto his head, peeling off the protective layer covering the sticky surface. In the gaps, he painted a thin layer of glue with a soft brush, avoiding the scars. The glue needed a smooth surface to stick to.

With the ease born of repetition, he pressed the front of the wig to his forehead before smoothing it back over his head. His natural eyebrow colour was light brown, but mascara enabled him to match the black wig. The eyes that stared back from his transformed face remained his familiar dark green. Contact lenses could alter their colour, but this was one feature he would not consider changing this time. For the four people on his list, those eyes would be the last thing they ever saw. He wanted them to recognise him.

He put on the leather jacket and scooped up the black helmet. When he put his hand on the keycard in the slot on the wall, he caught sight of himself in the mirror. Upright now, six-foot-three, with a heavy, powerful body.

Tom might hunch to avoid drawing attention to his bulk, but not Jimmy Blue. Now that Tom's slack features were animated by intelligence and purpose, even without the wig he would be almost unrecognisable to his fellow workers. His mouth twitched into a smile. His expression didn't offer comfort, empathy, or forgiveness. He had seen horrors most people never dreamed of. A child who shouldn't have lived, but who held onto the thinnest of threads, clinging to life with a tenacity no doctor predicted.

He knew the secret to his survival. A junior nurse had put her finger on the truth the day Tom Lewis was discharged from hospital.

"No one thought you would pull through. You should have seen the look on the doctor's face when you first opened your eyes. You were saved for a reason, Tom. I truly believe that. One day you'll find that reason. No one comes back from an injury like yours. No one."

She'd patted Tom's shoulder when the car arrived for him. "Good luck. Find out why you were saved."

Poor, gentle, silent Tom, smiled up at her, but didn't understand.

Jimmy Blue understood. He wondered what the nurse would make of the purpose he had found after twenty long years. He remembered the crucifix dangling from her neck. She probably wouldn't be best pleased.

Blue smiled at his reflection, noting the cold fury in his eyes, the commitment, the lack of fear.

Time for someone to die.

"Looking good," he said.

CHAPTER FIVE

MARTY INTENDED to spend the evening working. He clumped down to the workshop at six and boxed up the latest batch of polymer ten pound notes. Face value of fifty thousand pounds. Winter bought them at ten percent of that. Winter didn't sell them on, so any risk of exposure was negligible. The boss was too smart for that. He only used the fake notes to pad out his working capital. That way, they slotted into circulation slowly. Smart and cautious.

Not that Marty's notes had ever been exposed. His forgeries were good enough to pass all but the most thorough tests. He'd never got greedy, kept the counterfeit side of the business small, and built up a nice little nest egg over the last decade.

Once he'd sealed the box, Marty sat at his workbench. No banknote printing tonight. He had a fresh pile of number plates to make up. Fake number plates were more satisfying to construct than counterfeit banknotes, because he got to use his hands rather than rely on a computer program. His number plates were indistinguishable from the genuine article. Because he copied the registration numbers from real black cabs, turnover was high. More evidence of Winter's caution. A single evening's work—two or three strays picked up in the taxi Winter's crew used—and they tossed the plates. Which meant Marty always needed to be four or five new numbers ahead of demand.

Two plates left in the drawer. Time to restock.

He opened WhatsApp on his phone and checked the updated list. Whenever any of Winter's people had a chance, they sent photos of black cab licence plates to Marty's WhatsApp group. He used the most recent numbers posted, checking first against his master list. Not a good idea to use the same plate twice.

He typed the first number into the laptop and waited for the thermal printer to warm up and spit it out. In the meantime, he got the aluminium baseplate and clear plastic faceplate ready. Sticking the number on and screwing it in place was hardly the work of a master craftsman, but there was a scrap of pride in a job well done. Also, he couldn't drive for Winter without them.

He pulled his stool back up to the bench as the printer hummed. The thin plastic strip emerged slowly, sliding onto the desk behind him. Marty prised open the fridge under the workbench with his foot and took out a cold beer. He took a long swig while he waited, using his other hand to excavate some stubborn debris from his capacious navel. He flicked the resulting clump of fluff into the bin. Marty liked a tidy workshop.

A selection of tools hung on the walls: hammers, drills, saws, screwdrivers racked in size order, chisels, planes, tape measures, Stanley knives, a sliding bevel, and a layout square. Metal drawers beneath held every size of screw and nail, glues, sandpaper, and some wood-turning tools. The latter items, plus two half-finished chairs and a standard lamp, were there in the unlikely event of a visit from the police. Best to have a plausible hobby to explain such a well kitted-out basement.

In fact, the basement workshop was the only tidy room in Marty's house. He ate off paper plates to avoid washing up, and when his microwave smelled bad, he'd drop it in the bin and buy another. His personal hygiene was as lax as his housekeeping. Years ago, Marty gave up wearing anything other than elasticated tracksuit bottoms and polo shirts. In winter, he added a hoodie. He only shaved when on a job for Winter. Why shave if you lived alone and rarely left the house?

There was Tay, of course, but Marty wouldn't change his bathing habits for that arsehole. Tay was, apparently, Marty's apprentice. Marty would have told the obnoxious little shit to piss off weeks ago, but he couldn't. Winter was Tay's uncle. Marty suspected that Winter envisaged a future where he wouldn't have to rely on his personal forger so much, if at all. Marty had been ordered to teach Tay everything. Tay was an inattentive pupil, more interested in boasting about his 'rep' as a dangerous gangster than learning the art of counterfeiting. Marty would have laughed in Tay's face at the gangster talk, but the kid carried a knife and his temper was short. Marty planned to teach him slowly and skip town before Winter made his move, or Tay shivved him over some imagined 'disrespect'.

Marty took the sheet out of the printer and lined up the number on the plate. He wrapped a cloth around a short length of dowel and pressed it against the still-warm numbers, rolling it left to right, careful to keep the pressure even to avoid bubbling.

Halfway through the job, he stopped. He had lost concentration. A wrinkle now spoiled the second letter. It was ruined, useless.

"Sod it."

He looked at the calendar on the wall—a freebie from a local tyre importer with a fresh, semi-naked woman every month. Marty knew what day it was. He didn't need to check. June twenty-ninth. No wonder he couldn't work. He shouldn't even have tried.

With a grunt of shock, Marty realised it wasn't just any anniversary. It was twenty years. Twenty years to the day. He had been a different man then. Keen, ambitious, ruthless. Or so he thought.

Not so fat then, either. Marty pulled the grey, stained polo shirt down over the swell of his belly and eased himself off the stool. No point thinking about the past. No point at all.

There were no mirrors in the workshop, but Marty caught sight of his reflection in the plastic number plate. At forty-four years old, he looked the wrong side of sixty; the stubble on his pale, soft chins flecked grey-white, and his greasy hair retreating up his flaky scalp.

He paced up and down, his thighs rubbing together. Talcum powder stopped them getting raw. A shower might help distract him. Two decades. Shit.

First things first, though. Marty was hungry. Friday was pizza night. He fished his phone out and opened the pizza place app. A large meat feast, garlic bread. No. Two large meat feasts. Tay sometimes turned up uninvited and helped himself to Marty's dinner without asking. The cocky bastard.

He pressed the order button. Estimated delivery time seven-forty. Marty checked his watch. Six fifty-five. Enough time to shower first.

Before leaving the workshop, he opened a drawer and took out a tin box full of old keys. They all looked the same, unless you knew to look for a particular pattern of scratches. Marty lifted one of the hanging saws from the wall, revealing a hole cut into the MDF beneath. When he pulled on it, the panel hinged outwards, exposing a metal door concealed behind. The key turned in the lock, and Marty pushed the hidden door open, standing in the doorway.

When he had the basement converted to a workshop, Marty added this small room. He'd got the idea from Winter's house. He didn't know why Winter needed a soundproof basement and he hadn't asked. Especially since he referred to it as the dungeon.

It wasn't a big room. The bed filled most of it. It had no pillow, duvet, or blanket, just a stained elasticated sheet stretched across the mattress. A bucket stood in one corner. Marty sniffed the stale air. He'd been planning on changing the sheet, but the stench wasn't too bad. Various dried and pungent body fluids gave the stale air a unique tang. It had been a while since the last girl. Winter wasn't as generous with the cast-offs as he used to be. More evidence of time running out. Still, Marty might get to play with one more before he ran.

Marty stared at the room. He would miss this place when he escaped. It distracted him. And a distraction would have been welcome tonight, of all nights. He pictured the last girl; an addict, half-starved, her face slack and prematurely old. The kind of woman no one wanted. The only kind Marty deserved.

He sighed, shut the door, backed into the basement, then climbed the stairs to the kitchen. Flies buzzed around old takeaway boxes on the surfaces. He tore a black bin bag off the roll and swept most of the rubbish inside, tying the top and placing it in the corner. He'd had a cleaner once, but she'd stopped coming months back. Said she wouldn't do it anymore, not for any money. Stupid bitch. Still, what did it matter now? A month or two—six months, tops—and Marty would be gone. Thailand, or the Philippines. He hadn't decided yet.

He grabbed a handful of clothes from the dryer and went upstairs for a shower. Maybe he'd watch a movie later. A comedy. Something to stop his thoughts returning to what happened on June twenty-ninth, twenty years ago.

The shower was hot. He closed his eyes under the water, not letting himself see the layers of grime, limescale, and mildew. As he lifted his heavy paunch with one hand to soap it underneath, it growled. He was ravenous.

Marty hoped Tay stayed away tonight. He could eat both meat feasts, easy.

The bell rang just as he was pulling on a fresh polo shirt. He checked the front door cam on his phone. Was there any better sight on a Friday evening than a motorbike delivery guy carrying a bag full of freshly cooked goodies?

Yeah. Pizza, movie, the vodka from the freezer, and a couple of joints to relax. He wouldn't think about what day it was anymore.

CHAPTER SIX

JIMMY BLUE KNEW Marty Nicholson's routines well. Pizza Friday was sacrosanct. The tiny cameras outside the Forger's house in Ilford recorded every delivery.

Blue had watched the footage, making notes on Marty's habits.

He'd stolen a motorbike to follow Marty one evening, keeping the Forger's old Peugeot in sight until it pulled into an industrial estate. When a black cab left the estate ten minutes later, Blue recognised the silhouette of its obese driver and pulled in behind him. Marty stopped outside a newsagent. When he returned to the cab, Jimmy was ten yards behind, pretending to be texting. Marty fumbled in his pocket for his keys, and Blue's right hand dropped to the throttle, ready to open it up, roar onto the pavement, and end Marty's sick, murderous life by sending his body careening down the street like the last pin in a bowling alley.

Striiiiiiiiiikkkkkkeeeeee!

Jimmy got as far as engaging first gear, his fingers finding the biting point of the clutch; scar burning, eyes burning, body burning, the thought of Marty's broken and bloodied corpse almost too good to resist.

Almost.

But Blue had come too far, worked too hard, to allow lack of discipline to spoil his plan now. He'd relaxed his grip, watched Marty drive away, and followed. When Marty picked up a young bearded man on the way into the city, Blue hung back. Twenty-five minutes later, a middle-aged woman helped a confused, skittish girl into the cab, shutting her in with the bearded man. Jimmy kept his distance. When Marty dropped his two passengers at a terraced house in Romford, Blue stayed behind to place a camera on a lamp post opposite.

Jimmy Blue's method for placing cameras had proved undetectable so far. Even if he was observed, no one guessed what he was really doing. He carried rolls of stickers in his messenger bag. Some protested climate change, others promoted obscure bands. While he placed a sticker on a lamp post, telegraph pole, or wall, he positioned the camera with his other hand. He'd found a supplier of fake bird shit online, tucking the camera and battery behind the rubber excreta. If anyone checked, they'd find the stickers. No one got too close to the wet-looking white and black streak nearby.

To date, he'd followed Marty on six occasions. He'd bailed out twice, when he couldn't stay close without making it too obvious he was tailing the black cab. The other occasions yielded a second address, another girl taken the same way, helped into the cab by the middle-aged woman. And, in a stroke of luck Blue might have attributed to divine providence if there was a god, one of the photos on his phone caught the woman's face perfectly. Despite the wig, the glasses, and make-up that darkened her pale complexion, he recognised her immediately.

Rhoda Ilích. Auntie Rhoda. He planned to visit her soon, but that unexpected glimpse brought on such a powerful reaction that he'd pushed his helmet's visor up, gulping the air.

That had been six months ago. Since then, Blue had honed his plan, keeping it flexible, making sure to cover every known contingency. He could deal with unknowns as they arose.

Six weeks before the anniversary, he was ready, but he waited.

Jimmy Blue wanted his first visit to occur on June twenty-ninth. Twenty years to the day. That way, someone on the list might realise the significance of the date. Probably not after the first death. Maybe after the second. Surely by the third. He hoped so. He wanted them to know who was coming.

And now the day had arrived.

Jimmy Blue waited in a narrow side street often used by bikers and cyclists to cut half a mile out of the one-way system. He wore his black motorbike helmet and stood next to an industrial bin, looking at his mobile phone. Staring at a mobile device was a superb method of urban camouflage. The pizza delivery rider didn't give him a second glance as he puttered towards him.

Blue turned away from the approaching rider as if getting out of the way. The rider blipped the throttle, then came to an abrupt stop before flying backwards as an arm like a tree trunk swept him off his moped and tossed him into the open bin.

"Phone."

The rider lifted his visor, eyes wide. "What the hell? You can't do this!"

"Give me your phone. I won't ask again."

The rider realised he was in no position to negotiate and held out his device. Blue flicked it onto silent.

"I'll be back in an hour or two. I'll let you out and return your bike. Your phone too. Sit tight."

Jimmy Blue slammed the lid, clicked a combination padlock in place, wheeled it round a corner, and pushed it down a concrete ramp. It came to rest against the back door of a furniture shop, underneath a noisy air conditioning unit loud enough to cover any shouts for help.

The moped lay on its side. An old man walking a dribbling bulldog was standing next to it. Blue started limping.

"I'm all right," he said to the unasked question. "I'll have a nice bruise to show for it."

He lifted the moped and got on. The suspension creaked under his bulk as he rode to the end of the street, turned right and pulled back into the Friday evening traffic.

The pizzas smelled good.

Eight minutes later, he rang Marty's bell, smiling behind the dark visor when he heard footsteps approaching the door.

CHAPTER SEVEN

OVER THE MONTHS, Blue had only seen Marty from a distance. He'd never been this close to the man who'd shot him in the head. It was a disappointment.

Two decades ago, Marty Nicholson had been a fit, handsome man in his twenties. Well-dressed, designer clothes, he'd kept his walnut-brown hair tidy, using mousse to style it into a Tintin-like curl. His preferred aftershave was Fahrenheit, and he used too much of it.

Jimmy Blue knew this because Marty had been kneeling behind him, arms wrapped around his chest, pinning him in place, while Tom Lewis's father was executed. A single bullet, point-blank, head shot. The Executioner had shot his mother in the stomach next, leaving her alive, tied to a chair. Soaked in petrol. Winter and his crew burned their house to the ground. They used Tom's mother as kindling.

When the Executioner killed his father, Tom smelled blood, bone, and shit, but the Parma violet and leather stench of Marty's neck had dominated even that.

The man who opened the door tonight to get his pizza didn't look like he used aftershave. He sported three or four days' worth of stubble, darkening in lines as it followed the rolls of fat on his neck. Marty

Nicholson wore his thinning hair long, as if having enough for a ponytail might compensate for the growing expanse of skin on his forehead.

The eyes. The eyes were the same. Deeper set, watery, but the same. The last time he had seen them had been twenty years ago, when Marty caught up with Tom, dragging him back from the open window of his bedroom.

Tom had looked into Marty's eyes because he didn't want to stare into the blind barrel of the silenced gun. For a second, Marty had looked back. Tom saw hesitation, indecision.

"Time to break your duck, Marty." That's what the Executioner had said just before Tom had bitten hard on Marty's fingers, wriggled free, and run for the stairs.

Blue hadn't understood the phrase the Executioner used back then. He did now. And, in hindsight, he understood the reason for Marty's indecision. The Forger had never killed anyone before. And there he was, pointing a gun at a terrified twelve-year-old kid. Hesitation. Indecision.

Then Marty had broken eye contact, the line of his gaze moving fractionally upward.

The old adage wasn't true. Tom Lewis heard the shot that killed him.

"Oh, bollocks. Come in, will you? Stick the pizzas on the table." Fat, old Marty patted the pockets of his tatty elasticated trousers and turned his back.

Blue followed him into the kitchen. The floor tiles were sticky. A rotten, sweet smell suggested a rat had died in a cupboard. Marty opened a drawer and pulled out two twenty pound notes. He looked up at Blue and frowned, as if just noticing that the man he'd invited into his house was built like a heavyweight boxer.

Blue lifted his visor. "Print those yourself, Marty?"

The sharp intake of breath may have been the shock of hearing his name, or the fact the intruder knew he was a forger, but Blue hoped it was recognition.

His gloved right fist caught Marty on his left cheekbone. Not hard enough to break it, but that wasn't Blue's intention. The jab just needed to knock Marty off -balance. He followed it up by grabbing him by the throat, pushing him back three feet, and smashing the back of his head into the greasy fridge-freezer behind him.

Marty exhaled, and his legs gave way. He fell sideways. Blue stuck out his foot to prevent his skull smacking into the tiles.

"Uh-huh. Not yet, you don't."

He grabbed a fistful of polo shirt and dragged Marty through the door to the basement, kicking it closed behind him. Marty moaned and tried to stand. Blue let him get to his feet, the fat man's expression more confused than afraid, then marched him down the steps to the workshop.

There was a wild exuberance about Blue as he reached the bottom of the stairs and pushed Marty into a chair. He removed his helmet and placed it on the worktop. Marty looked at him and moaned.

Blue was joyous, alive, and full of adrenaline. He sang as he took off his gloves and jacket.

> *"Still I sing, bonnie boys, bonnie mad boys,*
> *Bedlam boys are bonnie,*
> *For they all go bare and they live by the air*
> *And they want no drink nor money"*

The Forger's eyes filled with tears. He held his hands up as if begging, without a hint of recognition in his eyes. "Please. Take whatever you want. You know about the counterfeiting, right? Do you want me to print some money for you? It's top quality, I promise. I have about ten grand in a box. Take that."

Blue held up a hand, and Marty stopped babbling.

"You don't remember me, do you?"

Marty's mouth worked as if it might spit the right name out by itself, without his brain getting involved.

Blue leaned in close. "Want a clue?"

Marty nodded, and Blue dropped his voice to a whisper. "I'm

dead. I died twenty years ago today. How could you forget, Marty? You've hurt my feelings."

As Marty stared in shock, Jimmy Blue took two vices from a shelf, attached them to the bench, and opened both a couple of inches. He grabbed Marty's right hand, shoved it into the first, and tightened it. Not enough to break fingers, but enough to cause considerable pain. As Marty hissed and swore, Blue did the same with his left hand.

With Marty pinned in place, Jimmy Blue squatted in front of him and peeled back enough of his wig to reveal the mass of ridged, pink scarring on his scalp. The man responsible for the scar gaped like a fish and started hyperventilating.

"In case you're wondering, Marty, yes, I am here to kill you."

CHAPTER EIGHT

TAY WAS LOOKING FORWARD to this. He'd hung around Marty for months now, pretending he gave a shit about anything the greasy pig man said, giving him respect. Enough was enough.

Tonight was payback for all the, "Yes, Marty, no Marty," bullshit. As if Marty Nicholson had anything to teach Tay. Any idiot could print money and number plates or construct a fake ID. You didn't need a degree. You didn't need a six month apprenticeship with a coward who hid in his basement.

Not just a coward. Not just a failure. A month earlier, while Marty drove the cab for Rhoda, Tay let himself in. He was a housebreaker for years before his uncle invited him to join the business. Tay knew where people hid the quality stuff. It took him fifteen minutes to find Marty's fake passport, twenty grand in cash, and cards for a bank account in a new name.

Uncle Robert—Tay called him Winter now—had praised his initiative, giving Tay the opportunity he'd been angling for since doing odd jobs for Winter as a green seventeen-year-old. In the intervening three years, he learned to keep his eyes open and his mouth shut. Tay paid attention, worked hard, and, earlier than expected, joined the crew full-time. Winter kept numbers low. Marty, Rhoda,

Penny—his housekeeper—made up the inner circle. Working for Winter was that rarest of things: a job for life. Not in the 'shares in the company, pension plan, and gold watch when you retire' sense. More the 'think about leaving and we'll kill you' sense.

Tonight was the night Tay got to hand Marty his P45, personally. Strickland, Winter's hitman, had loaned Tay the gun. It weighed heavily in the messenger bag slung over his shoulder. He didn't own a holster, and Strickland hadn't offered him one. So the piece went into the bag along with his favourite knife.

Tay had never killed anyone before, but he'd been in some fights. He'd won all of them. Tay held no reservations about sticking a blade into his opponent, and he'd been quick to do just that. It bought him a reputation. Winter warned Tay not to search out trouble. "Trouble will find you soon enough. Strickland will teach you how to use a weapon. Never forget, if you work for me, even if you're the one doing the stabbing or pulling the trigger, it's only on my say so. Or you'll upset me. You got that?"

Tay got it. No one upset Winter, ever.

Here in Marty's kitchen, Tay felt desperate to use some of Strickland's knife moves. Not that Marty would be a worthy opponent. It would be like butchering a stunned animal. Still, at least he'd get to fire a gun at something other than a beer bottle.

Tay's heartbeat rose from dub, through hip-hop, to drum and bass in the thirty seconds after entering the kitchen. Adrenaline mixed with the line of coke he'd done off the dashboard before coming in.

He took the knife out of the messenger bag and slid it out of its sheath. Five inches long, serrated blade, wicked sharp.

Muffled sounds from the basement. Good. That's where Marty would die. Tay's plan was simple. Persuade the fat wanker to cooperate by sticking him in the shoulder. Not too deep. Enough to bleed a bit. Enough to scare him. Then march him through to the soundproof room. Tay shuddered at the thought of what the pervert might have done in there. Tay reminded himself not to underestimate Marty. He'd been a killer once. The point of Tay's knife must never leave Marty's back. Once in that soundproof room, all bets were off.

Tay could take his time, try some things he'd been daydreaming about for years. Like shooting someone in the kneecap. Was it as painful as people said? Would the bone explode, bits going everywhere?

He had the whole night to indulge himself. He intended to make the most of it. It was ages since he'd done something for himself, something fun.

Tay held the knife with the butt resting on his curled right fingers, the blade flat against his wrist and forearm, hidden from view.

With his hand on the basement door handle, he paused, looking back at the two unopened pizza boxes on the table. Marty never waited to eat. Tay backed up and opened the first box. The pizza inside was a mess—squashed up at one end, most of the topping smeared along the cardboard lid.

Tay frowned at the pizza. Something wasn't right, but he struggled to put a series of events together that would explain the uneaten pizza in Marty's kitchen. The puzzled expression remained on his face for a few seconds, then he shrugged and returned to the basement door, dismissing the mystery as unimportant.

Halfway down the stairs he realised he'd been wrong—it was very important. By then, the knife was in his hand, and he was operating on pure instinct, heart thumping even faster.

Tay heard Marty whimper like a baby. An enormous guy was standing in the workshop, and his back blocked Tay's view of everything else. The size of the guy was good news. Big guy, big target. And Tay's position on the stairs gave him a tactical advantage. He held the higher ground. It meant he could reach the guy's neck. Didn't matter how big you were, five inches of steel in the side of your neck made you deader than dead.

Two more steps and he'd be close enough. As he drew back his arm, ready to strike, Tay grinned.

CHAPTER NINE

JIMMY BLUE KNEW his body was human, constituted of bones, blood, veins, ligaments, muscles, and skin. Go deeper and cells provided the building blocks. Deeper still to the particles that make up the cells, and a strange landscape appeared, where matter itself occupied a tiny proportion of the surrounding space. Blue had scanned a few books about it, but put them aside for their lack of practical information. His outlook on life was pragmatic, and—unlike almost everyone else alive—he had a clear, achievable purpose. Four people were responsible for the murders of his father and mother. Four people needed to die.

If not for Marty Nicholson's incompetence, Tom Lewis would have died twenty years ago. And without Tom, there would be no Jimmy Blue.

Jimmy Blue—born singing, ready to stab, shoot, strangle, slice and dice—had sprung into existence like the best magic trick ever seen. He had a touch of the demon about him. He was a creature of shadows. He never slept, instead fading in and out of existence. When awake, he burned with a black flame that, rather than banishing shadows, deepened and darkened them.

His body was big and strong—that much was down to genetics.

The muscles, combined with a litheness surprising in such a large frame, were a product of Blue's will, and of years of training. The long period of preparation served a single purpose: to ensure he would be ready when the time came to visit the four names on his list.

And he was ready.

Jimmy Blue knew he had huge gaps in his education, but he had devoted a great deal of time to subjects that mattered. Subjects that would ensure he prevailed when he visited the names on his list. Practical subjects. Combat tactics, for example.

That was why, before tightening the vices onto Marty Nicholson's fingers, he had picked up one of the blank, plastic-coated number plates, leaning it against the laminating machine.

A reflected movement had caught his eye seven seconds ago. A wiry man in shorts, knife in hand, descending the workshop stairs.

It was all he could do not to laugh aloud at the exaggerated way the man crept, trying each stair with his toe before transferring his weight to it.

Blue sang a folk song silently to himself as he watched the man's progress in the number plate.

I went down to Satan's kitchen, for to beg me food one morning
There I got souls piping hot, all on the spit a turning

———

He waited patiently for the man to come within range. If he acted too soon, his attacker might run. He looked like he could beat Blue in a race. Jimmy was quicker and lighter on his feet than he looked, considering his bulk, but his body was all wrong for sprinting. So he waited. Closer, then closer still. Waited until the man brought his arm back and up to attack. Then, swiftly, and with a brutal economy, he spun on his left toe and unleashed a backhand slap that should have seen the wiry man knocked off his feet into the unforgiving concrete wall.

Only it didn't. His opponent had excellent reflexes. He flinched backward the moment Jimmy Blue moved. Even so, the tips of Blue's fingers caught his chin, snapping his head back, and pulling something in his neck, judging by the tortured howl he let out. Still, he didn't give up. As Blue prepared to follow up with a jab from his clenched fist, his attacker surprised him again by dropping into a squat and slashing the knife up and across.

Despite Jimmy Blue's dodge, the tip of the knife, slowed by the leather jacket, pierced skin and opened up a long gash in his side, half an inch deep.

Ignoring the pain, Blue stuck to his plan, delivering a brisk jab that caught the wiry man squarely on his breastbone, slapping him down into the steps behind him hard enough to hurt, but leaving him conscious, and still dangerous.

Jimmy Blue drew back his right hand for a punch that would finish this, but a sound behind made him half-turn. He had just enough time to register Marty pulling one vice away from the workbench before it smashed into the side of his head, sending him reeling.

Blue watched the fat man, the wiry man, and the workshop disappear down a long tunnel.

No. *No.*

He slept.

———

Tom knew he must be dreaming. He was in the hotel room, fast asleep. His dreams were never like this. The ones he remembered featured visions of his parents, and he knew they weren't real. Not like this. This was different. A fat man with something metal clamped onto his fingers was screaming at a second man, thinner and smaller.

"Finish him! Kill him! Fuck's sake, Tay, kill him. Now! What are you doing?"

The smaller man held something shiny. It was a knife, and it had thick red blood on its tip. Tom looked away, feeling sick. The sight of blood scared him. Pain now. He didn't know there was pain in dreams. Looking down, he pulled his jacket to one side and saw the fresh wet red stain on his T-shirt. He looked at the men, frightened. The fat one was still shouting.

"He's only dazed. Stab him, you stupid bastard."

The younger man rubbed his neck without taking his eyes off Tom. "Shut up, Marty. I've got a better idea."

"Mm. Mm." Tom wanted to wake up. If this was what other peoples' dreams were like, he wanted no part of them.

The man with the knife laughed. "Check out this poor bastard. How hard did you hit him? He can't even speak."

The man waved his hand in front of Tom's face. "Anyone in? Hello? Hello?"

He threw the knife down, reached into the bag, and pulled out a gun. It was dull black, ugly, with a long barrel screwed on to the end.

The fat man snorted when he saw it. "Where did you get the piece, Tay? You trying to tell me Winter trusts you with a gun now?"

The gunman—Tay—looked away from Tom, his eyes flicking towards the fat man. And everything changed.

Tom disappeared.

———

Jimmy Blue took two fast steps forward. Tay reacted, but Blue moved faster, pinning the gun between their two bodies. He brought his hand up to cover the other man's fist, finding Tay's finger on the trigger, the barrel pointing towards Marty. Marty realised the danger a fraction of a second before Blue squeezed and the gun popped, the long barrel jerking as the bullet left the chamber.

Marty grunted in surprise, then wheezed and dropped to one knee. Blood gushed out of the wound in his thigh. He tried to staunch the bleeding, but the vice still gripped his right hand, and his left hand was attached to the workbench. He settled for screaming.

Tay joined the chorus when Jimmy Blue twisted his gun hand one hundred and eighty degrees anticlockwise, tearing three ligaments and snapping his ulna and radius.

Blue pulled the gun away from him. Tay went for the knife, dropping into a fighting stance when he had it in his left hand. He froze at the sight of the gun barrel pointing at his chest.

Tay wasn't on Jimmy Blue's list. He was young. Maybe even in his teens. He probably hadn't been born when Winter and his crew executed the Lewis family and burned their house to the ground. Tay carried a knife and a gun, and—judging by what Marty said—worked for Winter, but that didn't mean he deserved to die.

Tay was sweating. His useless hand hung at his side. The slightest movement made him gasp in pain. In between gasps, he ground his teeth. His pupils were black dots.

"Mate," he said, slowly moving his knife hand over the bench and dropping the blade onto the surface. "Think we got off on the wrong foot, yeah? When I came downstairs, I thought you were robbing the place. But I was wrong, wasn't I? You came here to kill Marty, right?"

Blue was silent. Tay took that as encouragement to continue. "Right? Yeah. Me too. That's why I'm here. Funny, right? We both came here to kill the twat. If I'd known, I'd have left you to it."

Marty spat blood onto the concrete floor. "You little scumbag. Where's your loyalty? Do you think Winter won't find out about this? You're finished, you piece of shit."

He took a ragged breath, wincing and pushing down on the hole in his thigh. He eyed Blue. "You too, you freak. You should have had the sense to stay dead. Do you have any idea who you're messing with? Winter will take everything you love when he finds out you're alive. Then he'll kill you piece by piece, and you'll be begging him to die the whole time. He'll cut out your liver, he'll—"

Tay raised his eyebrows at Jimmy and nodded towards Marty. "All right if I...?"

Blue responded with a tiny nod. Tay kicked Marty in the side of the head, and the Forger yelped, falling to his side and curling up.

"Shut up, Marty."

The man on the floor started crying. Tay turned his left hand palm up, his right still hanging by his side.

"Listen, if you let me go, I'll tell my boss I killed Marty. That way, he won't even know you were here. It's the perfect crime, see? Sorry I stabbed ya, mate. But—" He raised his twisted and broken right hand. "Quits, right? Right?"

Jimmy Blue said nothing, and Tay took a single pace sideways towards the stairs. When the gun barrel moved from his chest to point at his head, he stopped. When he opened his mouth to speak, a tiny shake of Blue's head persuaded him to keep quiet.

Blue was thinking. He was only interested in the names on the list. Tay wasn't on the list. But his promise to say nothing was a lie. He was leaving without his weapons, and there would be no hiding the injuries to his hand. No. More likely, Tay would go to Winter and describe what he'd seen. He would probably exaggerate Blue's size, maybe add extra assailants to explain his defeat.

Jimmy Blue had planned this too long to allow anything to spoil it. He wanted Winter to know who was coming, so he could feel the fear as Blue stalked him, killing his people, getting closer and closer.

But not yet. It was too soon.

"Sorry," he said, and shot Tay through the forehead. The bullet entered at the bridge of his nose, and he dropped without a sound.

"Jesus," said Marty, "Jesus. Oh god, oh god. Please. Please don't."

Jimmy Blue put the gun on the workbench and watched Marty Nicholson as he tried to drag himself away, leaving a streak of blood on the floor to mark his progress. He didn't get far, as his left hand was still attached to the bench. When Jimmy Blue put a boot on Marty's back, the Forger sighed and passed out.

Blue rolled Marty over and reattached the other vice, making sure it was secure this time.

While he waited for the Forger to regain consciousness, he examined the knife wound where Tay had stabbed him. Not deep, but bleeding, and it would probably need stitches. He checked the workshop for something to use as a makeshift bandage. Finding a roll of duct tape in a drawer, he tore off two pieces to close the wound, then wrapped a layer around his waist to hold it in place.

Marty groaned. Blue waited until the Forger's eyes focused on him.

"Now," he said, "where were we?"

CHAPTER TEN

"WHAT DO YOU WANT?" Marty's voice sounded weak and flat. He looked behind Blue, where Tay's corpse lay in a heap at the bottom of the stairs. Blue smiled.

"That's how you shoot someone in the head, Marty. If you want to be sure you'll kill them, that is. It's called the T-box." He drew a capital T on his own face, using his nose as the vertical, drawing the horizontal line across his eyes.

"At close range, such as,"—he nodded back towards the body—"or when you shot me, twenty years ago, if you aim for the T, it doesn't even matter what calibre you use. The trauma from the bullet's kinetic energy, transferred to vital parts of the brain behind the nose and eyes, will put anyone down."

He shook his head at Marty as if teaching a particularly slow child. "No good shooting the skull. It's thick, Marty. Designed to protect the brain. You will cause damage, but death is far from certain. Still, I don't blame you for messing things up. I blame Winter for that. Who showed you how to fire a gun? Didn't do the job properly. Strickland?"

"Yes, yes, Strickland. It was Strickland." Marty's skin glistened. His breath came in rapid gasps, and his lips had taken on a bluish tinge. "Winter ordered me to do it. I didn't want to. I begged him. Strickland gave me his gun, showed me what to do. I had no choice. You understand that, right? They would have killed me if I had refused. And you'd be dead. You're only alive because they asked me, don't you see? Really, you owe me. And I changed, I changed. I wouldn't touch a gun again. I couldn't stop thinking about you. If I could take it back, I would, I swear. Look, Tom, you don't need to do this. I have more money upstairs. Real money. I planned on leaving, anyway. Take the cash. I'll disappear. I'll tell you where to find the others."

Blue put a finger to his lips and shushed him. "I know where they are, Marty. I don't need your help. Do you have pen and paper?"

"Second drawer down. Please, Tom, don't—"

Blue whirled round and spat the words out, his face an inch from Marty's. "Tom is dead, Marty. You did that much right. You shot a twelve-year-old boy in the head and killed him. But that bullet planted a seed that grew in the dark, in the chaos, in the clouds of blood. And that seed became a sapling, and that sapling became a tree, and that tree produced one fruit, which hung from its branches for a very long time until it was ripe. Then it dropped to the ground and became a beast that crawled on its belly. One day, it found it had limbs, and dragged itself out of the dirt, prowling, hunting, learning. Later, it stood on its hind legs and its eyes opened for the first time in the darkness."

When Blue stood up, Marty's expression had changed, his mouth slack. "You're mad."

"Of course!" Blue pulled the notepaper out of the drawer and danced around the workshop, singing as he whirled between the benches.

"Well what is this that I can't see
With icy hands takin' hold of me
Well I am Death, none can excel
I'll open the door to Heaven and Hell"

Jimmy wrote four words on the notepaper, placing it next to the vice holding Marty's left hand.

Jimmy Blue is coming

He picked up the gun from the workbench. Marty's eyes were glassy and unfocused. It didn't matter to Blue. He didn't care about last words, changes of heart, expressions of regret. If Marty, rather than going into shock, expressed remorse, and admitted his life choices had caused more bad than good, so what? Nothing changed. The dance began with Marty; the first verse of the song Blue was born to sing.

He aimed the gun.

"T-box, Marty," he said. "Strickland should have told you."

Marty looked up at him.

"Did you bring me a girl?" Whoever Marty saw, it wasn't the man about to kill him. "You promised you would. Can you take her to the room?"

Blue shot Marty Nicholson between his eyes. The Forger's head sagged. If it hadn't been for one last exhalation, then silence, it might not have been immediately obvious that he was dead.

Before leaving the house, Blue closed his eyes and conjured up the image of Tom's home before the slaughter, before the fire. It was always clear in every detail whenever he wanted to visit. He walked through the empty living room, up the three steps to where Mother's desk waited, tucked underneath the staircase. He pictured the list on the desk's leather writing surface, written in black ink on yellow parchment.

Jimmy Blue lifted a heavy fountain pen and crossed out *The Forger*, before looking at the next name: *The Traitor.*

CHAPTER ELEVEN

BLUE SEARCHED MARTY'S HOUSE. He found a padded envelope containing thousands of pounds, but he wouldn't take fake money from the Forger. He left with Tay's messenger bag, which now contained the knife and the gun.

Over six consecutive nights a month earlier, Jimmy Blue had exited Tom's lodgings through the bedroom window and watched the change of shift at some of London's major hospitals. Following tired paramedics home, Blue noted the locations of those who lived alone. Two of them were in Southgate, only a few miles from the building site where Tom had worked for the past six weeks. One of them lived less than a mile away from another address he had memorised earlier that day. Perfect.

Blue stood in Marty's kitchen, eyes shut, and reviewed the moment Tom had squiggled what passed for a signature on his wage slip in the Hartnell's office. His recall was perfect, a pin-sharp image of everything Tom saw. Nothing on the desk was of any use, but an envelope in the wastepaper basket gave him a road name and number.

He opened his eyes and zipped up the jacket, wincing a little as it tightened on his injured side. Once the helmet was on, he slung the messenger bag across his body and left the house, closing the door quietly behind him. It was past midnight. No need to disturb the neighbours.

He wheeled the moped around the corner of the road before starting it up and heading for the North Circular.

He rode past the Hartnells' house twice before parking a street away and walking back. It was large, detached, set back a little way from the road. Les Hartnell lived well for an ex-con with a murder conviction. The house was newer than its neighbours. Blue imagined Hartnell had used the cheap materials and labour available to him to build his tasteless little palace.

As he walked up the short drive, he saw the telltale flickers of blue light between a gap in a downstairs curtain. Not in bed, then. Watching television.

Jimmy Blue smiled as the motion sensor picked him up, and harsh white light bathed the front of the house. Every warrior must think as fast as they act, improvising when necessary. Tay's appearance earlier had been a painful reminder of this necessity. Jimmy's plan for the next ten minutes was simple. It had to be, since he conceived it in the few seconds before banging on the door and shouting.

"Boss! Boss! There's a fire! Mr Hartnell? Are you in there? The site's on fire. Boss! Can you hear me? Are you there?"

He gave his voice a touch of East London, repeating the same words and thumping the door, until the hall light flicked on and he saw Les Hartnell's distorted form through the swirled glass of the front door. Blue stood side on, bending forward, disguising his bulk.

"What did you say?"

"The site, Mr Hartnell. It's on fire."

Hartnell came closer, putting his hand to the lock. A series of excited barks came from the living room. "Who are you?"

"It's Andy, Boss, Andy. Quick!"

There were two Andys on site, and a third turned up on busier days.

Mrs H's smoke-gravelled voice joined in. "Who is it, Les?"

Hartnell hesitated. Blue repeated his message, keeping his tone urgent and panicky. If he gave Hartnell time to think, he might wonder why someone had turned up at his door, rather than phoning him. He might even ask how this particular Andy knew where he lived.

As it was, he slid the security chain in place before opening the door an inch. "What's going on?"

It was all the invitation Jimmy Blue needed. He shoulder-barged the door, and it gave way with a splintering of wood, ripping the chain away and sending Hartnell flying backwards into the hall. No doubt he was now regretting using the same shoddy, cheap front door for his own house as he did for the homes on his sites.

Jimmy Blue stepped into the hall at the same moment the door on the left opened and a ball of fur and teeth pelted out, its claws scrabbling for purchase on the polished hardwood-effect flooring.

"Get him, Bobby, get him!" Mrs Hartnell, in a pink flannelette dressing gown with a cigarette dangling from the corner of her mouth, looked like she was auditioning for a sitcom set in nineteen seventy-seven. She ruined the effect by pulling a mobile phone from her pocket.

When Bobby reached the intruder's feet, he stopped, sniffed, put his head on one side, sniffed again, then leaped up to rest his paws on Blue's knees, asking for a head scratch. Blue obliged with his left hand. He used his right hand to discourage Mrs Hartnell from calling the police by pointing the gun at her.

"Put your phone on the floor and slide it towards me." No need to disguise his voice, as Tom had barely spoken during the weeks he'd spent on the building site.

Mrs H did as instructed. When the phone reached him, Jimmy Blue stamped on it. The glass splintered, and the screen flickered, then died. The Jack Russell sniffed, then returned to Blue for more attention.

"Bobby!" There was no missing the note of wounded betrayal in Mrs H's voice, as Bobby tilted his head to offer alternate scratching locations.

"Wha—what do you want?" Les Hartnell's conversational tone was famously abrasive and harsh. He was so tightly coiled that even the word "hello?" sounded like a threat. Not now, though. Now his voice shook.

Mrs H looked at her husband, sprawled in the corner. He was barefoot, wearing grey jogging bottoms and a white sweatshirt. There was a small pool of liquid on the floor, originating from his crotch. She narrowed her eyes.

"Jesus, Les."

He didn't acknowledge her, instead watching the big man with the gun.

"You want money? I have some cash. Not much. Friday, see? Payday. A few hundred, that's all."

The Hartnells were old school with money. Cash was king. Money that didn't go through the banks was bloody hard for the tax people to trace later. Blue laughed and extended his gun arm.

"Open your safe for me. Now."

Hartnell didn't deny the existence of a safe. He made a high-pitched sound somewhere between a hiccup and a sob, scrambled to his feet, and pointed at the door to Blue's right.

"It's in there."

Blue backed up and waved Hartnell over. He motioned Mrs H to follow. She did as directed, shaking her head at her husband as he scuttled into the room, stood by the safe in the corner and waited for further instructions. After searching for a suitable way to express her feelings, she repeated, "Jesus, Les."

They'd set the room up as an office with shelves and a desk besides the heavy safe. The curtains were closed.

Jimmy Blue directed Mrs H to the office chair. "Sit down."

She did as instructed, folding her arms. Blue pointed the gun at her husband.

"Open it."

Les Hartnell spun the combination with trembling fingers, making a mistake and starting over. "Sorry," he squeaked. Bobby sat on Blue's feet, head on paws, yawning. Mrs H looked between her dog and her husband in disgust.

The safe had three shelves. Two of them contained paperwork. The top shelf held rubber-banded stacks of twenty pound notes. Hartnell indicated one of these with a shaking finger. "That's a grand." When Blue didn't respond, he added, "Shall I bring the money over to you?"

"Oh, for god's sake," said his wife.

"Shh." Jimmy Blue held up a hand, and they were quiet. "Let me think."

The Hartnells had been ripping Tom off. They paid him half what they paid any other hod carrier and ignored the fact that Tom's custom hod held more bricks than anyone else's. They never paid overtime and had invented fictional fees to withhold even more of the money they owed him. Blue arrived at a fair weekly figure and multiplied it by the weeks Tom had worked before deducting the cash already paid. He took the messenger bag from his shoulder and threw it over to Hartnell.

"I want two thousand, six hundred pounds. Put it in there."

Hartnell opened the bag's flap. If he saw the knife inside, he gave no sign. He stuffed two cash bundles inside, then took the rubber band off a third and counted out four hundred pounds, putting the rest in the bag. He looked back at Blue.

"Don't you want the rest?"

Mrs H looked at him.

"No," said Blue, then paused. "How much is there?"

"Another nine grand."

Blue considered for a moment. "Okay. I'll take it. Keep it separate."

Eager to please, and, to all appearances, grateful that the armed robber in his house would take more of his money, Hartnell emptied some papers out of an envelope and put the original twenty-six hundred inside it, stuffing the other bundles of cash into the bag.

"Slide it back over here," said Blue. Bobby yielded his spot when Blue picked up the messenger bag, put the gun back in, and left the room.

"Les!" hissed Mrs H. Her tone suggested her husband should think very hard, and very quickly, about regaining some dignity and preserving his reputation before it was too late.

"Listen, pal." Blue turned in the hall to see Les Hartnell emerge from the office, a metal baseball bat held in a double-handed grip in front of him. "I don't know who you think you are, but you're messing with the wrong man. I put bigger guys than you in the ground when you were still in nappies, shithead."

As Hartnell spoke, his voice grew stronger, and he straightened up, as if remembering how intimidating, and how violent, he was rumoured to be. He pulled back his arm for a swing, aiming at Blue's kneecap.

"I'm gonna kill you, you thieving—"

Les Hartnell never finished his sentence. The arrival of a gloved fist in his face knocked four of his front teeth down his throat and sent his head snapping back into the door jamb.

Bobby followed Jimmy Blue all the way to the road before stopping, looking quizzically after the helmeted man with the familiar scent as he walked away. Then he cocked his leg at the gatepost before trotting back to the house.

CHAPTER TWELVE

THE PARAMEDIC'S NAME WAS GLEN, AND he wasn't at all happy at being woken up a few hours before his morning shift. The huge stranger on his doorstep came straight to the point.

"I have a cut that needs cleaning and stitching." He held up a messenger bag. "There's a gun in here. When you call the police later, tell them I threatened you with it. I'd rather not have to do that, if it's all the same with you. It's been a long night. What do you say?"

Glen glued the wound closed in his tiny kitchen, after cutting away the duct tape and cleaning and disinfecting the wound. In an average weekend in the ambulance, he handled multiple lacerations, heart attacks, overdoses. He'd stitched up three knife wounds last week and held a kid's hand as he bled out. A muscled giant wearing a motorbike helmet with a stab wound to his side wasn't enough to freak him out.

"All done." The stranger pulled down his T-shirt and stood up.

"Wait," said Glen. He opened a drawer. "Fresh dressings. Leave the bandage on for twenty-four hours. Don't let the glue get wet. If it does, pat it dry with a towel. Any sign of infection, go to hospital. You should be fine, though."

"Thank you."

"You didn't give me much of a choice." Glen eyed the clock. Three-ten. He'd be getting up in just over two hours. The stranger put a bundle of cash on the table and left.

"Hey!" said Glen. "I don't want your money."

"I don't care." The front door closed. Glen stared at the cash as the kettle boiled. It was a lot of money. He put it in a drawer. Half an hour later, he called the police.

———

At three forty-five, an industrial bin in North London was flung open to reveal a seventeen-year-old pizza delivery rider, who'd woken from an erotic dream involving his old science teacher, Mrs Thornton.

When he remembered where he was and how he'd got there, he froze. There was no sound other than footsteps, and they were getting further away. He risked standing, his legs shaking, in time to get a glimpse of the big guy who'd stolen his bike. He stood in the bin for another two minutes, listening.

When he climbed out, he nearly kicked over his moped, which was leaning against the bin. The pizza bag had gone, which meant his boss would try to take it out of his wages. The key wasn't in the ignition, either.

He looked at his watch. That big, lying bastard said he only wanted the moped for an hour. He'd been gone all night. And he'd brought it back with no sodding key. Where was his bloody phone? Shit, shit, shit.

Then he noticed the takeaway bag leaning up against the front wheel. He picked it up. Inside were his key and his phone. Also inside was four thousand, four hundred pounds, in bundles of crisp twenties.

———

The owner of the office cleaning company went by the name of Chesterfield.

"Chesterfield," he repeated, eyeing the big lad who'd come about the job. "Like the sofas."

"Mm," said Tom.

Chesterfield shook his head. "Don't get it? Never mind. You look like a strong boy. You gonna give me any trouble? Anything I ought to know?"

Tom pulled the bandana tighter onto his scalp and shook his head.

"Well, then." Chesterfield stuck out his hand. It looked tiny up against Tom's. "The agency said you can start next month. I'll start you with a week's trial. Fair?"

"Mm. Mm. Fair."

"Good lad. See you then."

Tom walked back to the hostel. On the way there, he thought he saw someone, or something, in the shadow of a doorway of a boarded-up hotel. He stopped and looked, but couldn't be sure.

In the hostel's tiny private room, he turned onto his left side in bed, fingers tracing the dressing over his latest scar. Through the thin walls, someone sang in a language he didn't recognise. The sound wove itself into his dreams.

As sleep claimed him, Tom thought he saw a list on an old writing desk, one side of it blackened by fire. The first words on the list had a line through them.

In his dream, he could write, just like everyone else. He took a fresh sheet of paper and wrote his words down, wielding the pen with a confident flourish.

Tom knew what the words said.

Jimmy Blue is coming.

CHAPTER THIRTEEN

Tom hovered on the edge of sleep. He didn't see the men get on the bus. He heard them, though. They talked to each other while they climbed the steps to the top deck. Something about their tone signalled danger. A bit too loud, with a harsh edge to their laughter. But they walked past Tom without comment on their way to the back, and their conversation became quieter, so he gave in to his tiredness, resting his head on a folded jacket to stop it knocking against the window.

The bus ride from Charing Cross to Barking took nearly an hour, but Tom didn't mind. He slept both ways, mostly. The motion soothed him, the hiss of the doors opening and closing. He even welcomed the moments when noisy passengers half-woke him, as they gave him the opportunity to slide back into sleep.

Three rows behind him, across the aisle, two women had been chatting since boarding at Canary Wharf. Their animated conversation was punctuated with laughter, and the burble of their voices became the ambient background to Tom's sleep.

When their chat became quieter and more hesitant, then stopped, he opened his eyes.

The front window of the double-decker made a good mirror, but the vibrations of the vehicle blurred the reflections. Tom picked out the four men. They had moved from the back of the bus, occupying the rows behind, and in front of, the women.

The women sat closer together now, their faces brown smudges in the glass. One of them kept glancing at the man standing next to their seat. Tom risked a quick look. The man wasn't steadying himself with the pole; his hand covered the button requesting a stop.

If people talked quickly, or when more than one person spoke at once, Tom struggled to follow. When that happened, he gave up trying to identify words, instead listening to the sounds like music. He might not understand, but he could hear tone, pitch, volume and timbre. Music could be comforting, exciting, teasing, angry. So could voices.

The music of the men's conversation was discordant and dishonest. The obvious sounds—the melody—suggested good humour, fun, flirting. But everything else made the melody a lie. Like a horror movie soundtrack, a simple tune subverted by dark, abrasive harmonies; a shifting soundscape underneath the men's words spoke of entitlement, lust, shame, and an easy, tribal violence.

Before he knew he had moved, Tom was on his feet in the aisle, facing the group behind him. His legs and shoulders ached, but he didn't know why. Pushing a mop around an office block every evening couldn't account for the tightening of the muscles across his chest, the burn in his shoulders.

One of the men sitting behind the girls leaned out. He raised his voice, directed something at Tom. The others went quiet. Now the soundtrack had faded, Tom tuned into the words.

"I said, what the fuck are you looking at?"

Tom was familiar with this sentence. There was no satisfactory response. Ignoring the man would lead to an angrier challenge. Whatever Tom said, the next words were either, "You calling me a liar?" or "What did you say?"

Despite knowing this, Tom didn't walk away. It was the same impulse that saw him move snails from the path outside the Barking house every evening. Even if he didn't accidentally stand on the snails himself, someone else would. He was the only one there. So he moved them. What else could he do?

"Asked you a question, boy."

The nearest man moved into the aisle, adopting a loose-limbed, wide-legged, leaning stance. He wore black cotton trousers and a white vest stretched tight over a shaved chest. Tattoos covered both his arms. He was young, possibly still in his teens, but his facial hair and studied, world-weary expression suggested he wanted to appear older.

Tom looked at the two women. They were silent, hands in their laps, all the fun gone out of them.

"Mm, mm." Tom wasn't sure of the correct words, but it didn't stop him from trying to form them. They were close, waiting to be strung into sentences. Clever words, words to paint a picture in someone's head, or commanding words that others would obey.

"Spit it out, retard." The others laughed. Not the women. Their lips formed thin lines, their eyes dropped away from Tom.

Tom shook his head, pointing at the women. "Mm. Mm. No. Leave alone."

More laughter. The bus lurched around a corner, and both Tom and the tattooed man steadied themselves, Tom grabbing a pole. As he took hold of it, he found the stop button. Without thinking, he pressed it, and a *ding* signalled that the bus would pull in at the next stop.

The bus slowed, moving across the road, branches scratching the roof. When it shuddered to a stop with a hiss of air brakes, the tattooed leader put a hand in his pocket and pulled out a knife. It looked like a magic trick, as his pocket couldn't have contained such a long blade. A picture flashed into Tom's mind; a knife strapped to the man's leg, the pocket slit. Holding the knife where Tom could see it, the man yelled down to the driver.

"Sorry, mate, pressed it by accident."

The bus rumbled back into motion. The leader shot a glance at the camera mounted above the steps. Tom did the same. Someone had sprayed the lens with red paint.

"That's right. Now go back to sleep. This has got sod all to do with you."

Tom knew the women were in danger. Someone needed to stop these men. Their soundtrack had been confident. Sometimes boys played at being tough. Not these boys. They had done bad things before; they liked doing bad things.

But what was he supposed to do? Tom scooped spiders out of bathtubs before releasing them outside, and rescued pollen-drunk bees from roadsides, seeing them safely to the shelter of a hedge. His instinct, rather than his confused thoughts, told him these men would only back down if confronted with greater strength than their own. And the thought of violence made tears spring into Tom's eyes.

"Bloody homo." One of the men pointed. "Look. He's gonna cry."

The leader sneered, casually waved the knife towards Tom. "Go on. Sit down. Cry yourself to sleep. We're getting off at the next stop. All of us."

The gesture he made included the two women, who stiffened, one of them sobbing. The leader laughed. "Now look what you've done. Upset my girlfriend. Sit the fuck down."

Shaking, Tom hesitated. His thoughts swirled like washing-up water round a plughole. One idea at a time was manageable. *Take the bricks from here to there. Mop that floor. Empty this bin.* More than that, and it became difficult to do anything, often freezing him in place.

The tattooed man took a step towards him. "I won't ask again."

The way he said *ask* sounded like *axe* and this confused Tom even more. He heard the word *axe*, looked at the knife, the mute women, the swaggering leader. His head was heavy, his legs and arms leaden. Too much. His mind full of rain.

Then, a light switching on. A ray of sunlight through the clouds. *Go to sleep, Tom. It's okay. Go to sleep.*

He looked away from the leader's grin of triumph and shuffled back to his seat. He didn't see the second woman squeeze her friend's hand, her own eyes now filling with tears.

The smeared streets slid by through the rain-streaked window.

Tom closed his eyes and slept.

CHAPTER FOURTEEN

CALLUM PERKINS HAD WORKED for Transport for London since his mid-twenties, driving buses throughout the capital. He enjoyed the challenge of the constant traffic, the rich soup of nationalities and personalities travelling with him every day. Best job in the world, his dad always said, and he'd driven buses in Northumbria for fifty years.

What Callum didn't enjoy was the aggro. There wasn't much; not as much as the papers would have you believe, but enough that he'd developed a nose for it. The four guys who boarded at Stratford reeked of trouble. They each boasted a pistol tattoo on the backs of their hands. They didn't pay when they boarded. Three of them walked past while the fourth rested his hand on the Oyster card reader, long enough for Callum to see three bullets on his wrist above the gun tattoo. According to his ink, this kid—eighteen, nineteen years old?—had already murdered three people. Callum let them on without a word.

He turned the radio off after the gang boarded and drove in silence. The CCTV system hadn't been working all week, and the camera upstairs was permanently vandalised. He knew which passengers were up there, though. One method of staving off tiredness on late shifts was to keep track of who was aboard. The big shy guy with the bandana had been on since Charing Cross. The two girls from Canary Wharf were on the top deck, too.

At the *ping* of the stop request bell, Callum pulled over and waited until someone shouted that they'd pressed it by accident. He hoped they were just horsing around. He didn't much like the look of those boys, particularly the leader. Hard-faced, like he hated the world and wanted an opportunity to prove how much. The eleven passengers downstairs had gone quiet since the gang boarded. Six of them got off when he stopped, deciding to walk despite the drizzle. Callum couldn't blame them.

When the bell rang again three minutes later, he checked the mirror. None of the remaining five passengers downstairs showed signs of moving.

In the silence, the voice from the top deck rang clear. "I warned you, retard. Should have stayed asleep. Now you're gonna bleed."

Another voice answered, and the sound of it lifted every hair on Callum's arms and up the back of his neck. It was a man's voice. And it was singing.

"It's when next I have murdered, the Man-In-The-Moon to powder
His staff I'll break, his dog I'll bake, they'll howl no demon louder"

Callum guided the bus to the kerb and stopped. The downstairs passengers scurried out. None of them looked back.

"Oh, thanks, off you go then, that's just grand." Callum picked up the radio to call in, but hesitated. There'd been no actual violence. Kids threatened each other every day. What was he going to report? Unsavoury characters having a singalong? They'd take the piss for months back at the depot.

The first voice again. "What the hell? That's right, sing on, you mad fucker, sing on."

The mad fucker in question did just that, but his voice got louder, and when he didn't sing, he laughed. Then the words of the song were punctuated by screams.

"Still I sing bonnie boys, bonnie mad boys,
Bedlam boys are bonnie"

The bus started to shake, rocking from side to side. There were hisses of pain, a horrible snap followed by shrieks of agony, then two thumps as something heavy hit the window. The third thump shattered the glass. A second later, the gang leader landed on the pavement alongside the bus.

Callum lifted the handset again. "This is 692. I'm at Roman Road Playing Fields. I need police and an ambulance."

A second gang member landed next to the first.

"Two ambulances."

Another thump on the pavement.

"Maybe three."

"*For they all go bare and they live by the air,*
And they want no drink nor money"

At the sound of descending footsteps, Callum dropped the radio handset and twisted round in his seat. The youngest gang member, sweating, eyes wide with terror, ran for the door. He ignored his fallen friends on the pavement, sprinting away.

The two women were still upstairs. Callum Perkins didn't consider himself to be a coward, but it took every bit of courage he possessed to slide out from under the steering wheel, unlock the glass box he called his office, and climb the stairs to the top deck.

The first thing he saw was a long-bladed knife impaled in a seat cushion. No blood on the knife, but smears of red on the floor, along one of the intact windows, and dripping from the edges of the broken glass.

The two women hugged in the row behind the knife, heads bent towards each other as if scared to look.

Other than the women, the bus was empty. Then he heard it - a creak of metal over his head. Callum looked up. Another creak, then another. Someone walking on the roof. When the footsteps reached the front of the bus, they stopped. The silence that followed was thick as soup. One woman whimpered.

"It's okay, pet." Callum sounded just like his dad when he was stressed. "They're gone now. It's over."

The next moment, he shrieked along with them as the whole bus shook with the noise above. The footsteps were running now, smacking the roof like a toy drum played by a toddler with a sugar high. Speeding up as they reached the back of the bus, the footsteps suddenly ceased.

A Transit van was parked beyond the bus stop. Callum saw a bulky shape plunge from the end of the bus, land on the van's roof, roll with the impact, and drop. Seconds later, the figure climbed a low wall and vanished into the park beyond. The van's alarm screamed, its indicators flashing. Sirens contributed their wail to the soundtrack, adding a dissonant note as they got closer, washing the horizon in pulsing blue light.

"Are either of you hurt? Do you want to come downstairs?"

The nearest woman raised her head. Before answering, she looked at the broken window, and at the streaks of blood. Her friend was still shaking, and the first woman stroked her hair as she replied.

"Police?"

"They're coming, pet, don't you worry. Are you hurt?"

She shook her head, her eyes fixed on Callum. "They'll arrest him, won't they?"

Callum didn't need to ask who she meant. "I expect so. I mean..." He gestured at the damage, and through the broken window towards the three men lying crumpled and bloody on the pavement. "Yes. They'll arrest him."

The woman nodded. She had glitter in her hair, some of it sticking to her wet cheeks.

"He saved us. They would have raped us. Or worse."

Callum thought about speaking, but something in the woman's expression stopped him.

"I didn't see what he looked like," she said, slowly. "Neither did you, did you, Suze?" Her friend sniffed and shook her head. The first woman looked back at Callum. There was no mistaking the steel in her expression. "What about you? Do you remember what he looked like? If the police ask you, could you describe him?"

Big, broad, early to mid-twenties. Jeans, grey hoodie, brown jacket. Plain black beanie. Quiet. Wouldn't meet your eye. Hunched over, awkward, shy. Always covered his head, even when it was warm.

If not a beanie, then a bandana. Dark green eyes, blonde eyebrows. He'd been a regular for a few weeks now. Took the bus to the end of the line, got off at Barking.

Callum thought about the gang, how they'd got on without paying, the leader showing his gun and bullet tattoos. Three kills. And looking for the chance of more.

"No," he said, with the faintest of nods. "Can't say that I could. Didn't notice what he looked like."

The woman returned his nod. The first police car came to a screeching stop alongside the bus. Callum led the two of them downstairs as a second police car and an ambulance arrived.

Later that night, after a cheese sandwich and half a pint of cheap whisky, Callum Perkins went to bed and stared at the ceiling. For once, he was glad of the city sounds beyond his window; the horns, the dull thump of dance music, the laughter, and the shouts. He listened to them as he drifted into a fitful sleep, but even then, he could still hear that voice on the top deck of his bus, as one man put another three into hospital. Not shouting. Not swearing.

Singing.

CHAPTER FIFTEEN

RHODA ILÍCH ASSEMBLED the ingredients for her thermos, humming to herself. While the milk warmed on the stove, she added cocoa powder, brown sugar, Rohypnol and a glug of gamma-hydroxybutrate. No need to measure anything. One look at a candidate told her if a whole teaspoon of Rohypnol would be necessary. Too much and those passing by would see the kid was drugged; not enough and the candidate might fight back.

As she stirred the mixture, Rhoda's tongue found the two capped teeth she'd gained after underestimating a dose in the early days. These days, she didn't make mistakes. She'd learned her business from the best, watching the way her mentor appraised potential candidates, how she approached them, how long it took to gain their trust. The only part of the process Irene had excluded her from was preparing the drugged drinks. Trial and error, plus two broken teeth, taught Rhoda how to estimate body weight and get the dose right.

Nearly half-past nine. Summer was over, and the newest batch of homeless kids were getting their first taste of cold nights on the streets. Rhoda aimed to pick up the candidate just before ten. Something else she'd learned from Irene. Too early and the city would still be busy. Too late, and you risked catching the theatre and pub crowd, plus the candidate might have succumbed to the lure of a bottle, or worse.

She heard the diesel rattle of the black cab before Andy beeped the horn. Time to go to work.

———

Andy drove in silence, which Rhoda appreciated. He wasn't as good a driver as Marty, but he was better company. No small talk. Andy stuck to his job and didn't eye the female candidates with Marty's greasy hunger. Rhoda always showered after working with Marty. She wasn't sorry he was dead.

They picked up her wingman twelve minutes after leaving Crouch End. She didn't ask his name. He was young, muscly, and used too much hair gel. He barely looked up from his phone the entire journey. The wingman made sure the candidate stayed in the taxi until they reached the house. An easy job for the strong, silent, morally vacuous type.

Winter had stopped everything for ten days after Marty and Tays' murders. Rhoda lost the candidate she'd been working on. Winter sent Strickland to visit her the evening after the deaths, asking questions. His reputation terrified most people, but during Rhoda's time with Irene she'd seen things that woke her in the early hours, paranoid, sweating. She could deal with Strickland. He left satisfied Rhoda knew nothing about the murders. It was Winter's way of reminding her he didn't trust her. And that was okay. She had a recording of Winter ordering an execution. It would keep her alive if their business relationship turned sour.

"Drop me here. There's building work by the bridge. Meet me there in fifteen minutes."

Andy pulled over. A white-haired man held up his newspaper to hail the cab, but Andy kept the orange taxi sign dark, shaking his head when the man approached.

"Mirror," said Rhoda.

Andy craned round in his seat. "You're fine."

It wasn't his call. She didn't move, waiting until Andy shrugged and tilted the rear-view mirror for her. Rhoda checked her face. She thought of herself as Madge this week, which meant a blonde wig, too much makeup, an ochre shawl, and a hemp shoulder bag for the thermos. She tilted her head, tucking away the last strands of her own hair. Another lesson from Irene. Any eyewitness would describe a woman that didn't exist.

This was her fifth encounter with Sunny, the new candidate. The first had been wordless, a concerned frown as she dropped a two pound coin into Sunny's paper cup. The second time she passed Sunny's doorway, she'd eyed the girl's thin jacket before handing over her burgundy shawl, nodding in response to the quiet, "Thank you."

The cocoa came out during the third visit. Not drugged. Not yet. Rhoda offered Sunny a cup. Sunny shook her head, dark eyes already suspicious after less than a week on the street. Rhoda drank alone that night. On the fourth visit, Sunny accepted a cup after Rhoda finished hers. Tonight was the night. She'd gained enough trust. No one would remember 'Madge' later.

When Rhoda found Sunny, the young woman was wearing the burgundy shawl. She offered Rhoda a shy smile. The girl looked thinner every time Rhoda saw her. Grimier, too. No doubt she didn't smell too fresh. Well, the parlour would feed her, clean her, and make her beautiful.

"Hello, Sunny. Chilly tonight, isn't it? How are things? Are you hungry?"

"I'm okay, thank you." Still polite, soft-spoken, vulnerable. Perfect. Leave her on the streets, and the reality of eking out an existence in the gutter would either turn her feral, or kill her trying. From the way she spoke, Rhoda guessed Sunny came from a middle-class home. A rare find. Maybe her father had started paying her visits during the night. Or she'd been grounded for stealing from Mum, fleeing to London to teach her parents a lesson. Rhoda didn't want Sunny to tell her how she'd ended up in a shop doorway. She doubted she was still capable of caring, but why take the risk?

"Hmm. Well, a snack never hurts. Hang on." Rhoda rummaged in the shoulder bag, pulling out a protein bar. "Here you are. I've overeaten today, so you'll be doing me a favour."

Sunny consumed the bar in three greedy bites.

Rhoda pressed her advantage. "Confession time. I couldn't wait. I'm cold, so I've already started on the cocoa. But don't worry, I left a cup for you."

She unscrewed the thermos and poured while she spoke. Sunny accepted it without a word, inhaled the sweet steam, then sipped. The sugar hit the spot, and Sunny gulped the rest down.

Rhoda took the cup back and replaced the flask in her bag. She kept up a stream of inane chatter, describing the plot of a new film, asking Sunny what books she liked. All the while, Rhoda watched the candidate's pupils and listened for the beginnings of slurring in her speech. Sunny lost her train of thought after a few minutes, patting the concrete underneath her sleeping bag as if to reassure herself it was there. She giggled.

Rhoda held out her hand. Sunny took it with the trust of a child.

"Tell you what, Sunny. There's a hostel half a mile away. The people who run it go to my church." The mention of church didn't work on every candidate, but a nice middle-class atheist like Sunny would associate the word with comforting images of harvest festivals, weak tea, and well-meaning old ladies.

Sunny stood up more unsteadily than Rhoda would have liked, but that might be a lack of sustenance rather than Rohypnol and GHB.

"Here. Let me help with your stuff." Sunny leaned against a wall while Rhoda filled the sleeping bag with the few items that made up the homeless girl's belongings. Two books, both poetry. A spare jumper, underwear, a hand towel, tampons and some soap in a plastic bag.

"Let me give you my phone number. In case we get separated."

Sunny nodded dumbly and fished a phone out of her pocket, nearly dropping it. Rhoda caught it as she fumbled and took it out of her hand.

"I'll put my number in. Come on, I'll do it while we walk."

Sunny let Rhoda take her arm as they made their way to the rendezvous. To anyone watching, they might have been mother and daughter. Rhoda felt a touch of professional pride in how well she'd judged the dose. Sunny remained docile. She would be unrecognisable when the parlour finished with her. Rhoda estimated her cut would be ten grand. Possibly twelve, with that lovely Home Counties accent.

———

From the deepest shadows under the bridge, Jimmy Blue watched Rhoda Ilích approach the girl in the shop doorway. He had followed Rhoda the first time she approached the girl. After that, one of his bird shit cams monitored the shop doorway where the homeless girl slept.

He hung well back as the pair walked to the taxi. Rhoda got in beside the girl and they drove away. Halfway over the bridge, the window went down and someone dropped a plastic bag in a bin. Blue guessed it contained the girl's phone. Her last link with family and friends.

The taxi's next stop would be a house run by Winter. Nothing good happened there. Intercepted phone messages and emails referred to them as parlours. Grooming parlours.

He pulled his hood over his head before breaking cover, jogging out onto the pavement, his route mapped out in his head. He would visit the Traitor tonight.

Blue grinned as he ran. Soon, Winter would find out what was coming for him. Winter showed no fear, but it was an act. You couldn't be intelligent and fearless.

Unless, Blue reminded himself, laughing out loud, you were mad.

CHAPTER SIXTEEN

IT WAS three in the morning when Rhoda got back to her ground-floor flat in Crouch End. She rinsed the flask, placing it on the drainer to dry. The wig and the shawl stayed in the shoulder bag, which she hung in the hall cupboard. Careless people ended up in prison. The taxi always dropped her somewhere different, a few minutes' walk from home. By then, blonde Madge had gone, replaced by Rhoda's short, grey hair.

She felt wrung out after delivering a candidate to the parlour. Part of her job involved a pep talk, acclimatising new arrivals to the reality of their situation. Rhoda drank cheap tea with the maid and two of the parlour crew until Sunny was in a fit state to listen. The maid's title didn't reflect her duties—it was a hangover from her days running a brothel. It said a lot for the woman's life choices that she saw overseeing the parlour as a promotion.

The talk with Sunny went as well as could be expected. Experience showed that candidates were less likely to resist, try to escape, or attempt suicide. But if Rhoda explained their situation. It would be best if they accepted their changed circumstances as soon as possible. Freedom brought them pain; why mourn its loss? Sunny, tired and dazed, wept silently as she listened, but Rhoda didn't detect much resistance. Whatever put her in that shop doorway had already taken the fight out of her. Good. If Rhoda hoped to clear five figures' commission, Sunny needed to be undamaged when auctioned.

In the bathroom, Rhoda eyed the packet of sleeping pills. She'd taken them for a decade, on and off. More on than off since Marty's murder. He'd been killed twenty years to the night after a night she'd never forget. A strong enough coincidence to send her back to the pills. She was weaning herself off again now, but it took all her willpower to close the medicine cabinet door and go to bed.

In the darkness of her bedroom, Rhoda counted her breaths, visualising her calm place. Such a cliché: a beach with golden sand, the fine grains trickling between her bare toes. Deep blue sky, turquoise sea kissing the sand, warm sun on her face. The other people in Rhoda's calm place never disturbed her, but they were there; playing in the water, fetching drinks from the straw-thatched bar, stretching out to bask. All keeping their distance. Rhoda didn't like to be alone, but she didn't trust anyone enough to enjoy their company. Her imagination provided an illusory paradise.

A tired smile crept onto her face as her body relaxed. Without the pills, her beach retreat soothed her mind, and Rhoda began a relatively untroubled descent into sleep. She couldn't remember the last time this had happened. Maybe there would be no nightmares.

She woke up an hour later. Someone was standing at the foot of her bed, watching her sleep.

———

Rhoda's bedroom was dark, but a deeper darkness began beyond her feet. An outline; a human shape.

She slept light. The odds were slim that anyone could get into her bedroom without waking her. Despite this logical piece of reassurance, Rhoda kept her breathing as quiet as possible. She stared at the shape.

One straightforward way to dismiss her paranoia suggested itself: reach out to her left and turn on the bedside lamp. The shape continued to stare down at her. She blinked to clear its blurred edges. The shape didn't move. It couldn't be real. Turn on the light. Take away its power.

She began by taking her left hand out from under the duvet, sliding her palm along the cotton sheet. The gap between the bed and the table was three inches, but her fingers found nothing. A knot of panic fluttered in her throat.

Be calm. Think it through.

Rhoda's head wasn't on the pillow. She was further down the bed than she'd thought. Reaching out in the wrong place. She moved her hand backwards, and her fingers brushed the smooth wood of the table. The knot in her throat loosened, but her breaths, despite her efforts, came short and fast.

Her fingers reached for the lamp's cable. She traced the plastic cord up the side of the table until her index finger encountered the switch.

Slide it up, the light comes on, and this is over.

The shadows who pursued her in nightmares were dead, buried, gone. Rhoda was in the bedroom of her flat in Crouch End. Alone. She refused to be terrified of an imaginary shadow. This stopped now.

She slid the switch. Nothing happened.

A strange, whimpering gulp broke the silence, such a pathetic sound that Rhoda barely believed she'd produced it.

She tried the switch again, then a third and fourth time.

The shape didn't move. Rhoda pushed herself up until her back rested against the headboard. The lightbulb must have blown. Bad timing, but nothing sinister. Okay. Her phone was on the table. She'd use the light from that to dispel the shadow figure. No more sleep tonight, she conceded. A bottle of Chardonnay, and plenty of shitty reality shows to catch up on.

Rhoda slid her hand back onto the bedside table, finding her glass of water. The phone was just beyond it. Except it wasn't. Rhoda's fingers explored the table's surface until she found something that stopped the breath in her throat. The end of the charging cable. She reviewed that night's bedtime routine, her mind flitting from image to image. Bathroom, no sleeping pill, bedside light on—working perfectly—plug phone in. Had she done that? Yes. Definitely. Her fingers squeezed the cable as if the action might summon the phone.

The shadow moved, stepping away from the foot of the bed.

"No." Rhoda's lips shaped the word without the breath to support any sound. Her neck prickled with sweat, but her body stayed cold.

Once the shadow figure was standing next to her, it bent over the bed like a parent watching a sleeping child. Rhoda became aware of her full bladder. She stared up into the darkness, telling herself no one could stand so still. She was imagining this. Some kind of waking nightmare.

But where was her phone?

When the shape spoke, sweat broke out all over her body, and her heart fluttered in her chest like a trapped bird.

"Hello, Auntie Rhoda."

CHAPTER SEVENTEEN

JIMMY BLUE DIDN'T NEED to break into Rhoda's flat. He'd lifted Rhoda's keys out of her handbag months ago, taken moulds, and replaced them before she knew they were missing.

Once inside, Blue didn't waste any time. One-thirty a.m., and Rhoda would be back within the hour. He walked through the flat, checking for weapons. A faceful of pepper spray might spoil his fun somewhat.

In the bedroom, he noted the phone charger on the bedside table. He walked the route he planned to take, listening for noisy floorboards, and memorising their position. A few drops of oil silenced the bedroom door's hinges.

Once he'd scoped the layout, Jimmy relaxed, humming to himself as he waited. The cupboard in the hall was deep, and a pile of old sheets on top of some half-used paint tins made a comfortable seat. He shared the space with a large wheeled suitcase. He took out his phone. The camera on her garden gate gave him a perfect view of the back door. He waited. Waiting was something Blue was very, very good at.

When he saw Rhoda walk up the path, he turned his phone off, zipping it into a jacket pocket. He listened to her move around the kitchen, stifling a laugh when she opened the hall cupboard door and hung a bag on a hook without looking. He almost yelled, "Boo!" but clamped a hand over his mouth to stop himself.

After an hour, the flat settled into a deeper silence. Jimmy Blue uncurled, stretching his limbs in the dark hallway to rid himself of any clicks or pops from bones and joints. He negotiated the flat from memory. The images in his mind stayed so bright and sharp, he might have been walking in daylight.

The kitchen cupboards clicked when opened, so he had left one ajar. Blue reached in, found the fuse box and flicked the master switch. The numbers on the microwave vanished, leaving a ghostly green after-image.

Jimmy Blue loved the darkness. They were old friends. He and Tom had lived without a shred of light for a year. When Tom found his way back, Blue stayed put, an idea slipping between twists of shadows, a formless, dark tumour buried in the ink-black hollows. He grew strong there. Even now, when he came out to play, he never forgot where he belonged. The dark tapestry, the ancient terror, the long night. Home.

Blue didn't breathe for thirty seconds after entering the bedroom. He insinuated himself into the darkness, listened to the sounds of sleep, then crossed to her bedside and unplugged her phone.

Once at the foot of the bed, he breathed again, each inhalation and exhalation long and controlled. He drew on a technique learned from a teacher in California during his years of training, maintaining his pulse at fifty-eight beats per minute. With each passing moment, Blue became more at one with the night, his edges bleeding into the familiar darkness surrounding him.

The power seeped into him like fresh cement into a trough. The dark, the stillness, the oneness—all of it fed him. As he drew the night into himself, he remembered the last time Tom had been this close to the sleeping woman. Auntie Rhoda, wishing young Tom good night, allowing him one more chapter before turning out his light. Hours later, a stranger pulled him out of bed, took him downstairs, and held him tight while his parents died.

She didn't stay to watch. Now Rhoda worked for the man who killed his family.

Blue hissed.

Her breathing changed. She was awake. He listened intently. Not enough light to see by, but a dozen tiny sounds told him her head had moved. She was looking at him. He smiled. The smile broadened at the click of the useless lamp. He waited for her to reach out for her phone.

When he moved, he came so close he could have touched her face. The contents of her medicine cabinet suggested Rhoda suffered from insomnia. Jimmy wondered if, when she did sleep, she had nightmares. He hoped so. If not, that would change now.

"Hello, Auntie Rhoda."

The woman in the bed didn't reply, but her throat made a dry sound as if trying to swallow something sharp. He leaned in close.

"It's been a long time."

Jimmy Blue didn't need to see Rhoda's face. Her terror was obvious in the rapid, trapped animal breathing, the clicks of her windpipe in her tight throat, the sour breath and fresh sweat.

The woman staring up into the blackness had just woken up to a world she didn't belong in, alone in an alien landscape.

Rhoda was in the dark. Blue was *of* the dark.

He allowed a lengthy pause to stretch out before he spoke again. Long enough for her to wonder if this might be a vivid nightmare.

"Do you know who I am?"

Rhoda's breathing returned to its previous gasps. She sounded like she was being fed oxygen from a teaspoon, sipping frantically at it to stay alive. Such a desperate sound. He enjoyed listening to it.

"Answer me."

She tried. Blue listened to Rhoda struggle. The voice that emerged was a harsh, painful whisper.

"You... you can't be. Can't be."

Leaning in close, his breath on her face, he spoke again.

"Say my name."

"No. It's impossible."

"Say it."

"You're dead, you're dead. You can't be here."

"I killed Marty, Auntie Rhoda. I killed him first. I made a list. Now say my name."

Whether the sobs were remorseful, or a by-product of her terror, Blue didn't care.

"Tom?"

Jimmy Blue giggled. "Mad Tom! Poor, mad Tom!"

He danced on the spot and sang.

"For to see my Tom of Bedlam, ten thousand miles I'd travel

Mad Maudlin goes on dirty toes, to save her shoes from gravel"

"Oh, Auntie Rhoda, Tom isn't here. Poor Tom. You answer to me now. And Jimmy Blue has questions. Have you led a good life? Will you leave the world better than you found it? Do you ever wonder what happens to those girls and boys you pick out for Winter? How many of them kill themselves? Do you think about the night you betrayed my family? Mum said she took you off the streets, just like you did for that girl tonight. But Mum didn't groom you and sell you to the highest bidder. She gave you a home. And you let Winter and his people into that home to kill us. Auntie Rhoda, I don't think you've led a very good life at all. Do you?"

Rhoda surprised him by rasping out an answer.

"No. No, I don't. Are you going to kill me?"

"Yes. Of course I am. You're next on the list. But..."

He paused. A bit theatrical, perhaps, but he liked it.

"But what?" Rhoda's voice was almost normal. Her breathing, too. The trapped animal comparison came to his mind again. Didn't snared rabbits do this - give up, stop struggling, when the hunter approached with the knife?

"But I want you to see me coming, Auntie Rhoda." He sat on the edge of the bed, and a moan escaped the woman lying there. "Remember playing hide and seek?"

"Yes."

"Can't tell you how much fun that was. You were always around when Mum and Dad were busy. In some ways, you brought me up, didn't you? Such lovely memories. But then I keep seeing Winter dousing my mum in petrol, or Dad's blood splattering the wall when Strickland put a bullet in his head. And I have to say that rather spoils those memories. Still, in honour of the years you spent caring for me before betraying my family to the man who murdered them, I will count to ten."

"What?" Her voice was colourless. Blue wondered when, or if, the shock would fade. He smiled at her in the darkness.

"You always counted to ten before coming to find me. When you got to ten, my heart would hammer in my chest. Exciting. Scary, too. Properly scary. I dreaded being found. When you did find me, we always laughed. You would tickle me, do you remember?"

"Yes." Still the drained, flat tone.

"Well, same arrangement now. I'll count to ten. You hide. You can go outside if you like. I'll count really, really slowly. It won't be any fun if I find you straight away, will it?"

Jimmy Blue reached out into the blackness, finding Rhoda's face. He rested his hand on her cheek, wet with tears. She trembled like that trapped rabbit. A sound like air escaping from a puncture came from her lips.

"Oh, and Auntie Rhoda? Just so we're clear. When I find you, I won't tickle you. You understand that, right? No laughing. Just—"

He made the sound every schoolchild knows how to make: that of a throat being cut.

"So you'd better find a fantastic place to hide. Right." He stood up, took two steps away from the bed. "Off you go. Ten."

Rhoda didn't hesitate. She bolted from the bed as if it were on fire. "Nine."

In the front room, she trod on the squeaky floorboard a moment before her shin smacked into the coffee table. Blue winced on her behalf, and called out after her, "Eight."

He pictured her dragging the wheeled suitcase out of the cupboard. Ready to run at a moment's notice.

"Seven."

The suitcase contained a pair of trainers, four changes of clothes, toiletries and make-up, a laptop, an external hard drive, a new mobile phone, and a fake passport in the name of Carla Outen. Jimmy Blue had used the time waiting for Rhoda to install spyware on the laptop and phone, plus tracking bugs in the trainers, the make-up bag, the suitcase itself, and all five pairs of shoes he'd found. The final tracker went in the sole of the boots she'd been wearing when she got home.

"Six."

Rhoda experienced some difficulty with the security chain. Blue pictured her scraping it back and forth, wearing pyjamas, her feet stuffed into unlaced boots.

"Five."

The chain came free, and she opened the door. Blue gave her a brief round of applause, which he doubted she appreciated. Wheels scraped along the gravel path. When she passed the wall, with just a brick's width between them, he said, "Four," wondering if she could hear him. She half-tripped, then moved faster, so he guessed the answer was yes.

The front gate smacked against the fence.

She must be out of earshot by now. He could cheat and stop counting if he liked. But no. That would make him as bad as her.

"Three."

He thought of his father's face, staring right into the barrel of Strickland's gun, his expression neutral. As if he'd already died. He didn't see his son struggling to get free of Marty.

"Two."

Rhoda had made quite a comfortable life for herself since that night. Tonight marked her return to the streets, where Mum found her before Tom was born. This time, it was different. She had clothes, credit cards, and five thousand Euros in the pocket at the back of the suitcase.

"One."

Blue opened a custom app on his phone. The screen showed a pulsating yellow dot on a blue map. Rather than aim for the main roads, Rhoda stuck to the side streets. His phone vibrated, and he opened another app. His screen now showed the screen of Rhoda's new phone. She was booking a car. It would be there in eight minutes. Ah. Smart. Rhoda changed the pickup location to a street bordering a small park. Somewhere for her to hide while waiting.

No hurry. Jimmy would find her when he was ready. He wanted Rhoda to be looking over her shoulder for a good while longer yet.

Blue let himself out of the flat, closing the door behind him. He walked to the gate, whistling. When he turned onto the road, he stopped for a moment, turning first left, then right, before following the route Rhoda had taken, albeit in no particular hurry.

"Coming," he whispered, "ready or not."

CHAPTER EIGHTEEN

On her twenty-second day in Paris, Rhoda called Winter.

It was thirty-three days since Tom Lewis came back from the dead.

Rhoda spent the first twenty-four hours getting as far away from Crouch End as possible. While waiting behind a hedge for the Uber to arrive, she stripped off her pyjamas, replacing them with jogging bottoms and a sweatshirt, convinced Tom's ghost would materialise any moment and kill her. In the back of the car, looking through the rear window and finding no one in pursuit, her rational mind broke through the internal shrieking of her superstitious subconscious.

What kind of ghost has breath you can feel on your face? Breath you can smell, too. And his hand was real enough. He's alive. Tom Lewis is alive.

Rhoda had never asked Winter about the night of the fire. She didn't want to know. But what remained of the Lewis house in Richmond had stood out like a rotten black tooth. It was one reason for moving north of the river, so she never saw that street again. But she couldn't avoid the news. Winter slapped a newspaper into Marty's hand months later. "Lucky you. You don't have to finish the job. The kid's dead." Rhoda hadn't been able to avoid the headline: *Tragic*

Lewis boy succumbs to injuries in hospital, after parents executed in suspected crime feud.

But he wasn't dead. The headline lied. Tom Lewis was coming after her. He had a list. And hers was the next name on it.

Rhoda used a cheap French burner phone to call Winter, blocking the number. She took the Metro to Gare du Nord and called from there. Since fleeing London, she preferred to be in busy public places. She struggled to sleep, never staying in the same hotel for longer than a night.

"Rhoda? Where are you?" Winter sounded displeased. Rhoda was glad of the three hundred miles and body of water between them.

"Away. I'm not telling you where."

"Like hell you aren't. Get over to the house."

"No."

The silence that followed meant she'd crossed a line. When Winter went quiet, bad things followed. She didn't wait for him to respond. "Did you read my email?"

The silence deepened. He had read it, then. Since working for Winter, Rhoda kept notes of dates, locations, names. Her written confession wouldn't be enough to destroy his organisation, but the attached audio recording from her phone would put him in prison for life.

Winter didn't scare her like Tom Lewis, or—what had he called himself?—Jimmy Blue. She had taken a circuitous route to Paris, heading across France by train towards Italy before doubling back by bus, cash only, staying in cheap guest houses. On arrival in the French capital, eight days after leaving home, she dared to hope she might be safe. On her seventh night in Paris, she saw him.

She was waiting for a train in Glacière station along with a knot of tourists and commuters. A bruised purple sky pressed against the glass roof and hanging lamps cast pools of light on the reflective floor. The eastbound train to Nation arrived on the far track. When it pulled away, its passengers making their way to the exit, she registered one figure on the platform opposite. Before looking up from her copy of *Le Monde*, she knew. There was an awful inevitability about it.

Even that first glance was enough. She'd tried to persuade herself that the voice in the darkness might have belonged to a stranger, but she'd watched Tom Lewis grow up. She'd know him anywhere. And this was him. The boy had become a man. He was tall. Bulky, too. His physical presence washed across her in a wave of fear. Inch by inch, her head moved to face him again. Rhoda wanted to close her eyes, but didn't dare. If she did, she was half-convinced he would be standing in front of her when she opened them again.

The figure on the opposite platform maintained a preternatural stillness. Big hands hung by his sides. He wore jeans and a white shirt, with a light brown jacket. On his head—and Rhoda only just prevented herself from giggling when she saw it—was a black beret. If she laughed, she might not stop.

The train approached with the usual metallic scream. Her body moved heavily, limbs clumsy, thoughts treacled to sludge. Then the clanking carriages, lit butter yellow inside, broke the physical connection between her and Tom. She jerked forward, almost falling through the doors. Rhoda sat facing front and told herself not to turn her head. But she had to. If he was still there, at least it meant he wasn't sprinting across the bridge to board her train. And maybe it wasn't Tom, just some tired Parisian on their way home. So she looked. And, as soon as she did, the man on the other platform removed his beret to show Rhoda an angry red ridge of scarring where, twenty years earlier, Marty Nicholson shot him.

Tom Lewis smiled at her.

"No. No. No." Rhoda put her face in her hands as the train jolted into motion. She told herself over and over that terror combined with lack of sleep had brought on a hallucination.

After that night, she changed hotels daily. She stuck to crowds when outside and kept moving. The anonymous millions gave the illusion of safety, but Rhoda knew it for an illusion. She began to think the creature following her wasn't human. She picked up a cheap rosary, but her belief in her supernatural pursuer was stronger than faith in an omniscient deity.

Winter was still talking at the other end of the burner phone.

Rhoda watched hundreds of passing faces in Gare du Nord, her eyes flitting from one to the next, checking. Winter's words, soaked in menace, might as well have been in an ancient language she'd never learned. His tone suggested he was threatening her. Rhoda screwed her eyes up, shook her head, and interrupted him.

"It doesn't matter what you say, Winter. I'm not about to email my confession to the police. There's something else. Something I need to tell you."

Since that night on the Metro, she had seen Tom—Jimmy Blue —twice.

For more than a week after the Metro sighting, she moved from hotel to hotel, sometimes more than once a day, using back exits where possible. She dyed her greying hair jet black and took to wearing headscarves. She replaced her clothes, choosing pastel colours that didn't suit her. Her shoes were the only items she didn't change—she was doing a lot of walking. She almost always wore her trainers, the most comfortable shoes she owned. Not wanting to admit she only wore them in case she needed to run.

She was crossing a road when a bicycle swerved to avoid her, its rider ringing the bell furiously.

"Sorry. Sorry." She stepped back onto the pavement. "Désolée. Excusez-moi."

"Pah!" A Parisian response. As the cyclist pedalled away, he looked back at her and she gasped, dropping her shopping bag and smashing the wine bottle inside. A bearded man with short, teak-brown hair. Unmistakable dark green eyes. Rhoda was left shaking and sobbing.

Three nights after that, she had been buying vodka in a twenty-four-hour shop. While she paid, a drunk man stumbled past, leaning against the shop window, singing incoherently, and laughing. He was dressed like an ageing skateboarder; black trainers, black trousers, white T-shirt, black baseball cap over his dirty long blonde hair. The shopkeeper banged on the glass, and the drunk held up a hand in apology, pushing himself away, staggering a few steps forward, then back again. He was big. Really big. And the song lyrics; not French. English.

"I'm Death I come to take the soul
Leave the body and leave it cold
To draw up the flesh off of the frame
Dirt and worm both have a claim"

Rhoda watched the drunk spin and twist, wheel and caper, steadying himself against bins, walls, or parked cars. She stood at the shop counter for five minutes after he was out of sight, muttering to herself. The shopkeeper didn't bother to hide his relief when she left.

Back in the hotel room, she sat on the thin mattress and drank warm vodka straight from the bottle until she passed out.

"Well? What do you bloody want, then?"

Rhoda had drifted off into her own thoughts again. Winter's voice brought her back to the Gare du Nord. She was doing this more and more, allowing her thoughts to become as real as the ground beneath her feet, the sounds and smells of the travellers in the echoing space, the plastic phone pressed against her ear.

"It's Tom Lewis."

"Who?"

"You know who." Even Winter, with his reputation, hadn't killed so many people that he'd forget slaughtering an entire family.

"He's dead, Rhoda."

"No, Winter, he's not. Or maybe he is." She laughed, smothering the sound when it threatened to get out of control. "I don't know. But he came to see me. He told me he killed Marty. He has a list. I imagine your name is on it. But I'm next."

"You've lost your mind. He's dead. They're all dead."

"Maybe. But I saw him, Winter. He spoke to me. He's playing with me now. He might kill me next week, or next month. But he'll do it. And he'll kill you, too. He's not human. He's..." She fished for a word, eventually snagging a memory from her native language. "He's a *bauk.*"

"A what?"

Rhoda had last heard that word while sitting at her grandmother's feet back in Serbia as a child. "*Bauk*," she repeated. "Demon." She remembered what he had called himself. "Jimmy Blue."

"Get a grip, Rhoda. I'll look into this Tom Lewis nonsense, all right? Call me back in a few days."

Something had changed in Winter's voice. She put the phone in her bag. She needed a drink.

———

In the kitchen of a six-million pound steel, glass, and brick house in Elstree, Winter took out a calfskin wallet and removed a piece of paper, unfolding it on the quartz worktop. He stared at the words until it was too dark to make them out.

Jimmy Blue is coming.

CHAPTER NINETEEN

EARLY OCTOBER, and an Indian summer kept the Paris streets busy well into the evening. At the end of each unseasonably warm day, the locals smiled, or rolled their eyes, at tourists shivering in shirtsleeves and thin dresses.

Friday night arrived cloudless and cold, with a full moon.

Rhoda was drunk. She had never been more than a casual drinker, but since seeing Tom Lewis on the Metro platform, she carried bottles of vodka in her handbag. A few days of experimentation, and she could maintain a level of inebriation that allowed her to function without drawing attention to herself. It numbed the fear. It was still there, but more like a persistent toothache than a twisting blade in her gut.

She stayed out every night until the streets got too quiet for comfort, then headed back to the latest hotel. Today's choice was a last-minute cancellation in a four-star near the Eiffel Tower, so she kept the famous landmark in sight as she hovered close to the tourists, taking a gulp from her bottle every few minutes.

It didn't take much for that numb fear to flare up into something more urgent. A glimpse of anyone over six feet tall would dry her mouth in an instant.

The *bauk* constantly occupied her thoughts. Her superstitious grandmother spoke of demonic creatures as matter-of-factly as she did members of the family. Baka Ana, knitting in the corner while Rhoda sat at her feet, told her *bauks* lived in dark places like caves or abandoned houses. The creatures loved the shadows, avoiding light and noise. The thing in her bedroom had appeared in utter darkness and, since then, only haunted her at night. Rhoda felt safer during the day. By spending her evenings in noisy crowds and public places, she hoped she might spot him coming, at least.

Tonight, she circled the Fontaine des Quatre Parties du Monde for over an hour, as visitors came and went. Her constant pacing, pausing to sit at every point of the compass, allowed her to watch for the *bauk*. This end of the Marco Polo garden abutted well-lit streets, giving her plenty of options if she needed to run. She spent time by the fountains most evenings. She didn't know what the statues represented—four women holding the world aloft; horses plunging through the water; dolphins and turtles. The energy and power of the tableau captivated Rhoda with its optimism, its celebration of life. It didn't make her happy. Nothing did anymore. But it distracted her. Sometimes, she forgot what was coming for a minute at a time.

She was perched on the edge, trailing her hand in the freezing water, staying close to a loud, laughing group of Canadian tourists, when she saw him. The light from the lampposts on either side of the fountain didn't quite reach the line of trees beyond, but passing cars lit the watching figure from behind. He wore a hooded top, and his sizeable frame looked even bulkier.

Rhoda got to her feet, squinting. It might not be him. But he stood so still, as still as the bronze figures in the fountain. She looked left and right, then back at the hooded man. It could be anyone. She fumbled in her bag for the vodka. Someone tapped her on the shoulder.

"Aaagh!" Rhoda scrambled backwards to get away, before registering the shocked expression on the woman who had touched her.

"Jeez, I'm so sorry. I didn't mean to startle you, ma'am. Are you okay?"

Rhoda nodded, coughing to prevent her body from unleashing a scream. "I'm fine. Fine. You surprised me, that's all."

"We're visiting from Toronto. A European tour. Paris is a beautiful city, right?"

"Right." Rhoda peered back at the trees. The figure had gone. She looked up and down the avenue. Nothing. "I'm sorry. What did you say?"

The woman held something towards her. A piece of paper. No, a ticket. "One of our friends is ill. We have a spare ticket to the Montparnasse Tower. You get an amazing view of the Eiffel Tower from up there. Very romantic. Seems a shame to waste a ticket. I wondered if you'd like it?"

Rhoda scanned the area for signs of the *bauk*. Gone. If he had ever been there. She looked at the tourists. There were two more couples besides those offering her the ticket, all in their twenties. Wholesome, young, beautiful, their entire lives in front of them. They laughed loudly and often. And the Montparnasse Tower was a busy tourist spot. She would be safe there. She forced a smile onto her face and wondered if they could smell the alcohol on her breath.

"I'd love it. Thank you. That's so kind. Are you going now?"

"Yes, we are. Wanna tag along?"

Rhoda hoped she didn't look as haggard as she felt. "That would be lovely. Thank you."

"Hey, it's our pleasure. I love your accent. Where are you from? London? What's your name? I'm Aileen."

The vodka bottle was empty. Rhoda left it on the stone lip of the fountain and followed her new friends.

The Canadians talked non-stop on the walk to the tower and didn't stop until the lift doors opened at the top floor. They climbed steps onto a busy rooftop with seating areas, coin-operated telescopes and a bar, surrounded by high glass safety panels.

Aileen winked and said, "I think you'll love it up here, Rhoda. It's romantic, isn't it?" Rhoda found it strange, even insensitive, that the woman put such a heavy emphasis on the word *romantic*. To all appearances, she was a single woman, alone in Paris. In her dirty trainers, leggings, jumper, and jacket, she hardly glowed with *joie de vivre*. But Aileen's smile had been positively conspiratorial. Rhoda thanked them again and left to explore on her own.

She wanted a drink. For the price of one glass of champagne here, she could buy a bottle of *supermarché* vodka later. She circled the rooftop in the same way that she'd circled the fountain, checking every big male, making sure the *bauk* hadn't followed her. The open area was dimly lit, but noisy with people. He wasn't here. Fresh groups spilled out of the lifts. Rhoda was surrounded by tourists. She relaxed fractionally.

She ended up on the opposite side to the Eiffel Tower. Fewer people lingered to admire the city from here. They wanted photos with the most famous building in Paris as the backdrop. Rhoda stared out towards the Seine, not really registering the view. Her thoughts returned to the Lewis family.

The *bauk* asked if she had lived a good life. He knew the answer, as did she. Rhoda had made bad choices. Helping Winter twenty years ago might have been the worst choice of all. But she'd only agreed to help when Winter swore he wouldn't hurt Tom. No, Rhoda realised, that was her worst choice. Choosing to believe Winter. The blood of that child on her hands. Or whatever that child had become.

A shape moved closer in the reflective glass between her and the Parisian night.

"Hey." The Canadian woman again. Aileen. She held one of the overpriced champagnes in one hand. Her expression looked familiar. A brow furrowed in concern, a warm smile, body language friendly and unthreatening. Oh. That was why Rhoda recognised it. She wore the same expression when approaching candidates for Winter. In Aileen's case, it was genuine.

The Canadian offered her a tissue. Rhoda realised she'd been crying. The woman stood next to her for a while without speaking, while she blew her nose and wiped her face. Then she leaned closer and put a hand on her upper arm.

"Rhoda, I shouldn't do this, shouldn't spoil the surprise, but you seem so sad."

"Surprise?"

Aileen looked over her shoulder. "Yes. Please don't tell him I said anything. I just wanted you to know it's okay. Better than okay. Between you and your boyfriend, I mean."

"My boyfriend?" Rhoda glanced past Aileen to the stairs leading down to the lifts. She didn't want to be stuck two hundred metres up with a lunatic.

"Yes. Our friend isn't really sick. Your boyfriend gave us the ticket. He's about to propose. He flew out secretly. It's so romantic, I could die. He'll be here any minute. Please, please, please, act surprised. God, I'm terrible at keeping my mouth shut. You're not mad at me, are you?"

"My boyfriend?" Rhoda repeated. She saw the future, visualising Aileen's next words as if they were printed on a ribbon spooling out of her mouth. If she got hold of the ribbon, stuffed the words back, the future might change.

Aileen must have seen something in Rhoda's eyes she didn't like. She backed up in a hurry, stumbling in her haste to get out of range.

"Got to go. Good luck. Jimmy seems like a lovely guy."

Rhoda didn't reply. She was back in Crouch End, the fear consuming her. She scanned the faces again. No Tom. Tourists, mostly couples, arms around each other, whispering, laughing, kissing. A maintenance guy in a hard hat fixing the machine that promised *Le Plus Haut Selfie de Paris!* The bar staff, nearing the end of their shifts, looked bored. She should leave. Now.

Then the maintenance guy turned around, and everything stopped.

The *bauk*.

CHAPTER TWENTY

JIMMY BLUE ATTACHED Rhoda's old phone to the selfie photo machine. When he'd secured it, he tapped on the camera icon, selected video, and started recording.

In a moment of satisfying synchronicity, he turned to Rhoda at the exact moment she saw him.

The anger that burned through his body felt different this time. Marty Nicholson was a would-be thug, willing to point a loaded gun at a twelve-year-old boy's head and pull the trigger. Tom Lewis had seen the agony of indecision crystallise into action as Marty chose the path that led to his own death twenty years later.

Rhoda Ilích was different. Rhoda had killed no one. Not directly. Her flat contained no weapons other than a can of pepper spray. But the Traitor's transgressions outweighed those of the Forger's.

Tom Lewis grew up with Rhoda as a second mother. When he fell and scraped his knee, Rhoda fetched the antiseptic cream and plasters. She did most of the cooking, too. Sunday night meant a rich stew, the precise ingredients of which Rhoda never divulged. Years later, walking back to the latest bedsit after a day's manual labour, Tom stopped short, catching the faintest scent of caramelised onions, garlic and herbs. For a moment he was back in the family kitchen, handing Auntie Rhoda vegetables to peel and chop.

Twelve-year-olds are quick to pick up on adult problems. Weeks before the night of his parents' deaths, Tom sensed Rhoda withdrawing. For months, an uncomfortable gulf had opened between her and his mother. They discussed domestic matters as if nothing were wrong. But his mother acted colder, and Rhoda withdrew, becoming distant. For the boy who watched and listened as the unspoken tension increased, it was a time of turmoil. Relationships he thought would last forever were in danger of failing.

Rhoda had betrayed them. That was the terrible, unforgivable truth. But Tom could have stopped it.

Biking home from school one afternoon, Tom took his turn to buy cigarettes from the newsagents. Harry bought the last pack, so they could crouch behind the concrete hillocks of the skatepark, sucking in hot sandpaper breaths and trying not to be the first to cough. Tom hated the taste, but that wasn't really the point of the ritual.

He left his bike with Harry and walked across the road to the row of shops; two-and-a-half miles from home, a part of London he rarely visited. Everyone at school knew the newsagent there sold cigarettes to school kids. Booze, too.

His voice hadn't yet broken, so Tom cultivated a harsh rasp that made him sound like a stroke victim with a sore throat. The middle-aged Indian man behind the counter had to ask him to repeat himself. When Tom did so, his voice emerged as a clear, piping treble. His face went red. The shopkeeper handed over the contraband without comment. Coming out of the shop, Tom stuffed his hands in his pockets and hurried back to his friend. As he passed the cafe next door, he slowed, then stopped, peered through the glass. A man in a suit, sitting in a booth at the back, talking to a woman wearing a headscarf. Something about the way the woman's head moved. Rhoda. He waited until he was sure. Rhoda had told him she was meeting a girlfriend to go shopping, not drinking coffee with a serious-looking man in a suit. A boyfriend? Tom's stomach tightened at the thought. If Rhoda got married, would she leave them? He would be thirteen in a few months, practically an adult, but the thought of Rhoda leaving made him pout like a toddler. He swallowed hard. But, looking at the man, his hard, fixed countenance, pale blue eyes as devoid of expression as a lizard, Tom surmised this was no romantic tryst. This was business. What kind of business?

Tom didn't tell his parents. He kept Rhoda's secret. What harm could come of it?

Less than a week later, his mother was dead, burned alive after seeing her husband die. And the man with the pale blue eyes watched it all with the same disinterested expression. Tom could have stopped it. If he hadn't been loyal to Auntie Rhoda. He could have stopped it.

He was responsible for his parents' deaths. Now Jimmy Blue would avenge them.

A light breeze carrying an autumnal chill whipped across the roof of the Montparnasse Tower, causing couples to huddle together, or solitary tourists to pull jackets over their shoulders and shiver. Rhoda didn't shiver. She looked straight at Blue as he approached, the trapped animal glaze in her eyes. She sank into her terror, all hope evaporating.

When he took her by the hand and led her away from the glass barriers, she complied wordlessly. The Canadian woman looked on, unsure how to react.

"He promised me he wouldn't hurt you," said Rhoda, her voice quiet and tired. "I would never have done it otherwise."

Her voice trailed away. She looked up into his face. "All grown up, Tommy."

Jimmy Blue fought an urge to correct her. No one had called him Tommy for over two decades. A dead name for a dead boy.

Rhoda squeezed his hand. "It was no place for a child. And she wanted to bring you into the business. Your father..." Rhoda stared through him. "Your father did as he was told. I didn't want that for you. I tried... I tried..."

Rhoda laughed. The wind lifted the cold, shrill sound away from the tower, thinning it further as it blew across the Parisian rooftops, losing coherence until it became a whisper.

"I'm sorry, Tommy."

Rhoda dropped Blue's hand. "I'm ready."

This wasn't how Jimmy had imagined it. During the months of preparation, the nights following Rhoda around London, as she picked up desperate young women and men, delivering them into slavery, he'd never imagined this.

He saw no fear now, no remorse, no emotion. Just emptiness. So be it. He twisted Rhoda to face away from him, then gripped her body with two hands, his left hand bunching up the material of her sweat-shirt at the neck, his right twisting the waistband of her jogging bottoms to get a secure grip.

She offered no resistance as he lifted her over his head. She had been such a solid presence in his life for so long, it surprised him how insubstantial she was when he hoisted her into the air.

Jimmy Blue had studied videos of sudden, unexpected violence in public places. A fight breaking out without warning, a gun drawn at a football game in America, a man producing a machete in a bar. He didn't care about the perpetrators of these acts. Who knew what drove them to breaking point? It was those around them that Blue watched. He needed to know how people reacted in an unexpected crisis. How fast they responded, what their instinctive first reaction was likely to be. And he found that, in almost every case, people followed predictable patterns of behaviour. The first stage was acknowledgement. Something happening that shouldn't be happen-ing. Conventional reality interrupted. Conversations stopped, heads turning. The threat evaluated. Stage two was frozen shock. If the threat was great enough, such as the appearance of a semi-automatic weapon, stage two moved to stage three: fight or flight. Jimmy Blue knew that flight was, by far, the most likely outcome. Oddly, the more people there were, the slimmer the chances anyone chose to fight. If a man draws a gun in a bar with six people in it, there's a ten to fifteen percent chance someone will try to take it from him. Make that sixty people, and the odds drop to less than one percent. The behaviour of crowds is comfortingly predictable.

There were ninety-seven people on the roof of the Montparnasse Tower. The seventeen people looking in his direction when he lifted Rhoda over his head moved quickly through stage one to stage two. Their reaction spread to others on the rooftop. By the time Blue had begun his run-up, thirty-four people were watching. No one moved. The usual predictable reactions were exacerbated by how unusual the situation was. Rhoda's lack of resistance added a surreal extra element. Most faces had adopted an open-mouthed, wide-eyed look of horror, but a significant minority looked on with something more akin to idle curiosity. Perhaps they thought they were watching a reality tv show. The camera on Rhoda's phone was recording everything, but the intended audience of the video was one man.

Six paces. He accelerated from a standing start, twisting his body to hoist Rhoda like a human javelin. Jimmy drew the woman back in readiness for the throw. The glass barrier—ten feet high—was there to discourage any tourism-unfriendly suicide attempts. No one had considered the possibility of a very large, very strong man throwing a small woman off the tower. It was quite an oversight by the architects.

Rhoda didn't scream. She fell in silence, lending another layer of surreality to the already unlikely scene.

In the pregnant seconds of awed shock that followed, Blue retrieved the phone and walked to the stairs, shrugging off his jacket as he did so.

CHAPTER TWENTY-ONE

JIMMY BLUE HAD PLANNED his exit, allowing an extra minute for unexpected contingencies. Happily, he couldn't have asked for a more accommodating group of onlookers. They moved aside as if choreographed.

With Rhoda's phone in his pocket, he made for the central stairwell that led to the lifts and fifty-nine floors of stairs. He took off the hard hat, hanging it on a door handle as he passed, his scalp hidden under a blue bandana.

The first scream came as he opened the emergency staircase door with André's four-digit security code. André had also supplied the hard hat and an excellent escape route. Jimmy was very fond of André.

The stairs zigzagged from the top of Montparnasse Tower to the bottom, twenty-four steps per floor, fifty-nine floors, fourteen hundred and sixteen steps in total. Blue was fit, strong, and motivated. He averaged seven seconds per floor. Even that was too slow: six minutes total. Enough time for a lockdown until the police arrived. In that situation, Jimmy's natural advantages—his height, bulk, strength, and intelligence—would be of little use to him. He would be identified and arrested. He needed a less predictable escape route.

Blue sprinted down twenty-eight floors. Three minutes. No sirens yet. In the next few minutes, the security staff would run emergency protocols, dispatching a guard to locate what was left of Rhoda. Blue had identified four locations where a body would be hard to spot from the street. Rhoda should have landed behind a display board advertising a Van Gogh exhibition.

They would find the body within five minutes, but the police would be on their way sooner.

As he climbed out of the window on the thirty-first floor, Jimmy Blue heard the first sirens. The wind whipped around his face as he jumped.

André managed a muffled scream as Blue's weight caused the window-cleaning cradle to rock violently, a hundred metres above the concrete.

"Sorry. Were you sleeping? I tried to be as quick as I could."

This prompted another muffled sound from the blindfolded, tied, and gagged man at his feet. Blue picked up the coiled mountaineering rope and dropped it over the side.

Jimmy stripped off the grey boiler suit, revealing a dirt-encrusted sweatshirt of indeterminate colour beneath. The jeans he wore were equally filthy. He stepped into the harness he'd left, then clipped the carabiner to the descender, looping the rope through the metal device.

He put a tatty rucksack on his back and bent down to give André a friendly pat on the shoulder.

"Sorry about tying you up. They'll find you soon. I'm glad your English was better than my French. It's so hard to threaten someone in a foreign language. Oh, and thank you for the security code."

The trussed-up window cleaner replied with a series of incoherent grunts.

"True," smiled Blue as if he understood perfectly. "But it might be better if you exaggerate when the police ask. Say I held a big, sharp knife to your throat. No one could blame you then. And I do have a big, sharp knife."

André squeaked.

"Au revoir to you too." He climbed over the side of the cradle, leaped into space, and rappelled the remaining distance to the ground in seventeen seconds.

Jimmy Blue unclipped the rope and ran to the street, ducking behind a shut-up news kiosk. He opened the rucksack, taking out a long, matted wig, dirt-brown streaked with grey. The bandana went around his neck, and he peeled away the non-stick side of the tape on his scalp before manoeuvring the wig into position. He rubbed his hands in the gutter and spread dirt over his face and neck. He removed the half-litre of gin in the rucksack, dabbing it on his neck like aftershave. Blue gargled and spat a mouthful. The final touch was a splash of gin onto his crotch.

Police cars and ambulances strobed coloured lights across the tower's entrance as tourists and locals honed in, desperate for information. The few people moving away from the tower stood out. Jimmy Blue knew police officers would watch those few, ready to act.

He waited behind the kiosk until a cluster of old women hurried past. He tagged along behind them to the front of the tower where two gendarmes discouraged the growing crowd from getting closer and refused to answer questions.

Four police cars and one ambulance blocked the entrance. Inside the building, confused tourists with tickets for the roof huddled in small groups, exchanging whatever morsels of information they had gleaned.

Blue waited a few minutes until he could see the young gendarmes' patience turning to irritation. Two more police cars arrived, and the gendarmes shouted at the crowd to let them through. As the growing number of bodies closed back in behind the vehicles, Blue pushed to the front, turned his back to the tower, the flashing lights, and the gendarmes, and began begging. He held out his grimy hands, cupping them together and muttering, "S'il vous plait," over and over. When he reached the end of the line, he reversed, asking the same people a second time. A few complied, dropping coins into his palm, but most ignored him, wrinkling their noses in disgust at the smell. The gin combined with the dog shit Blue had mopped up with the jumper produced a unique perfume.

The youngest gendarme acted just as Blue had hoped. A third pass of the crowd, and a gloved hand landed on his shoulder.

"Monsieur! Vous cherchez quoi, exactement? Passez! C'est une scène de crime."

Jimmy, shoulders slumped, and affecting a limp, turned to the officer and gave him the full benefit of his gin-soaked breath, enjoying the flinch that resulted.

"S'il vous plait?"

The gendarme pushed him away, wiping his hand on his trouser leg. Jimmy Blue disappeared into the crowd, which let him through more readily than they had the emergency vehicles. After counting to thirty, he pushed back to the front and repeated the procedure, working along the line towards the same gendarme.

The unwitting gendarme played his part perfectly, marching Blue away from the tower, accompanying the brief journey with a stream of rapid French. Jimmy's limited grasp of the language didn't prevent him from accurately interpreting the gendarme's meaning. He was to go away and not return. Should he return, he would be arrested. Blue thought he was being described as a 'tantalising squirrel', but conceded that might be a translation error on his part.

A last sharp shove in the direction of the Seine, and the young gendarme turned back to rejoin his colleagues at the tower, shuddering at having been so close to the stinking, incoherent beggar.

Jimmy Blue shuffled along the streets, smiling. In a skip alongside a scaffolded building, he retrieved the duffel bag he'd left under a layer of plaster and rubble. Five minutes later, a tall, ponytailed man emerged from the public toilets near Notre Dame. He wore olive chinos, a white shirt, and a corduroy jacket with leather patches on the elbows. Jimmy Blue checked his reflection in a shop window, wondering if the round John Lennon glasses were overkill. He looked like a geography teacher who'd mislaid his class. He laughed at his own reflection.

Back in his hotel, Blue packed his few belongings and booked a ticket on the first train to London in the morning. He connected Rhoda's phone to the hotel Wi-Fi, scrolled down to Winter's name in her contacts, and sent the video he'd recorded on top of the Montparnasse Tower. Then he turned off the lights and pressed record again.

CHAPTER TWENTY-TWO

SUVINDER PUSHED his brush along the middle of the platform, flicking the dirt and debris of the afternoon and evening into a pile. He tilted the metal dustpan to open it, swept the rubbish inside, and deposited the result in the sack he dragged behind him. He took pride in keeping his end of St Pancras International station tidy, but that wasn't his current objective. He wanted to take another look at the frozen man.

Suvinder's earbuds were in place, but no self-improvement podcasts offered inspiration to his receptive mind. No music played. He wanted to hear if the frozen man said anything. So far, there seemed little danger of that. He hadn't moved a muscle in the last four hours.

The cleaner pushed his broom a little closer. Not too close, though. The frozen man scared him. He was huge, for one thing. And he carried his own, clearly delineated, atmosphere around him. The platform often got crowded as trains arrived, and passengers occasionally headed for the far end of the station where the silent, immobile figure waited. But everyone who got within ten yards of the man experienced a sudden change of heart, avoided his bench, and allowed him to maintain his solitude.

Suvinder had come closer than most before succumbing to the same urge to divert. Close enough to experience the physical presence of the man. Also close enough to see the intelligent eyes staring straight ahead, unseeing, tears wetting his cheeks. For a moment, Suvinder had considered approaching the stranger. He believed it was important to show compassion to all. He was also, by nature, very curious. Another half step and the invisible energy coming from the frozen man increased threefold. He stopped. Compassion was all very well, but the famously curious cat had come to a sticky end which he'd rather avoid.

He had been struck by the agony on the man's face. Whatever might have led to this personal tragedy, Suvinder pitied this individual. He had a noble quality, like a hero from an ancient myth.

With the crowds gone, and the station quiet, the silent figure became more eerie. It was getting cold. Surely the frozen man must have somewhere to go? He had luggage, a big rucksack on the bench beside him. Was someone supposed to meet him? Suvinder wondered if he were witnessing the end of a doomed relationship. An epic, operatic, doomed relationship.

He brushed imaginary dirt over the lip of the platform onto the track, then swept his way back towards the bench. Apart from his size, nothing about the frozen man drew attention. He dressed in loose, grey tracksuit bottoms and a hoodie. Old trainers on his feet, a black wool cap pulled over his head. Suvinder recognised the outfit, as he'd worn the same many times. Some people dressed that way to go jogging, or to lounge around the house. If you dressed like it every day, you were likely one of London's manual workers. Zero-hour contracts, long hours, low pay.

The invisible energy field wasn't there. Suvinder stopped short, far enough away to avoid any violent reaction should there be an unfortunate misunderstanding. The head had dropped a little. The frozen man's bench stood between two overhead lamps, and their light didn't stretch to illuminating the heavy face.

Another step forward. The man's eyes were closed now, the broad chest swelling and falling with sleep. Good. A kind of peace, even if it could only be attained through exhaustion. The beginning of healing, perhaps.

The big head dropped further, then the body sagged like a discarded puppet. Suvinder jumped in shock. He wished the illumination was clearer. As incredible as it appeared, he believed the frozen man was changing shape. Gone were the noble features, the agonised intelligence, the sense of danger. This was no apex predator to avoid. This was someone else. Someone broken; diminished. Someone Suvinder wasn't afraid to help.

"Sir?"

The man's eyes opened, looking around him in slow bewilderment before settling on the friendly, open countenance in front of him. He reached up to adjust his bandana. For half a second, Suvinder glimpsed a hard mass of scars on the shaved head.

"You were asleep, yes? Perhaps you missed your train. Can I help you?"

"Mm." A shake of the head. Then the man looked across at the station nameboard on the opposite platform, frowning.

"S-," he sounded out. "P?"

"Yes, sir. St Pancras International station. That's right." Suvinder couldn't work out what had happened. He looked up and down the platform, as if to identify the frozen man's whereabouts. Because this couldn't be him.

When the man stood, Suvinder took an involuntary step back. The lost expression remained on the man's features as he moved, stretching out his legs, bringing some flexibility back to his numbed muscles. He reached into his pocket and pulled out some euro notes, looking at them blankly. Then he tried another pocket and found a credit card holder. He produced an Oyster card.

"Tube."

"Yes. Let me show you. Don't forget your bag. Where do you want to go?"

"Mm. Mm. Soho, Soho."

"No problem. It's a five-minute walk to King's Cross. Take the Jubilee line to Oxford Circus. This way, sir."

Suvinder set off down the platform, checking to confirm that the man was following. The big man carried the heavy-looking rucksack as easily as if it were stuffed with bubble wrap. They followed the King's Cross Underground signs, stopping at the main glass doors.

Suvinder put a hand on the man's shoulder. He wouldn't have dared do the same twenty minutes ago. "Do you need help getting there?"

"Okay. Mm. N-no. Mm ... thank you."

A shy smile, then he pushed the door open and headed out onto the street. Suvinder watched until the bulky figure rounded the corner. He knew he'd just met someone extraordinary, but his emotional response—which one of his self-improvement podcasts had encouraged him to monitor—remained all over the shop.

Part of him wanted to hurry after the frozen man, make sure he was all right, as he seemed vulnerable and confused.

The other part of Suvinder, the part that won the silent argument at the ticket barrier, wanted to be far away from the individual who had sat on the bench for the past four hours. Because there was something compelling and terrifying about the frozen man. Something fundamentally wrong. Something that bypassed the frontal cortex, finding the most ancient part of Suvinder's brain and issuing a clear warning: keep away.

———

At a dinner party in Shoreditch, Winter excused himself, taking his phone outside. He hadn't been expecting to hear from Rhoda again, especially from this number. She'd used a burner when she'd called him last.

Her message had come in last night, but he hadn't opened it straight away. Making her wait for his response might remind Rhoda exactly how far down the food chain she was.

He downloaded the message and pressed play on the video, which was sixteen seconds long. When it had finished, he played it again, paying special attention to the man who'd lifted Rhoda over his head like a sack of potatoes. After throwing her from the building, her killer walked directly past the camera before turning it off, holding his hand to shield his face.

Winter stayed where he was for a few minutes, his expression unreadable. A methodical man, his response to what he'd seen would be measured and well-planned.

There were two more messages from Rhoda's phone. The first was text only.

I have an audio recording that would interest you. I'm not in it, but you are.

So Rhoda hadn't been bluffing. That complicated things.

The second message was another video, too dark to make anything out. Winter increased the brightness. Someone spoke. He started the video again, holding the phone's speaker to his ear. The voice wasn't speaking; it was singing.

"The children prayed, the preacher preached
Time and mercy is out of your reach
I'll fix your feet 'til you can't walk
I'll lock your jaw 'til you can't talk"

When the singing stopped, Winter took the phone away from his ear. Twenty-two seconds remained. He listened again. Silence, then a sound that lifted the hairs on his spine. A low chuckle. Then the voice of a dead man.

"Poor Tom. Poor, poor Tom."

Silence. The voice came closer. Whispering in Winter's ear.

"See you soon."

CHAPTER TWENTY-THREE

ROBERT WINTER, in as far as he ever loved anything, loved his house.

He never married. Aged fourteen, his father took him to a brothel and showed him what money could buy, which turned out to be almost anything. Young, old, fat, thin, male, female, any nationality, any personality. The best whores were excellent actors, faking nymphomania, or the frigidity of an upper-class virgin. Winter preferred the genuine article. As he got older, he discovered his tastes were not unique, and he recognised a business opportunity. A talented escort might be able to act the part of a well-educated middle-class girl forced into a life of sexual humiliation, but she would never be perfect. Far better if the girl underneath you genuinely graduated with a 2:1 from York and owned an Irish setter called Giles.

Sexual relationships, for Winter, weren't indicators of affection or commitment, but a release valve. He had no doubt that, were most people able to access the same well-stocked sexual larder, the societal norms of marriage and monogamy would fall apart like wet tissue.

Winter had no children or pets. He considered friendship an interesting concept, although only if it might benefit him. Winter enjoyed the clarity of self-knowledge. He was a narcissist and a psychopath. The labels didn't upset him. He doubted either condition put him at a disadvantage. Quite the opposite. It freed him from the sticky web of relationships holding most people back. Unencumbered by notions of loyalty, trust, or affection, he remained clear-sighted.

But he loved his house.

He'd commissioned it four years earlier. The architect, French, chic, and ridiculously expensive, came with a shelf-ful of awards and the fees to match. The architect was surprised to start with no restrictions, as the existing dwelling had been flattened. He mentioned planning regulations and building control, protesting when Winter showed him the pile of rubble that remained of the original Edwardian house. But a phone call from the local authority convinced the architect to go ahead. The head of planning, a mother of two healthy children, assured the architect that Mr Winter had done everyone a favour by pulling the old house down. She encouraged the architect to do anything Mr Winter asked. Anything at all.

Winter wanted a post-modern castle. The ideal of one man, a leader, in an echoing fortress was appealing. Not literally. There would be no draughty stone halls in Winter's castle. It would be concrete, fully insulated, with vast triple-glazed windows. The architect made his vision a reality, down to the modern dungeon below ground level. On that part of the blueprints, the prim little Frenchman marked it as a *playroom* and winked when discussing it. Winter let him call the soundproof room whatever he liked. *Playroom* wasn't entirely inaccurate, after all.

The work itself progressed smoothly. No disagreements about money, no arguments over schedules. The house was furnished at the close of a glorious summer and, on the day Winter moved in, he enjoyed a glass of chilled Manzanilla on the south terrace, overlooking the city of London. His own hidden empire lay in Britain's capital, and his move to this modern castle was a symbolic moment.

Winter's organisation relied on men and women afraid of him. Fear was the most effective management technique. Appealing to greed didn't work. Those who could be bought would always be open to a higher offer. Respect was all very well, but find the right nerve to probe, the weakness to exploit, the fires of ambition to fan, and respect crumbled like stale cake. No. Fear worked. Easy to maintain, too. Punish mistakes with ruthless cruelty and make sure everyone knows about it. Don't just have someone killed. Skin them and strangle them with their own intestines, then post the pictures online. For example.

The only man who didn't fear him was Strickland, but they had an agreement. Strickland started out as Winter's enforcer, becoming so successful that he'd built his own lucrative business as a reliable and discreet hired killer. Winter recognised talent and encouraged Strickland to expand, taking on outside clients. Winter always came first, should he need to call upon his colleague's services. Strickland owed him.

When Marty Nicholson was found dead, Winter's nephew cold and stiff a few feet away, it looked like an ill-advised hit by someone who didn't know who they had targeted. No criminal outfit in London had the balls to take on Winter. If they did, they wouldn't start at the bottom with Marty. They'd come straight for Winter, knowing if they failed, they, and everyone they knew, died.

But then a contact at the Met passed on the note.

Jimmy Blue is coming.

Winter researched the name online, finding little of interest. A Scottish folk musician who died before the millennium. A pop song by a band he didn't know. Winter stopped wasting his time. He didn't need a search engine to track down the fool who'd killed Marty, Tay, and Rhoda.

When Rhoda called from Paris, he thought she'd lost her mind. She hardly mentioned the recording she intended blackmailing him with. She sounded paranoid, deluded, and scared. He made a mental shortlist of who he should send to kill her. Then she mentioned Tom Lewis. And, despite how unlikely it was, since every member of the Lewis family should have died that night, it made sense. If Tom Lewis survived, it meant Winter could stop looking over his shoulder, wondering which of his peers might be eyeing his organisation. This was nothing but revenge. Stupid, predictable revenge. In Winter's opinion, revenge wasn't a dish best served cold, but a dish best not served at all. Bad for business.

Rhoda wasn't stupid or fanciful. If she ever regretted leaving the Lewis family to join Winter, she didn't show it. She reliably procured candidates for Winter's organisation to groom and sell to the highest bidder. And yet she fled London in the middle of the night, convinced the man pursuing her was the dead son of Irene and Michael Lewis.

Any doubts ended with the video of her murder and the subsequent phone call from her killer. Winter viewed it multiple times, referring to Lewis family photographs, comparing the freeze-frame on his phone with pictures of the twelve-year-old boy. It might be him. If not, he certainly wanted Winter to believe it. So how did a dead boy come back to life twenty years later?

Today, Winter intended to find the answer. His thoughts turned to the man in the dungeon. Doctor Sanjeev Chandran, bundled into a car on his way back from the newsagent that morning. Winter's men left him, tied hand and foot, at nine-forty. It was now six o'clock. Eight hours would soften a civilian. Winter knew he could have shortened the process with carefully applied violence, but beating up an octogenarian retired GP held little allure. This way, the doctor's imagination would already have done the heavy lifting. Winter needed merely to play his part.

The steel door to the dungeon was four inches thick. To open it, you either needed to know the eight-digit code, or to have had your thumbprint registered on the system. Winter pushed his thumb against the screen. The door groaned theatrically as it opened. The sound added a certain gothic touch to the ambience.

The old man blinked rapidly when the harsh fluorescent lights blinked into life on the ceiling. His coat had been taken from him, and the dungeon was unheated, so he was curled up in one corner, miserable and cold. He pushed himself into a sitting position on the sawdust-sprinkled concrete, then stood, despite the obvious pain it caused him as his limbs stretched. He wore a white shirt dirty with dust and sweat, and his trousers were belted about an inch below his ribs. He held himself with such dignity as he could manage in the circumstances.

"Why am I here, sir? What right do you have to imprison me?"

"Shh." The doctor stopped blinking. He looked at Winter's face and did as he was told.

Winter was not a remarkable looking man. In fact, he would have described himself as average. Average height, a few inches shy of six feet. Average weight, or—possibly—a little under the national mean, which seemed to be trending toward obesity. Symmetrical facial features, white hair cut short, pale blue eyes, somewhat of a Roman nose. Looking perhaps a few years younger than his actual age, which was sixty-three. But Doctor Chandra wouldn't be the first person to fall silent and look away when meeting Winter. True strength of will, sureness of purpose, and unquestionable leadership were such rare qualities that many people experienced a physical reaction when encountering them for the first time.

"You signed some death certificates twenty years ago. I want to ask you about them."

The doctor coughed, bringing his tied hands up to cover his mouth. He didn't protest his situation. One look at Winter had persuaded him that cooperation was his only option. "I have signed hundreds of death certificates. I'm not sure I will be able to recall any specifics from so long ago."

"Oh, I think you'll remember these. A fire at a big house in Richmond. Three bodies. The father and child were shot in the head before the fire started. The mother was left to burn alive, with a bullet wound to her stomach."

The doctor paled, moistening his lips several times before responding. Winter knew that the details he had just given were more accurate than those released to the press. He guessed the doctor had just worked this out.

"I remember," he said.

"Good. Now then, I want you to answer this next question truthfully."

When Winter paused, the doctor looked up, his voice cracking. "I will. I will."

"I know. There was an anomaly with one of the death certificates, was there not?"

"Yes. Yes. I remember. The police, they told me, they wanted me to... I mean, they insisted—"

Winter waved his hands impatiently. "Take a breath, then tell me what happened."

The doctor did as instructed. "I pronounced two dead immediately. The child was taken to hospital with critical injuries. A gunshot to the head."

"Being shot in the head is usually fatal." Winter's tone was even and calm.

"Usually, true. Not always. The skull is remarkably thick, and the bullet, as I recall, hit the victim at an angle on the frontal bone. The impact sent fragments of bone into the brain, but the bullet itself did not penetrate the skull."

However badly Marty Nicholson died, considered Winter, it couldn't have been as badly as he deserved, the incompetent coward. Winter had been too soft back then. Letting Marty stay in the organisation, working on the counterfeiting side. The forger had lost his taste for violence after killing a child. But he hadn't even managed to do that properly.

"What happened to the boy?"

"I don't know. Some months later, the police told me he had died, that he had never come out of his coma."

"And you were happy to sign his death certificate without checking for yourself?"

"I... I... well, no. I refused, initially."

"And what changed your mind, Doctor Chandra? Ah. They wanted to put the boy in the witness protection programme. And a death certificate would keep him safe."

The doctor nodded.

"There you go. Wasn't so hard, was it?"

Winter reached under his jacket, bringing out the Glock. The doctor's eyes widened. Winter had no interest in scaring the man. He shot him twice in the heart, putting a third bullet in the back of the head when the body was on the floor.

That's how you shoot someone, Marty.

He checked his watch. Time for an hour's reading before getting ready for the auction. Self-improvement was so important.

CHAPTER TWENTY-FOUR

THE AUCTION TOOK place at Excelsior Warehouses in northwest London, on an industrial estate owned by Winter.

In the middle of the huge, empty building, gaffer tape on the concrete floor marked out a space for a makeshift TV studio. The stage was dressed like an intimate cabaret performance space, complete with a professional lighting gantry.

Four motorhomes acted as dressing rooms for the performers. They arrived in a convoy of SUVs, which drove into the building through a shuttered entrance wide and high enough to admit a private jet. Once the stars of the show had been dropped at the dressing rooms, the vehicles left, parking two hundred yards away. Make-up, rehearsals, and soundchecks followed. The final touch, after the stage, lighting, and mics, were the cameras. Five of them, broadcast quality, three focusing closeup on the stage, two for wide shots. Operated by members of Winter's crew, trained by a moon-lighting BBC cameraman. Each camera broadcasting live on the internet.

At ten-thirty, Winter arrived. He sat in the darkness at the back with a laptop.

At eleven-forty-five, the fourteen guests received emails with the auction's IP address. They logged on through *4freeker,* a labyrinth of international servers with an exit node chosen randomly. The technical side was down to Penny, his housekeeper and assistant. Winter grasped the basics, but it was Penny who'd provided the means for the masterstroke he'd put in place at the first online auction a decade ago.

Before then, those wishing to bid at the auction sent proxies. Now, guests downloaded the itemised menu for the evening in advance from a secure server. Out of context, it looked innocent enough, like a casting list. Potential buyers bid in person, from the security of their scrambled, encrypted connections. And they thought they were safe to do so.

The red lights on the cameras glowed, and the screen of Winter's laptop divided into white squares, each one turning blue when a guest logged in. The squares were numbered one to fourteen.

At midnight, the music level dipped and Penny stepped onto the stage, veiled to preserve her anonymity. After a quarter of a century running his household, anticipating his needs, and fading into the background, she knew Winter better than anybody and, as far as he ever trusted anyone, he trusted Penny.

She was Ron Capinsky's widow. Winter beat her husband to death in the early days of his rise to notoriety. Capinsky's prominence in London's criminal underworld had been a mystery. He seemed to have been born lucky, always in the right place at the right time. He moved from armed robbery to white-collar fraud at the same time Winter was eying the human trafficking trade. Fraud, when the victims were bankers and CEOs, was a largely victimless crime. Capinsky's problem was that he missed the old days, the violence of the robberies. He started throwing his weight around, picking fights with the wrong people. Winter was one of them. The last one. He'd shot Capinsky through the neck and watched him bleed out.

Penny had come to him a week later. Not with a burning thirst for revenge, but a business proposition. A morning in her company proved enough to convince Winter that Capinsky's unlikely success was entirely due to his wife's savvy.

"So why do you want to help me?"

"Because organising a complicated criminal empire, and spotting business opportunities, is what I'm good at. Better than good, actually. And you will pay me well."

She named a figure that made him laugh out loud.

"I just murdered your husband," he said, "so I'll ask you again. Why do you want to help me?"

She answered by taking off her blouse, revealing a network of old bruises, scars, and burns covering her upper body.

Winter paid the salary. Over the decades that followed, she'd proved to be worth it many times over.

Penny stepped up to the mic. No stage presence, her manner brisk and business-like rather than entertaining. The remote bidders were there to spend money. They wanted to see what they were buying, and the lights and set gave the evening a Hollywood sheen.

"Lot One. Emma."

Winter imagined the billionaires in their offices perusing their menus.

1. Emma. 22. 5'7". Educated at Cheltenham Girls School. Brought up in the Cotswolds. Primary language English. Fluent in French, Spanish, Italian. Dropped out of Durham University, where she read English Literature. 50.

The last figure was the reserve.

Lot One climbed the stairs and moved to the centre of the stage. A dark red dress. Winter frowned from the back of the room. A little too obvious for his tastes, that dress. Lot One was blonde, and—had her diet not been controlled by her handlers for the past months— Winter suspected she might go from curvy to plump.

The girl, on Penny's instructions, twirled. Winter knew his customers. He looked at square twelve and saw the first bid come up on-screen. A strong opener. Winter may have been wrong about the clothes choice. Sonia, who ran the groomers, taking charge of costume and make-up backstage, understood how to bring out the best in each girl. Lot One's Rubenesque figure filled the dress. The eighty-four-year-old financier behind square twelve loved an hour-glass figure, especially when combined with a cut-glass accent.

Penny gestured at the downstage mic. Lot One coughed daintily into her fist—good—and introduced herself. Emma wasn't her actual name. She didn't hesitate, reciting a Blake poem and smiling when she finished. She spoke like someone born into money. Sonia's team produced top of the line specimens. A process refined over many years. Two decades, mused Winter, realising the anniversary of his taking on this part of his business had passed earlier that year. It took a careful, methodical approach to maintain such consistency. The candidates needed to be weaned off any substances before being introduced to the particular melange of drugs that would make them pliant, dependent, and desperate to please.

The bidding got busier, but Winter knew square twelve was committed. Lot One fetched a hundred-and-fifteen thousand. Not a bad start. Not a bad start at all.

Winter's auctions, featuring candidates hand-picked by Rhoda and groomed by Sonia, were the only game in town for top-end sex slaves. Not that Winter would ever use that phrase in front of his clients. To them, he provided companions. Permanent companions. Once they left the premises, they became the property of the successful bidder. What happened after that, Winter neither knew nor cared.

The rest of the auction went well. A tall brunette woman sold for a disappointing sixty thousand after bursting into tears during a poor rendition of Adele's Hello. But the loss was more than made up for by a young Indian lad, whose limpid eyes caught the attention of squares nine and three, pushing the price into high six figures.

All in all, a successful night. Rhoda's swan song, thought Winter, as each square winked out, unaware that their host had been capturing their details for years, to prepare for their eventual blackmail.

Winter's phone rang. Unknown caller. It would be Blüthner. Winter had expected this. The German, now living in America, was, even in this evening's company, the richest by some margin. He'd started out as a pimp in Berlin, setting up shop and aggressively expanding his territory in the months after the Wall fell. He moved into heroin supply, as trade routes opened up following the fall. These days he bought and sold corporations. Tonight, he paid three hundred thousand dollars for Lot Six, a tall blonde Danish girl whose muscled body didn't suit Winter's taste. Blüthner often bid on lots who showed signs of spirit. Perhaps he preferred to complete the breaking-in process personally.

"I heard about Miss Ilích. Unfortunate. How will you replace her?"

Not much of a one for small talk, Blüthner. That suited Winter. The German's mention of Rhoda's surname and her fate was a demonstration of power. Rhoda's body had been identified by the false name from the passport in her Paris hotel room. No one ever referred to her surname.

"There are one or two possibilities."

"Really." Blüthner's sceptical tone was understandable. Rhoda had been exceptional at identifying promising candidates, befriending them, and abducting them without a trail for the police to follow. She learned her trade from the woman who developed it, and, over the years, the disciple became more successful than the teacher. Winter had always been alert to the danger of being too reliant on one person, and tried—without Rhoda's knowledge—other procurers, other methods. Nothing else came close to her consistency.

Winter's thoughts turned to retirement. He could hand over the cocaine side to Gregor. Strickland might take on the munition smuggling. That left the most lucrative product—humans. The bread and butter part of the business remained steady—mostly Syrians these days, already displaced, easy to lure into the back of a lorry with the promise of fair pay and a new home. But margins tightened every time a lorry was searched, or a shipment arrived spoiled because some idiot didn't remember to check the air holes. Then there were the high-end 'companions' that went to auction, valuable not just for the excellent return on investment, but also for Winter's longer game —his retirement.

"Yes. Short-term, we'll see a dip in supply, but I expect to have the operation running smoothly again by early summer. Some people say anticipation provides much of the enjoyment."

"Some people are fools." Blüthner rang off. Winter wondered if he'd been insulted. Blüthner was hard to read. It would be a pleasure to blackmail him.

Blackmail would provide Winter with an excellent income during retirement. As a young man, Winter found the notion of extorting money sordid. Not so now. The clarity of thought which had seen Winter build his own criminal empire had also revealed flaws in his own logic. Money was money.

Winter's phone pinged with notifications as the deposits arrived in one of his offshore accounts. He took a hip flask from his pocket and toasted a good night with a mouthful of fine Calvados. He was in a reflective mood.

With age came wisdom, as the ideals of youth were variously tested, found wanting, and thrown away. Respect, obedience, adherence to laws. Tolerance. Empathy. All drummed into individuals during their formative years to protect the prevailing economic and political system. And, mostly, it worked, churning out unquestioning cud-chewers who did as they were told, thought as they were taught, and voted to keep the creaking control apparatus functioning.

Most citizens played the game without ever questioning their lack of agency, but society needed rebels. Those who flouted, or broke, the rules were crucial to maintain the very system they attacked. Punishing criminals shored up confidence in the restrictions on freedom that the majority bought into.

Which left a gap for the Winters of this world. Truly free, autonomous individuals who broke the rules but got away with it. There were plenty of pragmatic politicians and police officers on the payroll, prepared to look the other way.

Winter had flourished for a long time and was nearly ready to get out.

The means by which he captured his blackmail information was so simple, Winter had laughed when Penny first explained it.

"And you think they'll fall for that?"

"Most of them are men. I know they will." She'd been proved right.

A simple hack meant the video link cut out for individual bidders at a crucial moment. The 'reconnect?' dialogue that appeared didn't offer paranoia-level anonymous access through 4freeker, but they clicked it without thinking. Or, at least, eight of them had, so far. Including Blüthner. Meaning Winter had evidence of the bidders' involvement with a sex-trafficking ring. And a means to fund his long and comfortable retirement.

If he died, they were exposed. If they failed to maintain their quarterly payments once he claimed them, they were exposed.

His thoughts turned to Rhoda Ilích. Her own attempt at blackmail had taught Winter a valuable lesson. Because she had handed him the Lewis family, and had taken on the procurement role efficiently, without complaint, he had let himself trust her. Not for the first ten years. He wasn't a fool. But who could have guessed Rhoda would have the patience to appear loyal for so long? Eighteen years after joining his organisation, she'd used her mobile phone to record him ordering the execution of a mayoral candidate.

She wanted money, but—more than that—she wanted out, and for him to leave her alone. Rhoda proved more resourceful than he had expected. His only big mistake in forty years. Winter had suspected she was bluffing about the recording being emailed to journalists if she didn't log into a certain website and prevent it, but the risk had been too great. She was dead now, her bluff revealed. A good bluff. Well played. Unfortunately, the incriminating recording was now in the hands of an unknown quantity. Well, Jimmy Blue wouldn't be unknown for much longer.

Winter watched the guests depart, each square on the laptop going back to white.

His phone buzzed again. *The Twins.*

"Well?"

"Got him. One of Henderson's boys runs a construction company. Your guy worked on one of their sites last month. Hod carrier. Big, bald, scars on his head."

"What about his records?"

"Yeah, you were right. Not much to find. A bank account, wage slips. Nothing from his childhood at all. No permanent address. We ran his name, filtered out everyone over forty and under twenty, then filtered again to get rid of anyone with a permanent job. That left—"

"Do you have a point?"

"Sorry. Yeah. Found him. Working at a warehouse in Hounslow. He's the right age, he always keeps his head covered. We took photos last night, checked them against the screenshots you sent."

Winter had supplied the freeze-frames from Rhoda's murder that offered the best view of her killer. It wasn't much to go on—but there was no concealing the height and bulk of the man.

"And?"

"Yeah, the build fits. He's big enough."

The Twin—Winter had never bothered differentiating them— sounded unsure. Winter pressed him. "What aren't you telling me?"

"You said he was dangerous. Not this guy."

"Explain."

"He's slow. Learning difficulties. Severe. Can't read or write. We found someone who worked with him two years ago. He said this guy can barely speak."

Winter was silent.

"Boss? You still there?"

"I'm here."

"What do you want us to do?"

Whoever killed Marty and Tay and planned the Montparnasse Tower murder didn't have learning difficulties. He was capable and dangerous. One way to find out if this was the same man.

He'd chosen the Twins for their physical talents.

"Hurt him."

CHAPTER TWENTY-FIVE

TOM LIKED WORKING at the Hounslow warehouse. He enjoyed being indoors when it was so cold outside. At Christmas time, everyone became more friendly. Tom noticed this every year and made sure he always worked in December. The holiday itself meant little to him, having no one to celebrate with. Television programmes showed families, which made him feel like his insides had been scooped out. But the week before Christmas remained his favourite time of year.

The warehouse job paid cash, with fair wages, and Tom helped himself to free cups of tea whenever he wanted as long as he washed up his mug afterwards. Sometimes the boss left a packet of biscuits or cake in the canteen. The biscuits were broken, but they tasted the same. It was like getting a present.

It must be close to Christmas because everyone wore red hats, and the radio stations played the same few songs. He hummed along to some of them. Tina said he had a good voice. Tom blushed at that.

Mr Cracknell, the manager, offered him overtime tonight. A big delivery, delayed because of an accident on a motorway. Tom said yes. The same amount of work for more money sounded good, and the warehouse was warmer than the attic room he rented, where any heat from the two-bar electric fire rose straight up and out of the uninsulated roof.

At ten o'clock, Tom—muscles aching from stacking pallets—clocked out and put on his heavy black coat. Viv called it a donkey jacket, but Tom thought it must be a joke because you didn't make jackets out of donkeys.

At the door, he stopped when Mr Cracknell called his name. If a boss wanted to see him at the end of a shift, it usually meant they didn't need him anymore. They called it 'letting him go', which confused Tom, as no one had locked him up and he didn't want to go anywhere.

"Mrs Cracknell's Christmas cake, Tom."

The warehouse manager held out a brown paper bag.

"Mm? Cake?"

Tom took the bag and looked inside. A rich aroma emerged, white icing on a dark slab. He tried to remember the last time someone had given him a gift.

"Thank you." Tom didn't get stuck on either word, and smiled while looking at his boss's face rather than his feet.

"You're welcome. See you tomorrow."

"Mm. Tomorrow."

The night turned icy cold, a thin wind sending scraps of paper tumbling along the front of the warehouse. Tom buttoned the jacket and turned up the collar. He pulled his wool hat over the bandana, making sure it covered his ears, then set off towards the path that cut through Lampton Park to the shops and houses.

It took two minutes for the contented glow to fade. Mr Cracknell was a kind man. The other workers—Viv, Tina, Ali, Manu, even Terry, who called him slow—treated him well, but it was nearly over. Tom never stayed long. All his jobs ended after a few weeks; a couple of months at most. He needed to keep moving. Tom knew the urge to leave would come soon. Impossible to ignore, like a sneeze.

But the urge hadn't come yet, even though he had worked at the warehouse for ten weeks. Tom woke up every morning expecting it to be there. Its absence confused him.

And Jimmy Blue was missing. No trace anywhere. Tom was alone, anxious, and scared. He worked all the hours he could to stop himself thinking about it.

Blue had called twice in the summer. After the first time, Tom had woken up injured, a stitched cut on his right side. The second time, he had slept for weeks, waking on a London railway platform with no memory of where he'd been.

But, unaccountably, he buzzed with an optimism and joy he couldn't express. Jimmy Blue's recent visits left behind a sensation of fierce happiness like the scent of strong perfume in a small room. Tom worked the usual menial jobs, kept his own company, stammered when spoken to. But something had been set in motion, he knew, and it brought Tom a temporary sense of peace he'd never experienced before.

Now that peace was threatened, because Blue had disappeared.

Tom walked into the alleyway that cut behind the backs of the warehouses and led to the park. He was hungry. He considered opening the bag and eating the cake. No; it would be more special back in his room with a cup of tea.

Halfway down the narrow, poorly lit passage, he heard footsteps behind him. Tom looked over his shoulder and saw the silhouetted figure of a man.

Tom kept walking. He reached the halfway point of the long alleyway, and the security light on the warehouse wall came on. Another five steps and he was back in darkness.

A second man appeared, this time at the far end of the alleyway, walking towards him. Tom became acutely aware of the wall on one side and the high wooden fence on the other. Boxed in. Constricted.

He looked back again as the first man triggered the security light, and saw him clearly for the first time. Tall, about Tom's age, maybe older. His stare a challenge. Tom hurried forwards. The other man was twenty yards away. Fifteen, ten... Tom stopped. It was the same man. How could the same man be behind him and in front of him?

He stopped, not sure what to do. It was dark here.

"Jimmy Blue, mm, loves the dark," he murmured, but no one watched him from the shadows. No one responded.

The two men were close now. One of them took something from his coat pocket. Some kind of truncheon. Tom spun around. The second man held an identical weapon, and the two men looked exactly the same.

Tom moaned, backing up until his spine was pushed up against the warehouse wall.

The first blow caught his upper arm, and he cried out, instinctively hunching over. The second man's truncheon cracked on the base of his skull and he stumbled forward.

The first man stepped in close, punching Tom in the stomach. He coughed and retched, grabbing his attacker's jacket to stop himself falling over.

Where are you?

Even as he thought it, the familiar *fade* came over him, and he welcomed its embrace, falling away into unconsciousness.

When Tom came back and opened his eyes, there was time for him to register a sick sense of horror and despair before another blow from a truncheon sent him to the ground.

He was still here, still in the alley. The men were hurting him.

He couldn't wake up from the nightmare. Jimmy Blue had come, he was sure of it. But he hadn't stayed, hadn't helped. And now Tom was on the floor as the men punched and kicked him. He curled into as tight a ball as he could and started to cry.

He heard them leave. They chatted to each other as if nothing unusual had happened.

When Tom rolled onto his back, it hurt to breathe all the way in. He ran his fingers along his ribs, pushing carefully and wincing. His arms and legs hurt, his cheek ached where a boot had caught him. When his fingers encountered something soft and warm on his side, he recoiled. It didn't feel like blood.

He sat up and looked at his hand, coated and glistening. It was Christmas cake.

Back in the rented room, Tom didn't even get undressed. He

rinsed his hands and face, kicked off his work boots, and laid on top of the sheets, sore, scared, and empty.

———

"John, let me put you on hold for a second. I have to take this."

Winter looked out of his first-floor study towards the moonlit lake, where a fish flipped out of the cold water, sending ripples across the surface.

He didn't have to put Strickland on hold. He could just as easily call the Twins back. But small reminders of their respective positions in the hierarchy were never a bad idea.

"What happened?"

Winter didn't use names when talking to the Twins. He assumed they had first names, but they only ever referred to themselves— collectively, and individually—as the Twins.

"We did as you asked. He'll be sore for a few days."

"What about you?"

"What about us?"

"Your injuries." Winter had sent the Twins in without any prior information about their target. If Tom 'Brown', the itinerant manual worker with the scarred head, was actually Tom Lewis, this so-called Jimmy Blue, he doubted the Twins would be unscathed.

"Injuries? Right?" A low chuckle followed. "He didn't even try. He's never been in a fight before."

"How do you know?"

"His first reaction. You can't fake it. I was watching him when he clocked us. I came in swinging and he practically shat himself. No idea how to defend himself. He started crying."

"Maybe he was faking it."

"No way. He was bloody hopeless, Mr Winter."

"Yes, so you said. Give me some supporting evidence for your assertion."

"Come again?"

Winter tried again, with fewer syllables. "What makes you so sure?"

"Oh, right. His footwork, mostly. If you've had any kind of training, even if you're just a brawler, you get your footwork right. If someone comes at you, you don't want to end up on the floor. If you go down, it's pretty much all over. So you keep your stance wide, knees bent. You do it without thinking. When I went for this guy, he froze. His feet didn't move. No way you can fake that. He was bloody hopeless. I could have taken him on my own, pissed, with both hands tied behind my back."

"Thank you. I'll be in touch."

Interesting.

Winter returned to the waiting call.

"Apologies, John. You were saying?"

If Strickland was irritated by Winter keeping him waiting, his tone didn't betray it.

"I found a perfect match for the physical description you gave me. Similar M.O., too. Remember that urban myth doing the rounds about a monster chucking people off the top of a bus? Turns out it's real. The victims were Reaperz Crew boys. I found one of them."

Winter grunted. The Reaperz Crew was the biggest gang in east London. They'd kept their drug business confined to a handful of postcodes around Walthamstow, but they were big enough to be on his radar. Not big enough to be a concern. Not yet.

"Bring him in tomorrow, John. We'll have a chat." The tiniest hesitation from Strickland. Winter realised it had sounded too much like an order. "I assume that's what you were calling to suggest?"

"Of course. Is the dungeon free?"

Winter looked out at the lake. Its surface was mirror calm now. Twenty feet down, Doctor Chandra, diving weights hooked onto his body, was beginning the slow process of transformation from human being to fish food.

"Yes. It's free."

CHAPTER TWENTY-SIX

JIMMY BLUE SNAPPED awake in the darkness of Tom's room. He rolled off the bed and stripped naked. The curtains of the tiny attic room were open, and the moonlight revealed his silver, grey, and dark blue body reflected in the long mirror on the cupboard door.

His injuries were superficial. The ribs looked the worst, but they weren't broken. His lip was split, and an ugly bruise shaded his left cheek. Legs, arms, shoulders, and back were scuffed, grazed, and sore. Another twenty-four hours and his body would be a patchwork of bruises.

The first aid kit in the bathroom yielded a bandage roll. He bound his ribs. They'd heal faster without the binding, but, for tonight, he didn't want the pain to distract him from his work.

He got dressed again, putting on a hooded sweatshirt under the jacket, adding a black fleece neck warmer. After lacing up his running shoes, he pulled out the wallet he had lifted from his attacker's jacket pocket. Cash, credit cards, gym membership, a coffee shop loyalty card. No address, but enough information to get one.

He descended the stairs without a sound. The first time he had climbed them, he noted every squeak, and knew which steps to avoid. He ducked into his landlady's bedroom. Her snores continued as he walked across to her dressing table. He found what he needed and retraced his steps.

Outside, Blue jogged to the high street. He kept his pace slow, wanting to warm his damaged muscles.

One-twenty a.m. The internet cafe was quiet. A couple of gamers with headsets trading insults with their virtual opponents. Blue paid for thirty minutes and sat at the back.

Tom Lewis didn't own a smart phone. His Nokia could make calls and send and receive texts. Not that he could read them. But its big rubber case provided more than protection. Jimmy Blue used his thumbnail to peel the back of the case away, revealing a USB drive in a tiny compartment.

The drive rebooted the PC with Jimmy Blue's custom Linux operating system, running anonymous browsing software.

The wallet had two bank cards, which helped narrow the search. The name, Mark Adams, was so common he assumed it was fake, but triangulating bank locations with the gym membership gave Blue three addresses in Twickenham. The first was a children's entertainer, and his face was all over social media. The third was eighty-three years old.

The second Mark Adams was notable for his lack of internet presence, and his bank was among those hacked three years earlier. Everyone changed their passwords as advised, but not so many moved house.

Address memorised, Blue logged off, leaving the cafe's computer free of any evidence he'd been there.

It was three miles to St Margarets, where Mr Adams lived. He set off, hood up, jogging at an easy pace.

Mark Adams and his twin were, Jimmy Blue concluded, likely just cheap muscle with no formal connections to Winter. But he didn't doubt for a second that the crime boss had sent them. With Marty and Rhoda dead, and after the personal threat on the recording he sent to Winter, it was a question of when, not if, the boss would find Tom Lewis. There were weak points in any plan, even one as carefully constructed as Blue's. The next stage was crucial, and events had to follow the correct pattern for him to triumph. If Winter deviated too far from his predicted behaviour, if the potential exposure of the incriminating recording wasn't enough leverage, then Jimmy Blue's entire existence would be for nothing. Everything hung in the balance. For once, his lips didn't twitch with a smile.

When he reached Adams' street, Blue jogged down it without pausing, looking both ways. Adams lived in a mid-terrace house. Jimmy Blue turned right at the end of the road. The back gardens led down to a footpath, then onto allotments.

Two streets away, a skip full of bricks and rubble stood in front of a scaffolded house. Blue picked up three bricks, tucking one under his arm, then jogged back.

Nothing moved on the street apart from a fox, which looked at the interloper with a frank, open curiosity. It followed, watching from a distance when the hooded man stopped in front of a house, placed one brick on a low wall, and pulled his arm back. The fox didn't move until the first window exploded, the crash of breaking glass sending it scurrying back to the allotments. The second and third crashes followed the first in the time it takes to draw a breath.

Blue was running before the third brick reached its target. He sprinted to the end of the street, turning left this time. Halfway up the parallel terrace, he turned left again, entering the narrow alleyway he'd noted on his first pass of the street. A wheelie bin at the far end provided ample cover. He sat behind it and waited, watching the houses opposite.

The door of the first house was open. A woman in a thick towelling dressing gown stood in the garden, looking at her broken window. She lit a cigarette, shaking her head. As Jimmy Blue nudged the wheelie bin forward to get a better view, the door of the third house opened, and two men came out, one cradling a pug. While the other hung back, checking the shattered window, the man with the pug walked over to his neighbour. They were too far away for Blue to hear their conversation. The middle house's door remained shut.

A handful of residents were on the street to discuss the incident, but most had drifted back inside by the time the police arrived, twenty-five minutes after Blue lobbed the first brick.

The police officers inspected the damage and took notes. Three minutes after arriving, the female officer knocked on the door of the middle house. The hall light came on, and when the door opened, Blue recognised one of the men who'd attacked Tom. Tall, barefoot and bare-chested, saying very little, looking past the police officer to scan the street.

"Hello, Mark Adams," Blue whispered, then ran back down the alleyway and onto the parallel street, taking a roundabout route back to the terrace to make sure he wasn't spotted.

He approached the back of the houses through the allotment, climbing the fence and dropping into the small paved yard. At the back door, he listened, his ear pressed up against the keyhole. Adams was still talking to the police officer. Good.

Any burglar knows that back doors are generally not as secure as front doors. Strange, really, since front doors are generally overlooked by the neighbours, so it would be a bold thief who tried to break in that way. Adams's back door was solid enough, but the lock was a simple pin cylinder.

Blue reached into his pocket and brought out the hairpins he had borrowed from his landlady's bedroom. He poked the key out of the lock, hearing it hit the mat. The lock clicked open seventeen seconds later. Once inside, he replaced the key and locked the door.

He breathed in deeply. No pets. Curry for dinner, something with fresh green chillies. One plate in the sink. Three empty beer bottles on the side. Adams lived alone.

The kitchen door hung open an inch. Blue put his eye to the gap. At the end of the hall, the front door was shut, but on the latch, Adams still talking to the police officer in front of the broken window.

Jimmy Blue moved through the hall and up the stairs like a shadow. He went straight to the bedroom, took a pillow case, then moved quickly from room to room, removing every lightbulb before placing them carefully inside the case.

Back in the bedroom, he put the pillow case on the floor and used his heel to break the glass bulbs. He tipped them out onto the polished floorboards, then stood behind the door and waited.

The conversations outside stopped, and the front door latch snapped back into place as Adams came back in.

Blue melted into the darkness, his heart rate slowing. He had learned to detect the presence of another human being nearby through non-visual clues, but the ability was a rare one. He doubted Adams would even register his scent, as subtle as it was. But a stray movement, however tiny, might alert his attacker to the presence of a stranger in his house. Jimmy Blue's pulse dropped steadily, and he relaxed into stillness, his stance a variant of T'ai Chi's *mountain*.

Click. Adams's footsteps on the stairs stopped when the landing light didn't come on. He waited. He was, Blue knew, thinking and listening. The footsteps retreated. Good. It meant he was checking the back door. When he found it locked, it would allay his suspicions.

Sure enough, the footsteps returned a minute later. At the top of the stairs, he hesitated before coming towards the bedroom. Blue maintained a state of relaxed readiness.

The bedroom light clicked. When nothing happened, Adams went across the hall to the bathroom and tried that. He was cautious and thorough. Maybe further up the order than a basic thug. If none of the upstairs lights were working, a blown fuse was the obvious culprit. Check now, or wait until morning. If the former, and if the fuse box was downstairs, Jimmy Blue would follow. The latter would be more fun, though.

Adams chose the latter.

He took two steps into his bedroom. His right foot, with all his weight on it, landed on a jagged broken bulb, sending a shard of glass two inches into the flesh of the arch. The shock and pain made him lurch sideways, and his left foot stamped heel-first into more glass, puncturing the skin in multiple places.

His momentum took him forward, so Adams tried a kind of crippled hop, hoping he could leap clear of the lethal carpet. He was off balance when Blue broke his jaw with the small truncheon he had taken from the jacket hanging behind the door.

Adams spun, hit the wall, and came down on his left side, landing on the shattered glass. His instinctive gasp turned into a groan of pain as the movement caused the broken bones of his jaw to grind together.

"Don't pass out," said Blue, stepping out of the darkness. He grabbed Adams's wrist and dragged him out of the glass, causing hundreds of fresh lacerations. Adams looked up at him in fear. He knew he had lost this fight before it had even begun. Blue wondered how much he could see in the darkness as a hooded man, a scarf over the lower half of his face, bent over him.

Blue tossed Adams's wallet onto the floor. "You attacked the wrong man. Do me a favour. Please pass on the following message to your brother."

The Twins' assault on Tom Lewis left no injuries requiring hospitalisation. Blue had no such inhibitions. He broke three of Adams's ribs, shattered his left hip, and continued raining damage onto that leg until certain his enemy would never walk without a stick.

He picked up the beside phone, dialled 999, and requested an ambulance.

"Yes. I'm calling on behalf of Mark Adams. He and his brother are violent criminals. I've just done the local community a favour and beaten the living shit out of him. Multiple fractures, some deep lacerations and a broken jaw. Concussion too, I'd imagine. If you could send someone over. No hurry, as he really is a piece of lowlife scum. Thank you."

He gave them the address, stepped over the whimpering Adams, and left.

It was still dark when he got to Hounslow. He ducked into an alleyway close to home, unwound the bandage from his ribs, and threw it away.

In his room, he changed back into Tom's work clothes and lay on the bed. The success of all his plans might come down to what happened in the next twenty-four hours.

He had made his play. Now it was Winter's move.

———

The call came at lunchtime the next day. Winter was watching an investment programme. The stock market rose or fell depending on the fear and greed of shareholders. In another, more boring, life, he believed he might well have prospered as a trader, given his ability to manipulate those emotions in others.

His phone rattled on the desk. *The Twins.*

"Yes?"

"Mark's in hospital. He was attacked last night. In his house."

Mark? Winter was blank for a moment. It was the first time he'd heard a first name.

"Who did it?"

"He doesn't know. But he lost his wallet when we beat up the bald guy yesterday. And whoever attacked him returned it. Warned us off."

"The same man?"

"Can't be. I told you, he was bloody hopeless. But this bastard, whoever he is, knows him. His mate or something. And he destroyed Mark. His leg is completely busted up. Why didn't you tell us about this other guy? My brother's in a bloody hospital bed, they're about to operate, and—"

"Don't forget who you're speaking to." Winter's voice was calm. The Twin stopped talking for a few seconds.

"I'm sorry, sir. It's just, my brother... the shock. They say he'll need metal plates and rods. This guy took him apart."

Winter rang off. Interesting. It seemed Tom Lewis, if that was who they'd found, had a protector. Either that, or his personality was one big fake, and he was a dangerous killer out for revenge. No matter. It would be easy enough to find out which.

He messaged Strickland on the encrypted app they used.

Once you've brought in the eyewitness, I have another job for you. Irene Lewis's boy is alive. I'll give you the details when I see you.

Time to find out who they were dealing with.

CHAPTER TWENTY-SEVEN

DETECTIVE INSPECTOR DEBBIE CAPELLI, long divorced from a philandering Italian she'd met at a multi-car pileup in Croydon, broke her husband's nose but kept his surname. Her maiden name was Smith. *Debbie Smith* evoked beige walls, sensible shoes, weak tea, and not getting ideas above your station. *Debbie Capelli* was different; a mix of exotic and silly. She could have a guest-starring role in a daytime soap, a brief spell in the charts with a breezy, upbeat summer hit, or, as ex-colleagues sometimes pointed out, her own page on Pornhub. Debbie Capelli was dangerous, exciting, unpredictable. Debbie Smith kept her favourite recipes in a folder, sliding each one into a clear plastic pocket to stop it getting stained.

The truth was, Debbie conceded, slowing her Fiat on Fulham High Street, ready to dive into any available parking space, her surname had become a lie. Or, at the very least, false advertising. Her life was more Smith than Capelli. Thirty-three years in the police, and her only car chase had ended as soon as it started. The Ford Mondeo belonging to a crackhead drug dealer rolled to a stop three seconds after he stamped on the accelerator. He'd forgotten to fill the tank. West London police work didn't live up to *Luther*. It didn't even live up to *Juliet Bravo*. As for the recipes, she'd started her own folder two decades ago.

She found a parking space on a side street near Putney Bridge. Tom Lewis's file was in the glove compartment. Debbie knew the contents of the file backwards, but she scanned it again anyway. His case was the only one in her career where she'd failed to maintain a professional distance. She'd long since given up trying. When she saw the picture of twelve-year-old Tom, smiling at the camera alongside his dad, both holding ice creams, the familiar maternal instinct kicked in. Childless herself, she supposed it was inevitable she would bond with the boy who had nothing, not even his memories. His case was the only reason she didn't want to retire when the option came up in four years' time. While Robert Winter walked free, she owed Tom Lewis.

Tom entered the witness protection programme over nineteen years ago. When he was transferred to a private hospital, it was Debbie who announced his death to stop Winter coming back to finish the job. Everyone knew Winter was behind the killings. Trouble had been brewing for months, although most of the organised crime team would have put money on Winter losing that particular fight.

Debbie was on duty the night of the Richmond attack, arriving behind the fire engines, the heat pulsing at her face like a living thing. The ambulance crew watched with her. No one expected survivors. They stood talking in emergency service demarcated groups, with no sense of hurry; just a depressed air of resignation accompanied by the usual black humour.

As dawn broke, the chief fire officer waved the two paramedics forward. The forensic team waited, ready to photograph any charred remains, before sifting through the rubble, categorising the evidence.

It took the paramedics a few minutes to identify two shapes among the twisted, blackened, smoking remains as human. The wind changed direction at one point, and Debbie suspected the smell had guided the paramedics to the corpses. She still couldn't eat at barbecues.

The paramedics called the forensic team over once the smoul-
dering husks had been officially declared dead. The first paramedic
returned to the ambulance while her colleague lit a cigarette and
strolled around the edge of the garden. Before joining the police,
Debbie wondered why so many health professionals smoked. It
didn't take long to realise that being surrounded by pain and death
produced a fatalistic attitude in those who stuck it out. They met
Death every day, and justice or compassion didn't feature on his
agenda. On a typical shift, they shut the eyes of a ninety-year-old who
died in her sleep, then did the same for a three-year-old run over
outside his house. Each cigarette said, *I know you're coming, but up
yours, sunshine.*

When the smoker yelled from the far side of the burning house,
Debbie reached him first. The body lay face down, half-concealed by
a hedge. Thin legs poked out of the undergrowth. Dirty bare feet and
pyjamas. Debbie traced the kid's route through the dew-wet grass
back to the house.

"He's alive. Broken leg, dislocated shoulder. Minor burns.
Christ!"

The paramedic pushed the hedge aside to get a proper look at his
face. His colleague arrived with a wheeled stretcher. At the press of a
button, it concertinaed to the ground.

"On three," said the first paramedic as his colleague squatted
beside him. Debbie saw Tom's face for the first time. Her first thought
was that he wouldn't survive the stretcher journey to the ambulance,
never mind get to hospital.

The boy's features were obscured by blood, which seeped from a
bullet wound in his head. She couldn't guess the colour of his hair,
matted in crimson clumps like alien plants sprouting from his skull.
His eyes were closed, chest barely moving under pale blue cotton
pyjamas. The last time Debbie saw anything so graphic was on the
cover of three thousand pirated horror DVDs in a warehouse. The
gaping wound on that cover had been laughable. This one not so
much.

Back at the station, Detective Chief Inspector Stevens twitched with excitement. "The boy survived. Once we get his witness statement, Winter is finished."

Debbie thought of that face, fragments of smashed-meringue skull in his blood-soaked hair. "I wouldn't get your hopes up, Sir."

According to the neurosurgeon who'd operated on him, Tom would likely never speak again, his synaptic network irrevocably damaged. His brain had suffered significant injuries. Surgery mitigated that damage, but could only go so far. Neuroscience, explained the surgeon, was the Wild West of medicine, every frontier leading to new mysteries. They understood so little of the brain that it was impossible to predict the long-term results of serious trauma. Debbie asked him when Tom might be able to make a statement. "If you forced me to guess? Never."

Tom's progress had surprised everyone, but it only went so far. He could speak, after a fashion, but his medium and long term memory were severely compromised. The witness statement had never come. Tom couldn't remember anything of that night. He remembered little of his childhood.

Debbie had volunteered as Tom's liaison in witness protection. He knew her and trusted her. They'd met regularly ever since.

The worst time for her had been the missing years. Between the age of twenty and twenty-seven, Tom stopped coming to their meetings. She tried to track him down, but he had vanished. After finishing a building site job, he'd left his room in a shared house and dropped off the face of the earth. Six months with no news, and the police stopped active work on the missing persons case. After a year, Stevens called her into his office and ordered her to give it up. He thought Tom was dead. It took Debbie another twelve months to believe him. After seven years, Tom turned up at the station. When she asked where he'd been, he said, "Asleep."

Since then, Tom had never skipped a meeting. He wouldn't talk about the missing years. But whatever he'd been doing, whatever had happened to him, he came back changed. Not just physically—somehow he had grown even broader—but something deeper. Something buried. He'd been easily agitated before, often upset and confused. That had gone. His lack of communication stayed the same, but there was a calmness behind it now. His life didn't change —the same menial jobs, the drifting from place to place. But he was centred. If Debbie hadn't known better, she would have described Tom as a man who had discovered his vocation.

Debbie put the file in her shoulder bag and walked to the cafe. She approached it with the river in front of her, knowing Tom always sat somewhere where he could look out at the water. He couldn't read, but he once told her he enjoyed watching the patterns made by moving water, the way they constantly changed.

He wasn't at his usual table. Tom always turned up early. His struggles with reading, writing, and short-term memory loss made keeping appointments a challenge, so he over-compensated. The cafe wasn't busy. Debbie waited by the counter, expecting Tom to emerge from the toilet. When he didn't, she asked the barista, but no one had seen him.

She took her cappuccino to the window table and swivelled in her seat to watch the door. Ten minutes later, she called him. No answer. After her third cup, she left.

Her phone rang as she was getting back into the car.

"Tom?"

"Mm. S-sorry. Mm. Forgot."

He was a terrible liar. She'd left the usual voicemail that morning.

"Not to worry, Tom. Are you okay?"

"Mm. Okay."

"We can rearrange. Or skip this meeting and put one in the calendar for April."

"A-April." He didn't hesitate. Debbie's stomach turned and her throat constricted. She knew it was ridiculous to feel hurt. Tom enjoyed their meetings. She knew he did. Was he going to disappear again?

"Okay. If that's what you want. But if you need me in the meantime, for anything at all, you call me, Tom. Got that?"

"Mm."

"Good. Well. Happy Christmas. I'll see you in April."

133

"Mm. Bye."

Debbie started the Fiat, then turned the engine off again, staring out of the windscreen. She reminded herself that Tom was an adult, with his own life. After this many years, their meetings weren't mandatory, but she thought he enjoyed them as much as she did. She made a note on her phone to check up on him at the start of January.

Something was going on. She knew it.

CHAPTER TWENTY-EIGHT

THE MAN on the back seat of the SUV looked through the high iron gates towards the building they guarded. The house beyond might have belonged to a banker, a professional athlete, or a TV chef. Perhaps a bestselling author. From the road, which wound between the A1 to the east and Elstree to the west, nothing could be seen other than a gravelled drive snaking out of view downhill behind high walls and iron gates.

It was seven p.m.; the car pinned to the dark tarmac by security spotlights while cameras mounted on the gate swivelled to film it.

Two sizeable men in tight suits approached the SUV. The car's driver, a small, trim man in his fifties, his grey hair in a military-style crewcut, sighed.

"Why is it that steroid-injecting, protein powder-swilling, weight training-obsessed, closeted gay bodyguards always buy suits that don't fit? It's not that no one makes them big enough. But they buy jackets that won't quite button across their coconut-oiled pecs. Why is that?"

One of the two men inspected the vehicle with a thermal-imaging camera. The other leaned down to the driver's window, nodding when he recognised the man behind the wheel.

"I don't know, man." The voice of the man on the back seat was thin and croaky. He coughed.

The bodyguards held a key fob to a smaller pedestrian entrance and walked through as the main gates swung open.

The driver twisted round on the leather seat to face his passenger. "What?"

Up until an hour ago, the man sitting behind the driver had considered himself above his peers, above the law, above everyone. His clothes and tattoos marked him out as untouchable in the few square miles of London where he grew up. He was a killer. Not scared of anybody. He swallowed hard before he could speak.

"I said I don't know. I don't know why they do it."

"What's your name? Daz? Gazza?"

"Tariq. It's Tariq."

"Tariq. Right. Here's the thing, Tariq. Ever heard of a rhetorical question?"

Tariq examined his cable-tied hands, his eyes flicking up to the driver's, then away again when he met that unblinking stare. Three months ago, he, and two gang members, had been badly beaten up. By one guy. He'd lost three teeth, broken a leg, two ribs and his wrist, and suffered a concussion. From invincibility to fearful and paranoid in one night. He was still a leader, still a killer, still someone people crossed the road to avoid, but Tariq knew the truth. He was a coward. Only a matter of time before some chancer called him out. His authority had been irretrievably damaged when two of his lieutenants witnessed him getting thrown out of the window of a double-decker.

This old fart in his shiny German SUV hadn't even raised his voice to get the better of him. He arrived in his gleaming car, parked it by the row of shops where Tariq and the boys sold wraps of crack in between putting the shits up pensioners buying groceries.

The old guy got out of the car and walked up to them, stopping five yards away, arms by his sides. Polished boots, suit, buttoned black winter coat, cashmere scarf. Even his haircut looked expensive. Tariq and the guys smirked.

"You the boys who got the crap beaten out of them on a bus?"

Tariq couldn't let that pass. Not without losing what little face he had left. He unfurled himself from the wall and approached the old geezer with a rolling gait. This style of walking was part studied menace and part necessity; trousers as low as Tariq's would end up around his ankles if he walked normally.

He eyed the interloper with an expression of lazy threat, getting right into his face before answering.

"What the fuck did you s—"

An open-handed smack; hard, shocking. It came so fast, so unexpectedly, he didn't even flinch. The *crack* of it echoed off the walls and bounced from the grey council houses over the road. Tariq took a step back. The old geezer's hands were by his side, and he looked unruffled. "Yes or no?" was all he said.

Tariq's ascendance in the ranks of the Reaperz Crew had been assured until that *thing* on the bus had beaten him to a pulp. Tariq was still clinging onto the slim hope that he could recover his credibility, given time.

Now this. A slap from an old geezer. The world went quiet. And, just like that, it was over.

"Yes," said Tariq. He didn't look behind him, didn't need to clock the faces of those witnessing this humiliation. There was no fight left in him. Some people were properly dangerous, properly crazy. Predators. The monster on the bus was a predator. This old geezer wasn't at that level, but he was closer to it than Tariq ever would be.

"Put your hands in front of you."

"What?" Tariq spiralled into a state of fatalistic apathy. His body ached, and his tongue found the pink gums where the three teeth were missing.

"Imagine I'm a copper. Hands in front."

Tariq obeyed and heard the zip of the cable tie's teeth as his wrists came together.

The old geezer didn't even bother grabbing Tariq's arm. He turned his back, opened the rear door of the car.

"Get in."

Tariq complied without looking back, knowing that, whatever happened, he wouldn't be running things anymore.

Now he was somewhere near Elstree, where every house cost millions, about as far out of his comfort zone as he'd ever been, and the old geezer wanted to chat about rhetorical questions. A sputter of defiance flared up in his gut.

"Yeah, actually, I—"

Crack. Tariq didn't see that slap coming, either.

"I think you're missing the point, Tariq. You're a lowlife piece of shit. My car will have to be valeted to get rid of your stench. I don't want you to speak. At all. Not unless I make it very clear I expect you to say something. Do you understand?"

Tariq pressed his knees together to stop them knocking against each other. He thought it might be safe to nod.

"Good."

The gates shut behind the car as it purred down the drive. The forecast had predicted icy roads, but the gravel supplied plenty of grip as the SUV rounded the long bend, forked to the right, and drove behind the house, then beneath, the underground garage door sliding closed behind it.

CHAPTER TWENTY-NINE

IT WAS lunchtime when Tom woke up. He blinked into the pillow, wondering why his body ached so much. Had Jimmy Blue come back? For a moment, he believed it, sitting up with a smile on his face. Then the smile faded as he remembered why he ached.

In the bathroom, he angled the mirror to check his body. Blue-black and purple bruises on his ribs, arms, and legs. His right eye puffy and sore, the cheek below a swollen, angry red.

His phone had the two circles on the screen that meant he had a message. He pressed the right button and picked up Mrs Capelli's voicemail. They were supposed to meet. But she would see the bruises on his face. She would ask questions. Tom didn't trust the police—Blue would never go near them—but Mrs Capelli was different. Debbie had always been there. Always.

His finger hesitated over the button to call her number. He hated talking on the phone even more than talking in person, but it was okay with Debbie. She never prompted him or interrupted, but gave him all the time he needed to find the right words and say them.

He put the phone down. Something much more insistent—and far stronger—than instinct told him not to call her, and not to meet her. It could only be Jimmy Blue. Maybe this meant he would come back. He hadn't protected Tom against the men who had hit and kicked him. But the attack might bring Blue back. Tom missed seeing him in the shadows, knowing he was nearby. The last time had been so long ago, it scared him.

When the phone rang, he nearly dropped it. Debbie. She wouldn't give up easily. He lied to her about forgetting, agreed to a meeting in April. Put the phone down, face flushed with the shame of lying to his friend.

He went back into the bathroom, splashed water on his face. Something wasn't right, but he couldn't understand what. Blue felt so close, like he was standing in the next room. But, at the same time, he kept his distance. Almost like he was hiding.

Had Tom done something wrong? Jimmy Blue was all he had. Blue would never leave Tom. Would he?

———

At work, everyone looked at his bruised face, but no one said anything. No one except Mr Cracknell, who took him into the canteen for a cup of tea. He even opened a packet of unbroken biscuits.

"You in trouble, Tom?"

Tom shook his head. "Fell. Mm, f-fell over."

"Right. Well. Do you want a lift home tonight?"

Tom wanted to say yes. He even started to form the word. Before he could do it, his mouth opened. "No, thank you, Mr Cracknell."

The words came out easily. Blue. He must be coming. He must be. Tom nodded his thanks and left before his boss asked him what had happened to his stammer.

Tom avoided the alleyway tonight, taking the long way round to the park, which lay between the industrial estate and his rented room. A mixture of fear and excitement coursed through him as he trudged through the gates. Jimmy Blue might be here, waiting for him.

The path wound through trees, and the shadows there lay deep and dark. Tom slowed as he passed each one, waiting for a shifting blur, an invisible face turning to look his way, a glint of starlight reflected in Blue's dark eyes. Nothing. No one.

On a bench, a silhouette. Tom stopped, squinted. Then a red dot glowed, illuminating a beard inside a hood, as a stranger smoked, his head tilted towards Tom.

"Problem, pal? Jog on, will ya?"

Tom stared at the man. There hadn't been any anger in the stranger's challenge, but it would be best to keep walking, not provoke him. He shuffled on, moving to the far side of the path to pass the man, who continued to watch him. After another twenty yards, he looked back, but the man was on his phone. He stood as he talked, then walked in the same direction as Tom.

Not following, just leaving the park. Even so, Tom's pulse quickened. Still no Jimmy Blue.

Tom understood, at a deep, basic level, that his existence, his hollowed-out, fractional, daily life, only had meaning in that it enabled Jimmy Blue to do his work. And Blue's work, while beyond his understanding, would be great and glorious. When he woke from a nightmare of his mother screaming, he didn't panic. He waited. He waited until a sense of calm, an unarguable assurance that everything would be made right settled over him like a warm blanket. That was Jimmy Blue. He brought Tom happiness. Or, at least, an absence of sadness.

No Jimmy Blue in the shadows. No contact from him since moving to Hounslow. Impossible that Blue had left him. Impossible. What would Tom do when the warehouse job ended? Tom had no plans. Blue always took care of things.

Ahead, the streetlights were out. Tom looked up hopefully. Jimmy Blue drew strength from the darkness. Tom scanned the empty street, the front gardens' grass replaced by concrete for parking. The opposite side of the street lined with cars and work vans. Narrow vertical shafts of light from drawn curtains.

Something... something was wrong. Tom hesitated, looked over his shoulder. The smoking man flicked the cigarette away. Still on his phone, still walking behind Tom, not hurrying.

A movement along the park fence to the right. A second man, big, squat, coming from the south side of the park. Hard to make out in the darkness. Still no Jimmy Blue. The two men met and walked together without a word. They both looked at Tom. He moved faster.

A distant part of his brain signalled something about the scene in front of him. Tom swung his head from left to right as he walked, but whatever information his brain had picked up, Tom couldn't interpret it. He swallowed. His spit tasted funny, like when he'd put two pence on his tongue pretending to be a magician.

Tom started humming. He stumbled across to the side of the street, past the parked vehicles. With them between him and the two men, maybe he could run and turn the corner before they noticed.

The first van was a light colour, dirty, a few years old, the sort of vehicle a million small businesses used. Tom looked at the number plate, sounding out the first letter. T. T for Tom. T for tomato. T for television. T for terror. The distant part of his brain sent up a flare now, but too far away. Tom paused by the passenger door, his forehead creased in thought.

He'd seen that number plate before. But the memory made no sense, because it was nowhere he remembered visiting. In his mind, the number plate lay on a workbench. The letters and numbers meant nothing, but he recognised the pattern they made. And the pattern on the front of the van matched the one on the workbench.

Whatever else it meant, Tom understood it meant danger. He turned. The two men closed in, crossing the street.

Tom ran.

As he passed the back doors of the van, they opened and two more men emerged. Tom moaned, dodged to the side and, head down, put all his effort into sprinting, his big boots smacking hard onto the pavement. He heard the others pursuing him. His sudden break caused confusion, the two men from the park tangling with those coming out of the van. It bought him a little time. Not much, though. They ran faster than him. Tom's only chance lay in reaching the main road. An orange glow promised working lampposts ahead. Even this late, there would be cars, taxis, people. Witnesses.

Fifteen yards from the turning, Tom knew they wouldn't catch him in time. Safe soon. Call Debbie. She would help. Debbie said call her day or night if he needed her. Well, he needed her now.

The last car at the top of the street was a dark German SUV, parked on double yellows. Half a second after Tom noticed a shape sitting behind the steering wheel, the door opened, and a smartly dressed middle-aged man stepped out, extending a hand towards Tom.

Not a hand. A gun. And the man who held it was the man who shot Mum and Dad. Tom was twelve years old again, looking at a gun, knowing he would never get to drive a car, drink a beer, or see a girl naked. He screamed and put his arms up to his head, cradling his own skull as if trying to protect it, then dropped to the hard, cold pavement, where he curled up, moaning, crying, snot mixing with drool as it puddled under his face.

He hardly registered the many pairs of hands that took hold of his shoulders and feet, picked him up like one of the big boxes on the warehouse pallets, walked him back to the van, and threw him inside.

The doors slammed and the engine roared. He rolled across the space, hitting the other side as the van U-turned and accelerated back up the street.

The dark inside the van gave him hope, and Tom tried to say Blue's name. "B ... b ... mm... b." Even if he could have settled his scattered, terrified thoughts for long enough to speak, even if he had managed to say the words, Tom knew the bitter, horrifying truth.

Jimmy Blue had gone. Tom was on his own.

CHAPTER THIRTY

WINTER WATCHED the van from the monitor on his study desk. Locked inside, tied up, was little Tom Lewis, if it was really him. Still very much alive. Calling himself, and Winter shook his head in disbelief when he first heard it, Tom Brown. What kind of idiot kept the same first name in the witness protection programme?

And there was the problem. According to the paperwork and his fellow-workers, Tom Lewis really was an idiot, a classic idiot, the 'somewhere there's a village missing an idiot' variety of idiot. One or two sandwiches short of a picnic. Not the sharpest tool in the box. Lights on, but no one at home. Well, someone was at home, but that someone was an idiot. In short, the man cable-tied and moaning as Winter's men dragged him out of the van and marched him to the dungeon had, as the liberal elite would no doubt call it, severe learning difficulties.

Actually, Winter mused, the politically correct term was apt in this instance. Tom Lewis hadn't yet learned the consequences of crossing Robert Winter. But that omission could be remedied.

He pushed the intercom. "Penny."

"Sir?"

"Show Strickland straight in when he comes up. A pot of Darjeeling for me. Double espresso for my guest."

While he waited, Winter switched the view on the monitor to the dungeon. The tattooed gang leader didn't look happy under the harsh lights; pacing and mumbling, biting his nails. For someone who styled himself a stone-cold killer afraid of no one, it only took twenty-four hours of captivity to turn him into a whimpering child scuttling into the far corner every time the door opened. Amazing how quickly, and effectively, a permanently lit room broke someone. Disrupting the sleep cycle softened a subject up. Almost as effective as removing fingers and toes, though not as much fun.

Winter propped the study door open. Expecting Strickland to knock would have been disrespectful. If Strickland walked in without knocking, that, too, would have been a problem. The showing of respect in violent criminal organisations was, Winter mused, as useless and frustrating a habit as knowing which fork to use for pâté. If you were supposed to use a bloody fork at all. The only significant difference being that making an error in dining etiquette might provoke a raised eyebrow, whereas not asking after the daughter of one of the Glasgow Italian bosses resulted in your courier being sent back in little pieces.

Strickland walked in, stuck out his hand for a brief, firm handshake with two seconds of eye contact, then sat down opposite his old boss.

"Good to see you, John," Winter lied.

"You, too, Robert. You're looking well," came the insincere response.

In his army days, John Strickland had topped an unofficial sniper leaderboard. He showed a rare talent for killing. His job options once back in Britain proved limited.

Organised crime was not short of violent men and women. The trade attracted certain rage-fuelled dissenters who, if they didn't end up in prison first, joined organisations like Winter's hoping to channel their anger into a lucrative career. Such individuals didn't rise far. They were the rank and file. Foot soldiers.

The leaders controlled their less socially acceptable urges. Winter's greatest strength was self-awareness. He enjoyed violence. Killing another human being—mostly vicariously these days—thrilled him to the core in a way nothing else could. But his self-control was iron-hard, and his predilections never influenced business decisions. Hence his rise to the top.

John Strickland was a different beast. He killed people for money, never for pleasure. As far as anyone knew, that was. He never, ever, talked about his work. Strickland joined Winter's organisation in the early days, when they were doing little more than shifting dope, crack, and MDMA in the clubs at weekends, plus running a few girls on the estates. Winter anticipated problems, noting how Strickland didn't fit in with the others, always quiet and undemonstrative. Only a few years younger than Winter. But Strickland was good. A tangle with a Romanian crew who accused them of straying into their territory—which was true—proved just how good.

The Romanians turned up at one of Winter's houses with enough heavies to send a message. When Strickland heard the door being kicked in, he didn't join the rush to confront the threat, instead taking his Beretta 9000 from its shoulder holster and screwing on a silencer. He used a Beretta type D, the model without a safety. Strickland subscribed to the samurai idea that, if a sword is drawn, it should not be replaced until it has tasted blood. He didn't point guns at people to scare them. He did it to shoot them. When the first Romanian burst into the front room, rushing its sole occupant with a blood and hair-matted hammer, Strickland shot him in his left knee. He stepped over the screaming man into the hall. Twenty-seven seconds later, Strickland had left a trail of five corpses—one in the hall, two in the kitchen, and another two in the upstairs bedrooms. He found the last Romanian in the bathroom as he ran out of bullets. What happened next had passed into legend.

"Here, hold this." Strickland held out the Beretta. The Romanian, who had a young prostitute by the neck and was forcing her head into the toilet bowl, took the proffered weapon with his free hand, confused. Strickland pulled out a knife, slashed his throat, took his gun back, and washed his hands while the man bled out on the floor beside him, the girl sobbing in the corner.

The Romanian with the ruined knee survived to tell his tale. They didn't stand in the way of Winter's planned expansion after that.

Winter's rapid rise owed much to his executioner. Without Strickland, he might not have been ready to move into the top division when the opportunity presented itself. When Rhoda Ilích came to him with her proposition.

After a decade during which Winter expanded the human trafficking side of the business to become the market leader, Strickland asked to be released. He had no interest in putting together his own crew. He just wanted to widen his net of potential employers. Even Winter couldn't keep an assassin busy week in, week out. The unspoken element of their severance deal was that Strickland wouldn't accept the inevitable job with Winter as the target.

Penny brought in the drinks. Winter didn't believe in small talk.

"You took him too easily. You sure it's him?"

Strickland shrugged. "It's been twenty years, and he's supposed to be dead. He's the right age—early thirties. He has a mass of scarring on his skull. An old bullet wound fits."

"It does." Winter sipped his tea. "So he's faking the learning difficulties?"

Unlike Tariq, waiting in Winter's dungeon, Strickland recognised a rhetorical question when he heard one.

"Well, then." Winter put his teacup down and stood up. "Let's make sure. I don't want to waste my time having the wrong man tortured."

Two of Winter's crew manned the dungeon's anteroom. The soundproof chamber beyond boasted security cameras, mics and speakers. Most visitors to the dungeon died there. Those who survived were transformed by their stay. Sometimes a politician, government official, or police officer in a pivotal position resisted joining Winter's payroll. Persuasion was employed. A few days in the dungeon worked wonders. If they were intractable, Winter took a spouse, a parent, or—ideally—a child. It required little actual violence to change someone's mind at that point.

"Open the door, Christopher. How is Rachel? And the boys? They must be at school by now." Winter liked to pretend he cared about his employees' lives.

Christopher, fit, capable, and with a temper rarely aimed at his wife since Winter trained him as a torturer, stood by the door.

"Yes sir. All doing well, thank you, sir."

The second guard pressed the button on the mic. "Turn around and stand against the far wall." On the monitor, Tariq jumped to comply.

"Thank you, David," said Winter. "Still running?"

"Training for an ultra marathon, sir."

"Good for you."

Christopher held his thumb against the panel, and the door clicked open. He drew his weapon before entering. "Clear."

Winter and Strickland walked in. The man standing against the wall trembled. "Turn around."

Winter had read the reports of Tariq's conversations with Christopher and David. He had answered their questions in full. They only needed to beat him the first time, after which he became keen to help. He even claimed to like the twenty-four-hours-a-day lighting. When he woke up at home in the dark, he often imagined the psycho on the bus hiding in his room. Amazing how quickly some people broke.

"Hello, Tariq. I want you to do something for me."

Tariq's eyes flicked to Winter, then across to Strickland. "Yeah. Yeah, fine. What do you want? Look, man, I want to help you. Wanna go home, that's all."

"Of course you do. I'm going to bring someone in. I'd like you to tell me if you recognise him. Then you can go."

"That's it? That's what you want? Yeah, sure. Yeah." Surely the kid realised he could never go home. Winter had noted this self-delusion in the face of death before. More evidence of the chasm separating men like him and Strickland from the common herd. Lying to one's self was a flaw no leader should countenance.

"Thank you." Winter nodded through the open door at David, who left his desk, returning with Penny a minute later. They brought a man built like a wrestler, hunched over, humming tunelessly behind a hood. His wrists were so thick there was only a spare inch of plastic where the cable ties were pulled taut.

Penny guided the prisoner inside. Tariq looked him over.

"This him? This the guy you want me to check out?"

"Yes," said Winter. "And I want the truth."

"Yeah. Yeah. The truth. I swear."

"Good."

Winter nodded at Penny, and she removed the hood. As much as Winter wanted to inspect the man who might have killed Marty, Tay, and Rhoda, he didn't take his eyes off Tariq. Only a fellow-psychopath or sociopath might be able to conceal a reaction under such duress.

Tariq, who took a tentative step forward when the hood came off, now retreated, scrabbling back to the wall, his breath coming in gasps.

"Fuck! That's him. Oh, shit, no, oh shit. You've got a piece, right? You need to shoot this crazy fucker, shoot him. Right now. I'm not kidding, man, he's not even human, I don't know what he is, but he's not human."

Tariq was as scared as anyone Winter had ever seen.

"Where do you know him from, Tariq?"

"The bus, the bus. Come on, shoot him, kill him, for fuck's sake, please, please, oh thank god ..."

Strickland had taken out his gun. Tariq pointed at the prisoner. "Make sure he's dead, man, make really sure, I'm not kidding, he's—"

Tariq stopped talking when Strickland shot him.

Winter put a hand on Penny's arm. "Have that cleared away. And make our new guest uncomfortable. Let's give him twenty-four hours."

Winter studied the man who had, apparently, survived being shot in the head, then—twenty years to the day after his family were killed —popped up out of nowhere to murder Marty, Tay, and Rhoda. Tom had gasped when Strickland shot Tariq and now crouched against the wall crying, streaks of snot hanging in front of his lips as he whimpered with fear.

No one was that good an actor. Who the hell was this guy?

CHAPTER THIRTY-ONE

THE MUSIC WAS the loudest thing ever.

Tom didn't want to wake up, but the bad men wouldn't let him sleep. Not properly. They watched him. They saw when he laid down, and when he closed his eyes. They waited until then to turn on the music.

He didn't recognise all the songs, but words came into his mind when they played, the beat pulsing through his skull even when he clasped both hands tight over his ears and hummed.

Iron Maiden. AC/DC. Black Sabbath. The names meant nothing to Tom—but he was used to that. Sometimes, passing a shelf in a library or bookshop, a sentence popped into his head and he pretended he could read again. Fantastic Mr Fox, Danny, The Champion of the World, Howl's Moving Castle, The Sword In The Stone... these combinations of words conjured an unnameable joy in Tom. But the words didn't pop into his head if he tried too hard. He shuffled between shelves until a title transported him or someone asked him if he needed any help and he fled.

The words he thought of when they played the loud music didn't transport him, they left him here in the grey room where they shot a man yesterday. Or the day before. With no windows and the lights always on, Tom wasn't sure.

The blood left a stain. Wood shavings soaked up most of the fluids, but enough seeped through to make a dark map. Older stains dried around a covered drain in one corner. The floor wasn't flat, so the fluid ran in that direction. Rooms with floors like this were usually showers or toilets. Wet rooms. This was a different wet.

There was no toilet here at all. When Tom asked, the taller man laughed and pointed at the drain, then a bucket. "Piss here, shit there." He laughed as if he'd told a joke, but he never showed Tom the actual toilet, even after he'd banged on the door to ask, so he used the bucket. They hadn't emptied it yet, and he held his nose while eating the cheese sandwich they threw in.

When he fell asleep, they woke him with the music. They wouldn't turn it off until Tom stood up to prove he was awake. The cycle repeated: Tom lay down, closed his eyes: BAM! LOUD LOUD MUSIC! He rolled into a kneeling position, covering his ears, and stood up. The music stopped. He walked around, stumbling, tired, sat down, slumping, lay down, eyes heavy: BAM! MORE LOUD MUSIC! Tom remembered the name now: Heavy Metal. He never wondered what that meant before. Maybe because when you needed sleep it felt like someone climbing into your ears with big metal drums and gongs and hitting them with shovels. Or the music was solid, hard, and heavy, like a hod full of bricks falling on your head.

After ten hours, a day, or a week, one man brought a wooden chair while the taller one pointed the taser at him. Tom knew the name now. The first time the man pointed the taser, Tom thought the man wanted him to take it. When he tried, the man pressed a button and wires shot out. They clawed at Tom, getting into his skin, burning him inside over and over and over until his head banged on the concrete floor. Now Tom kept away, and when the taller man said sit down, he sat, while the other man tied his arms and legs to the chair, pulling the plastic too tight.

The tall man stayed in front, the shorter man stood behind Tom. A voice came from a speaker on the ceiling.

"Hello, Tom. That's your name, isn't it?"

Tom nodded. The voice sounded familiar. Not the one who shot the gun and killed the tattooed man. The one who had watched him do it. Tom knew he had heard that voice, and seen that man, before, but the memory was hidden. The locked doors in his mind were there when Tom woke up in hospital as a child. He didn't want to discover what lay behind them, and he had stayed away so long, the paths leading there were overgrown, tangled, lost.

"Good. Now, your bank card says your name is Tom Brown, but that's not really your surname, correct?"

Tom was confused. Debbie Capelli said Brown was his name now. She said he would get used to Tom Brown, but he never did. Tom remembered his real name. He didn't want to forget. His name was all he had left of his family. So he tried not to say his new surname very much.

"Tell me your real name, Tom."

Mrs Capelli—Debbie, she told him to call her Debbie—would be upset if he said Lewis. He should use his new name: Tom Brown. Debbie said the name kept him safe.

"Before you changed it."

"Mm, mm." Tom shook his head. He had promised Mrs Capelli. Debbie.

"Christopher," said the voice from the speaker. Was he trying to guess Tom's second name? Christopher wasn't right. Not even close. A shadow loomed overhead. A dark object flitted in front of his eyes, something coiled around his neck. The shorter man's knee pushed hard between Tom's shoulders, but that pain meant nothing compared to gasping for air and not getting any. No air got into his throat. Pinpricks of light buzzed as the edges of his vision darkened. An irresistible pressure commenced, reaching inside Tom's skull and squeezing his brain, squeezing and squeezing until his teeth hummed and the bones behind his eyes ached, and the room wasn't there any more because there was no room and no men and nothing around his neck and—

The air rushed into his lungs, crisp and beautiful. Tom didn't think air tasted of anything, but now he knew different, although he could never have described it. His chest heaved, bringing more oxygen into his body, the pressure easing and the room returning.

For a time, the only sound was Tom panting and crying. The man spoke again.

"Your real name, Tom." And this time, before Tom answered, the knee was pushing into his back, and the pressure resumed; his windpipe pinched closed a second time. When his sucking lungs found no air, his brain seized up. Like a car he'd been in once. Something happened to the engine, and the driver put it in limp mode. Tom's brain went into limp mode.

When the shorter man released him, Tom sucked in the beautiful air again, crying with fear and relief. He begged them to stop, but only formed the first consonant. "Pl, pl, pl pl."

"What's that, Tom?"

The material tightened on his throat.

"Wait a moment, Christopher." The pressure loosened. Tom experienced a rush of gratitude towards the man in the speaker.

"You have trouble talking, Tom. Is that right?"

Tom nodded. "Mm. Mm."

"Very well. For now, let's make it simpler. I'll say a few names. When you hear your real last name, I'd like you to nod for me. To stop these men hurting you. Do you understand?"

Tom wasn't sure. He thought hard; nodded.

"Good. And Tom?"

Tom looked up at the speaker. The small white box with glass at the front next to it wasn't, as Tom first thought, a broken light, but a camera. Tom looked up to show he was listening.

"Don't lie to me. If you do, I'll know. And David and Christopher will hurt you. You don't want that, do you?"

He shook his head this time.

"Here are the names. Nod at the right one. Purcell. Maidment. Wood. Lewis."

Tom nodded.

"Thank you, Tom. David, Christopher, that will be all."

While David pointed the taser, Christopher cut away the cables.

Blood pulsed back into Tom's numb toes and fingers. The two men left with the chair.

He had told the man the truth. Now they knew his name.

Tom Lewis.

He hoped Debbie wouldn't mind.

Perhaps they would let him go now.

CHAPTER THIRTY-TWO

TORTURE PROVIDED A MEANS TO AN END. Winter took no pleasure in it, although he suspected Christopher enjoyed it. Violence could be as dangerous as sex in his business. Some men and women became ensnared by a need to inflict pain or to kill. Both had their place, but when it became an end rather than the means, it led to disaster. Unpredictable, savage criminals only rose to the top in movies. In real life, if you thought your boss might shoot you in the head when you said the wrong thing, you tried to shoot him in the head first to avoid the situation ever arising. Like everything else, it was a balance. Winter relied on fear to run his organisation, but the fear needed to be rooted in logic, in the expectation of a proportionate response. If someone insulted Winter, he'd have them beaten. If they tried to muscle in on his business, skimmed from the profits, or tried to cheat him, then they died. Reasonable. Logical.

Tom Lewis had been in the dungeon three nights and two days. By December twenty-fourth they'd got nothing out of him. Lewis was still the same stammering idiot they'd brought in.

Winter's men stuck to a simple list of questions. How did Lewis find Marty and Rhoda? What was he planning next? And what was this Jimmy Blue crap? Nothing got a response. Winter wanted those answers first before discussing Rhoda's incriminating recording.

The lads on dungeon duty alternated between asphyxiation and good old-fashioned beatings, but nothing worked. When they punched Lewis, he cried. Winter was astonished. In his early thirties, built like a fighter, Tom Lewis was one of the broadest-shouldered men he'd ever seen, his arms hard as oak. Shaved head, over six feet tall, he looked like he had stamina, like he could take punishment without complaint. Not so. When Christopher punched him in the gut, he folded to the floor and sobbed like a child. A couple of kicks later, and he stopped crying, becoming unresponsive. At Winter's order, they checked his breathing and his pulse. Deeply asleep. Snoring, sometimes. Slapping, pinching, or kicking did nothing. He became unreachable.

If they left him alone, Lewis would emerge from his catatonic state and sit up, snivelling. During the next beating, the same pattern of crying and withdrawal followed. They went back to the sleep deprivation.

Near the end of the third day, Winter admitted his doubts, if only to himself. Lack of sleep tripped up liars. It chipped away at the subject's sense of reality, slowing their thought processes, making it near impossible to dissemble. But Lewis's answers, and his demeanour, remained consistent. He had displayed nothing other than the same halfwit idiocy since arriving. Which left two possibilities. First, he was what he appeared to be, which meant—despite the strong resemblance Lewis bore to Rhoda's killer—that they had the wrong guy. The man downstairs was brain damaged, incapable of planning, and carrying out, three murders. The second possibility would make Lewis the smartest, most devious opponent Winter had ever encountered, able to hide a considerable intellect behind this dribbling cretinous facade. If the latter, Lewis began the pretence twenty years ago and had never dropped the facade since. Surely not possible.

If Winter was torturing the wrong man, the real killer remained at large, hunting his people, and still in possession of a recording that threatened to turn Winter's empire to dust.

Fresh thinking was called for. Perhaps a leaf out of the intelligence community's playbook. *Enhanced Interrogation Techniques.* That was how the CIA described it. Americans had a peculiar genius for euphemism.

He pushed the intercom for the dungeon's anteroom. "David?"

"Sir?"

"Waterboard him."

The downside of waterboarding was the possibility of brain damage or death. Who could judge what effect it might have on an already compromised brain? Only one way to find out.

Winter turned off the monitor when David and Christopher wheeled the modified stretcher into the dungeon, securing Lewis with two broad leather straps, his head six inches lower than his feet.

He wanted to see this in person.

———

When the taller and shorter men tied Tom up this time, they pulled a black hood over his face. He heard them come back, pushing something on wheels. When they guided him there, shoving down, Tom wondered if it was a bed, if they would let him sleep. He didn't like the hood; he tried to tell them, but, as usual, the words got stuck. The men weren't listening, anyway. They pulled straps across his chest and legs, tilted him backwards.

It was dark inside the hood, which gave Tom a moment of hope. He hadn't been in the dark since arriving in the grey room. Jimmy Blue called him from the dark, from the shadows. Now Tom desperately needed to find the companion who'd been with him since he woke from his coma. Blue lived in the dark corners; born in darkness, Tom knew, and only able to return the same way.

The hood didn't help. Dark, but the same dark as when Tom closed his eyes. Not real darkness. Jimmy Blue didn't come. Tom screamed out for him in his mind, but found no trace. Blue needed the shadows, but no shadows existed in this terrible place.

After they tipped him backwards, he heard footsteps. Tom recognised the voice from the speaker. This man was in charge. He might stop the bad things from happening.

But he didn't. He didn't stop it. He told the men to begin. And fifteen seconds later, Tom wanted to die.

Tom turned his mind away from what was happening. He tried to picture his mum and dad, the faces he saw in his dreams.

If he died, that would be okay. He'd been dead before.

———

He slept, after. Not for long. His face and neck were still damp. Someone shouted. The taller man.

"Get up, you stupid arsehole. Wakey, wakey. Happy Christmas, mong. Get up."

Christmas? Tom was sure he'd been in this room for weeks, and the holiday must have come and gone ages ago. His mind reeled at his skewed sense of time. Unless the man was lying. Tom didn't think so. Not this time.

He rubbed his fingers along the front of his filthy shirt, put his hand up to his head. No hood. Apart from a darker patch of sawdust where the water poured through the cloth on his face onto the floor, there was no sign of what they did to him.

"Enjoy that, Tommy boy? Bit of fun? Sounds like fun. Skateboarding's fun. Kiteboarding's fun. I bet waterboarding's fun too. Don't worry, we'll let you have another go."

Tom didn't answer. He had tried to understand what was going on since they brought him here. He'd listened to the men, answered their questions when he could. But Tom found it hard enough to speak when calm. When terrified and in pain, he didn't stand a chance.

He slumped against the wall, half-awake. The lights still blazed.

Even if he wanted to, Jimmy Blue couldn't come to him. Not without the darkness. He was going to die here.

CHAPTER THIRTY-THREE

WINTER WOKE at six Christmas morning.

He reviewed his schedule, eating porridge steel-milled from Irish oats with a sprinkling of blueberries and flaked almonds. Winter always ate breakfast standing, facing the rising sun. Studies showed the most successful leaders rose early and followed established routines.

He read his notes. A jog around the grounds, a review of the finances after the auction, a call to the parlours for an update on the latest candidates. It was a holiday, so perhaps some reading in the afternoon. Winter liked to keep up with the latest medical and psychological journals, and any interviews with, or books about, leaders. There was always something new to learn.

There would be no work this evening. He expected nine for dinner—members of his crew who didn't have families to sit down with. Strickland, too.

This kind of gesture was normal from employers at Christmas.

Goal-setting featured in the routine of every successful business person Winter studied. And he could vouch for its efficacy. The important thing was to specify your goals, breaking down the elements necessary to achieve them. No good saying you wanted a billion pounds. Too vague. Better to plan on earning your first hundred thousand by your twentieth birthday, half a million before the next, ten million by the time you reached twenty-five, and so on. Next, set annual, monthly, weekly, then daily goals. At the most granular level, you could decide how best to spend each half-hour period to maximise your potential.

When Winter set the goal of taking over the human trafficking business in London, he made a list of his rivals. Rather than trying to kill everyone in his way before forty, he broke it down into manageable chunks. His goal-setting meant he only needed to murder one-point-six people a month over a five-year period.

Winter also read psychological studies claiming that many successful people, once they reached the summit of their personal mountain, were unhappy, empty, unfulfilled. Rich but miserable. A footnote provided Winter with the exceptions to that rule: sociopaths and psychopaths.

Winter thought the psychologists rather missed the point. Psychopaths didn't indulge in the pursuit of happiness. It was pointless. He pursued results. He wanted to win. And he always did.

Before leaving for his run, Winter checked on Tom Lewis. And what he witnessed on his monitor led to a decision that meant nobody would ever forget this Christmas.

At first, Winter thought Lewis had lost what passed for his mind. Bare-chested, he held his shirt like a matador, stretched between his hands. Like he expected a bull to materialise in the corner of the room. He looked at the ceiling, back at the wall, angled the shirt.

He muttered to himself as he did this. From the way his lips moved, it wasn't the usual toneless humming. Winter turned up the volume. Lewis's voice rose and fell as if speaking in sentences. No. Too repetitive for that. The same short sentence, over and over. Lewis stood at the far end of the room. Two mics listened from the ceiling above the door. Even when Winter turned up the volume of his headphones, he couldn't make the words out.

Tom walked across to the opposite corner, looking over his shoulder, stretching out the shirt, still mumbling. He kept adjusting the position, looking up before holding the shirt a few inches higher.

After three-and-a-half minutes of what looked like an experimental theatre piece, Lewis moved to the front of the dungeon. He didn't take a direct route, avoiding the spot where the tattooed kid bled out. Didn't want his bare feet touching the dried blood. Squeamish, as well as crying when punched. No, this couldn't be the guy who shot Marty and Tay and threw Rhoda from the top of a Parisian landmark.

The cameras had fisheye lenses. Lewis's stupid, scarred bald head looked swollen, his body elongating and stretching beneath it. He flapped open the shirt again, looking up at the light, starting to make adjustments. Winter leaned forward. Lewis was using the shirt to block the light. This time, when Lewis spoke under the mics, his voice was clearer. He repeated the same phrase over and over, looking from the ceiling to the corner.

"Blue needs the dark, Blue needs the dark, Blue needs the dark, Blue needs the dark."

Blue? Jimmy Blue? Winter didn't know what Lewis's nursery rhyme chant meant, but it was the only sentence with a subject, verb, and object that had passed his lips in the dungeon.

He frowned at the screen. Sleep deprivation didn't work. Torture failed. Lewis had no dependents, no friends, no partner. And Winter wiped out his family twenty years ago. No leverage available.

After the Reaperz Crew kid had identified Lewis as the man who attacked him and his gang on the bus, Winter dropped the idea of an accomplice. But days of torture with no result left Winter, for the first time he could remember, almost out of ideas. The Tom Lewis downstairs could barely wipe his own arse, let alone carry out a complicated revenge strategy.

Schizophrenia? Multiple personalities? It was known as dissociative identity disorder these days, Winter remembered. He'd scanned a few articles, but Lewis didn't fit the diagnosis; there had been no signs of alternate personalities during his imprisonment. Switching between 'alters'—different personalities—was often triggered by stress, and he'd been given plenty of that.

A half-remembered psychology article nagged at him. There was something, some piece he'd read about a rare condition. He sat back, thumbs pressing on his forehead for a moment. No. It wouldn't come. He turned to the internet. Winter knew he was unusual in not liking the ease of finding information online. He treasured his autonomy, his self-reliance, and Google was a lazy way out. Still, on this occasion...

Three minutes later, he had found the name of the condition: nyctophilia. Love of the dark. There was surprisingly little information. Winter dug deeper, looking for examples of people who behave differently in the dark, but there wasn't enough research available. Some clinicians even dismissed it as non-existent.

Winter drummed his fingers on the desk. The concept of the carrot and the stick was not an unfamiliar one, but it hardly applied when you were torturing someone for information. In that situation, the alternative to the stick was just another kind of stick. Bigger, harder, electrified, or with spikes sticking out of it. The closest thing to a carrot was promising someone you'd kill them quickly if they told you what you wanted to know, rather than flaying them alive or making them eat their own body parts.

But, since nothing else had worked, perhaps giving Tom Lewis what he wanted was worth trying. He brought up the anteroom on the second screen.

"David?"

"Sir?"

"Turn off the lights in the dungeon."

David stood up immediately. No one questioned Winter's orders. The dungeon's cameras had no night vision. The only time the lights were off was when the room was unoccupied. Perhaps worth considering an upgrade.

Winter donned the headphones again and listened to the sounds coming from the dungeon.

"—the dark. Blue needs the dark. Blue needs the dark. Blue—"

The monitor went black, and the voice stopped at exactly the same moment. Winter closed his eyes and put his hands over the cups of the headphones, pushing them closer to his ears.

For a minute, there was no sound at all. Winter had the curious, and disconcerting, sensation that, as hard as he was listening to Tom Lewis, Tom Lewis was listening to him. There was no two-way traffic when the intercom was closed, but it didn't stop him feeling there was. When sound returned, Winter had to concentrate to make sense of what he was hearing. He thought perhaps Lewis was putting his shirt back on. Next, the sound of bare feet on sawdust. Four steps. That would take him into the middle of the room. Another scrunch of sawdust and a scraping sound. Had Lewis sat down?

Then nothing except the sound of breathing; each breath slightly deeper than the one before. When it settled into a steady rhythm, Winter timed each inhalation and exhalation using the minute hand of his watch. He did it for ten minutes to make sure. Each of Lewis's breaths lasted forty-seven seconds. This wasn't sleep. He was either meditating or lapsing into a coma.

Winter took off the headphones, placed them on the desk and stared, frowning, at the dark screen.

"David. Listen in on him once every thirty minutes. Let me know if there's any change."

He flicked through the other camera feeds from their positions around the house. Penny had come through from the annexe and was reviewing a list on her tablet at the kitchen table. Winter pushed the button to speak. "Earl Grey in an hour, Penny. Going for my run now."

Penny nodded at the screen before returning her attention to the list.

Winter went upstairs to change. He was setting off thirty-seven minutes later than usual. He ran towards the artificial lake he'd installed alongside the woods. He'd had it stocked with perch, chub, pike, and bass when it was dug and filled. One day, maybe he'd finally learn to fish. But fishing looked so bloody boring, and there were far more interesting ways to fill his time. Also, he was as likely to hook a body as a fish out of the water.

His thoughts kept returning to the man in the dungeon. He was intrigued. Lewis's medical records were full of gaps. The gunshot injury report showed that the bullet had hit the skull at an angle. Early reports suggested the boy's coma might allow his brain the time and resources to heal from the life-threatening injury. After that, the hospital reports became a lie, noting that Tom Lewis had never regained consciousness. His name was added to that of his parents on their gravestone in the cemetery.

Winter turned away from the lake and ran into his woods. A brief negotiation with the owner of the neighbouring property had secured the signing over of the land, so Winter had four acres of mature trees to himself. The negotiation had been brief because the neighbour had tried to up the price three times, before a meeting in a cafe with one of Winter's crew where he was shown a series of photographs that would have led to an abrupt end to his political career had they become public. A tawdry device, but effective. Winter had been privately impressed by the man's sexual appetite and stamina. Not surprised, though. When you dug around in anyone's life, you always came up with leverage. Except with Tom Lewis, it seemed.

What interested Winter was the gap in Lewis's history. He must have left hospital secretly, around the time his 'death' was announced. He had been thirteen years old. There were specialist facilities that looked after children recovering from serious injury or illness. Winter had no doubt that Tom would have been sent to the best the taxpayer could afford. The police must have thought they had a golden goose. A witness who could point at Robert Winter and testify he had ordered the murders of the Lewis family, personally soaking Irene Lewis in petrol before burning her alive.

If the initial medical reports were accurate, Tom Lewis's injuries, even if they didn't kill him, would be life-changing. In a case like his, that might mean round-the-clock care for the rest of his life. Even the most optimistic prognosis suggested the damage to his brain was severe enough to cause lifelong communication problems and learning difficulties.

All of which tallied nicely with the shuffling, humming cretin in the dungeon. But if that was Tom Lewis, where was Jimmy Blue?

CHAPTER THIRTY-FOUR

WINTER SPENT the rest of the day with the tasks and reading he'd planned. The caterers arrived mid afternoon, unloading boxes under the unsmiling supervision of the two gatehouse guards. As Penny transferred the contents to the ovens in the kitchen, the smell of roasting meat, potatoes, and parsnips drifted through the house.

By the time Winter and his guests sat down to eat, it was late afternoon, the thin sunlight draining out of a leaden sky.

At dinner, Penny told an off-colour joke that had the guys roaring around the dinner table. It involved a nun, a broken-down car, and a physically impossible manoeuvre with a gearstick. They were drinking a very expensive Australian Shiraz. Most of them usually drank wine from a box they'd picked up at Calais, but it was only once a year, so what the hell. Strickland was drinking beer, slowly. They were probably in the safest place in London, but old habits were old habits for a reason.

Penny was the sole female present. Rhoda hadn't missed a Christmas dinner for the last nineteen years, but only because she understood the message her absence would send. Winter thought of that last phone call from Paris, Rhoda babbling about demons and ghosts.

Winter made his decision as he watched them eat, drink, and laugh. It often happened this way. Something he'd been considering, weighing up variables, crystallised when he relaxed. The next year would be his last in the business. Quit while you're ahead. That was the cliché. Winter was ahead and always had been. Richer than most CEOs, and more consistently successful, although he would never feature in the Sunday Times rich list.

He sipped the wine, letting the flavours reveal themselves as they rolled across his tongue.

Christopher took a buzzing phone out of his pocket. Since he was on duty, Winter allowed it.

Christopher stood up as he listened. "What? He's what? Yes. Will do."

"Is our guest all right?" said Winter.

"Yes, sir. Still in the dark, sir. But David said you need to hear him."

"Is he talking?" Winter folded his napkin, dropping it on his chair. Strickland caught his eye and stood up, too.

Christopher joined them at the door. "Not talking, sir, no. He's singing."

———

Winter led the two men upstairs into his office, signalling them to join him on his side of the desk. The monitor was dark. He turned up the volume and unplugged the headphones. A male voice blared out of the speakers.

> *"It's when next I have murdered, the Man-In-The-Moon to powder*
> *His staff I'll break, his dog I'll bake, they'll howl no demon louder"*

Christopher's whisper broke the silence. "What the hell?"

Neither Strickland nor Winter displayed any outward reaction, but Winter noticed a tiny contraction of the muscles around the assassin's lips as his teeth clenched.

Singing in the dungeon was a first. A raucous rendition in a clear, strong baritone on Christmas Day made the experience positively surreal. The singer was locked inside a soundproof room with concrete walls and a steel door. Yet they heard a joyous confidence in his voice, and each line rang out like a personal challenge. The man should be broken, not celebrating.

"Interesting," said Winter. He had hoped a spell in the dark might produce results, but this was more dramatic than he had anticipated. Then the voice plunged into a different chorus, and Winter pretended not to feel the chill that raised goosebumps on his arms, and made the skin on his back prickle with cold sweat.

> *"I'll close your eyes so you can't see*
> *This very hour, come and go with me*
> *I'm Death I come to take the soul*
> *Leave the body and leave it cold"*

"David. Turn the lights on."

The three men in Winter's study waited. The second monitor showed David leaving his post. They saw his hand move, flicking the switch on the wall. The screen remained black.

"David. My monitor may be faulty. Check yours."

On-screen, David returned to his desk, tapped the keyboard, and checked the connections at the back of the screen.

"Monitor's fine, sir. But the lights aren't working."

The dungeon was twelve feet high from floor to ceiling. High enough for the most gymnastic occupant to fail to reach the cameras, speaker, or mics. Or the fluorescent lights. The plastic waste bucket was the only implement available. Even the most accurate throw would be unlikely to cause damage.

"Christopher. Get back down there. Take torches. Subdue the prisoner and restrain him."

"Yes, sir."

Winter stopped him at the door.

"Take Scott with you."

Winter offered Strickland a seat, and they watched the screens. The singing continued unabated.

"My staff has murdered giants, my bag a long knife carries
For to cut mince pies from children's thighs, with which to feed the fairies"

Neither man spoke as, two minutes later, Christopher entered the anteroom, followed by Scott—a short, broad man with a wine stain birthmark covering the left side of his face.

Scott had worked for Winter for six years. In other circumstances, Winter conceded, Scott might have become a pillar of the community, given his intelligence and self-discipline. A police commissioner perhaps, or an army general. He might have learned to control the rage that troubled him. Winter taught him to channel it. And a fine weapon he had turned out to be, treating violence as a vocation.

If Tom Lewis gave them any trouble, Scott would be more than a match for him. Not that Winter thought the sobbing idiot in the dungeon could really be a threat. Alzheimer patients sometimes recited long poems, or sang word-perfect songs from their childhood. This was probably something similar.

David took the taser from a drawer, and Scott stood four feet back from the door, holding a torch as Christopher pushed it open.

The moment the door opened, the singing stopped. The monitor remained dark. Winter had been expecting a grainy view of a few square feet as light from the anteroom spilled into the dungeon. It wasn't just the lights, then. Lewis had disabled the cameras. But he'd left the mics on. And he'd done it all in the dark.

They all heard the next sound. The men on the monitor looked at each other. In the office, Strickland and Winter stared at the screen.

In the dungeon, someone was laughing.

David handed Scott the taser. The younger man took it in his right hand, switching the torch to his left.

"Turn around and stand against the far wall." The laughter stopped.

He couldn't illuminate the whole room without stepping inside, but Scott angled the beam up to the ceiling.

"Lights look okay," he called. "Maybe it's a power outage."

Winter pressed the intercom. "Check the cameras."

Scott took another step forward, the taser held ready. He listened, and let the beam of light play around the room, then back to the ceiling and into the corner not obscured by the open door.

Winter was glad Strickland was here to see this. After years of mentoring, discipline, and preparation, training in multiple fighting techniques and mastering weapons, Scott was, in Winter's view, almost a match for Strickland himself. Winter allowed himself a small smile. The next few minutes would be a brutal demonstration of Scott's abilities. It would be a privilege to witness it.

Scott took another step.

"It's been... hang on, it can't be." His squat, broad frame filled the lower two-thirds of the doorway. He was looking up. "It looks like it's been shot out."

The interval that followed was the longest half-second Winter had ever experienced. The soundproof dungeon comprised four walls, a drain, and a bucket. One door. No other way in or out. To get through it without a registered thumbprint or an eight-digit code would take so much plastic explosive that the whole house would come down on top of it.

What Scott had just told them couldn't possibly be true, and everyone knew it.

Which made what happened next equally impossible.

Scott's body jerked backwards, as if pulled by an invisible bungee rope. Blood and gobbets of flesh hit Christopher, still standing by the door. The mics picked up the sound perfectly. Automatic gunfire.

Scott hit the floor. Or, rather, his corpse did, with bullets in the torso, neck, and head. He died with a surprisingly peaceful expression on his face, considering the circumstances.

A flywheel of sparks lit up the doorway. David, reaching for a shotgun from the rack on the wall, was driven face first into the stock of the weapon as a line of bullets traced a route up his back.

Christopher, frozen in place, remembered he was holding open a reinforced steel door. He tried to close it, but a hand emerged from the darkness and pushed back, sending him skidding away.

Winter didn't dream, so he'd never had a nightmare. If he ever did, he suspected, the figure who walked out into the anteroom would have a starring role.

Next to him, Strickland found his voice.

"Who the fuck is that?"

CHAPTER THIRTY-FIVE

WHEN THE LIGHTS TURNED OFF, Tom shuffled to the centre of the dungeon. He sat on the sawdust, more tired than ever. When his head sagged against his chest, he forced it up. He had to find Jimmy Blue.

In the past, he caught glimpses of Blue. A figure watching from a night-black window, a movement in the shadow of a building as someone turned to watch him. There was no mistaking the call. When Tom looked into those shadows, or up at the darkened window, a sense of rightness, of pieces sliding into place, descended. Like a child's puzzle, plastic squares sliding around a grid to make a picture. Except Tom didn't need to move the pieces into place. He just had to show up. His stomach clenched with excitement. Blue was close.

This was the strongest call, the clearest sense of his presence he'd ever experienced. It came on fast and strong. Jimmy Blue filled the room, expanding into every dark corner, intoxicated with freedom and power. Tom peeled away from himself, sinking into a beautiful nothingness with no bad men, no pain, no loud music. He slept. Blue would take care of everything.

Tom's memories of the past few days rose like smoke into wind, dissolving, thinning, disappearing. He followed, rising and expanding, senses fading. Touch, taste, smell, all gone. Only the silent dark.

———

Jimmy Blue stood up in the dungeon. Such darkness. Thick, inky, impenetrable. He stretched out his arms as if giving, or receiving, a blessing; tears brimming, then falling. Years of preparation to find the Forger and the Traitor. Now for the two remaining names on his list: the Executioner and Winter. So well protected, both of them. So experienced, wary, intelligent, and brutal. After Paris, they traced Tom in weeks, not months. Dangerous men; not to be underestimated.

But Blue was more dangerous. And they had underestimated him badly. They were about to find out how badly.

He couldn't see the walls in the dark, but he didn't need to. He knew the dimensions and layout of the room intimately. Not just because of Tom's time in captivity. Jimmy's knowledge went deeper. Deeper than anyone's, including Winter.

When his outstretched fingers touched the plastered concrete, Jimmy Blue walked sideways to his right until he reached the corner. He slid his hands up level with his face and rapped his knuckles on the wall. He had remembered the location perfectly.

Four-and-a-half years earlier, Tom Lewis worked for a building crew constantly in demand with the best London architects. It was a small company, and Werner, the boss, oversaw every project. He had a reputation for being one of the fairest bosses in the business and only employed the very best construction crews. Tom had already gained a reputation as the strongest hod carrier in the city, and the Elstree job was his fourth for Werner.

It took three weeks to dig foundations and another fortnight to assemble a steel superstructure. During that time, Jimmy Blue broke into offices, checked blueprints, withdrew a significant amount of money from his reserves, and made many illegal purchases.

The soundproof room, situated next to the underground parking garage, was the first to be finished. Werner never speculated about its use, but some labourers said the owner must be a music producer. When Werner's crew moved on to the next floor, Jimmy Blue waited until after midnight, and came back.

Security on the site meant a few lights with motion sensors, and a retired policeman in a hut. There would be nothing much to steal until the house was furnished and the so-called producer moved in with his platinum records and priceless guitars. Blue knew the real owner. Winter's twelve-month search for an architect drew his attention. It was why Tom Lewis currently worked as a hoddie.

The security guard proved embarrassingly easy to overcome. Blue tossed a brick into some undergrowth. When the guard came out to check, he sneaked in and spiked his drink with gamma-hydroxybutrate. In tiny doses, GHB makes people relaxed, euphoric, and horny. Larger doses, when—for instance—administered in the coffee of obese security guards, make them fall asleep within ten minutes, and start snoring in fifteen. After twenty minutes, the only response to a shove on the shoulder was a bubbly fart and the whispered word, "clipboard."

With the security lights off, and five hours remaining before dawn, Blue worked hard and fast. He used a pickaxe to smash through the newly finished concrete wall, hollowing out a compartment big enough to contain the items he had brought. Once everything was inside, he closed the hole with a wooden board and covered it with concrete from an airtight bag mixed with calcium chloride to speed up the drying process.

When the hidden compartment was flush with the rest of the wall, Jimmy Blue played the beam of a powerful torch over it. He couldn't see any evidence of his own work. He took the gear back to the stolen car. He turned the security lights back on before he left, dumped the rubble into a skip in Borehamwood nine minutes later, and replaced the gear in the Soho storage unit before breakfast.

Revenge was a long game. Four years after breaking into the site where Tom Lewis carried bricks by day, building the foundation of

Robert Winter's house, he was back. They brought him here. Just as Jimmy Blue planned.

Blue grinned into the darkness. Then he brought his enormous fists up and behind his head, bringing them forward to smash into the concrete wall which—in this precise area, and no other—was a finger-width thick. The board beneath splintered and sagged. Blue felt his way around until he found the weakest point. He pushed his fingers inside and pulled on the thin wood, plaster and concrete, grabbing handfuls of it to expose the compartment.

He took the handgun first. He doubted they listened in on him constantly. If they did, the tearing open of the hollow section of wall would bring the guards, and he needed to be ready.

No one came. He walked forward, bare feet exploring the floor. When the guards—David and Christopher—tied him up, the back legs of the chair fitted into two indentations. It stopped him moving while they beat him. Blue could picture the layout perfectly from that spot. When he found the indentations, Blue knelt, eyes closed, seeing what Tom had seen.

When ready, he raised the gun and squeezed off four shots: left-hand corner speaker, camera, right-hand corner speaker, camera. Shooting out the lights would be easy, but a man with no shoes didn't need a room full of broken glass. He kept his breathing slow and steady, lifted the gun, and fired three more times. Each row of fluorescent tubes was powered by insulated, plastic-wrapped cables on the ceiling, less than an inch in diameter. Three bullets, three severed cables.

Blue tucked the gun into the waistband of his filthy trousers. No need to shoot out the microphones. He wanted the guards, or—hopefully—Winter, to hear him next time they listened in.

Jimmy Blue didn't need any light to see inside the compartment. He remembered precisely where each item was placed. He removed the contents of the hidden shelf methodically, laying them out on the floor behind him. With the compartment stripped bare, he knelt on the sawdust in front of his treasure, picking up each item.

It took him twelve minutes to get ready. His grin broadened. He stepped under the microphone and started singing.

CHAPTER THIRTY-SIX

JIMMY BLUE STEPPED out of the darkness. Always important to make a first impression, and he'd thought about this outfit for a long time. He wanted to inspire fear in those who saw him, but he also wanted to have fun, and if a *what the hell* reaction bought him an extra split second, that was a bonus.

Mostly, though, he wanted to look badass.

He wore a samurai-style helmet, and a loose-fitting martial arts outfit that could accommodate some athletic moves. Everything black, of course. He carried the handgun in his left hand, and a sub-machine gun in his right. On top of the ninja suit, spare clips for the weapons crossed his body on a harness. The small rucksack was a concession. It spoiled the overall image, but its function was utilitarian. He had a serrated hunting knife in a sheath on his left hip. His wrists, forearms, and shins were covered with dull black polyethylene body armour pieces, 3D printed to Blue's specifications. Tool steel blades lined each piece of armour like lethal corduroy.

The first two guards died before getting a proper look at him. The smaller, stockier guard—Christopher, the one who administered the controlled asphyxiations—was granted a few extra seconds to appreciate the sight.

Fighters know their strengths and weaknesses. If they aren't cognisant of both before engaging an opponent, their education will be brief and brutal. Jimmy Blue's enemy, well-trained and aggressive, didn't hesitate. Christopher moved in close, trying to negate the extra reach of the taller man. A good play, usually. He grabbed Jimmy's right wrist with both hands. Wrist bones are delicate, and someone who knows how to manipulate them can bring the most powerful opponent to their knees. Again, usually. Not today.

Christopher screamed when his fingers closed around Blue's wrists. The rows of sharpened steel blades that ridged the armour sliced into his flesh, leaving vivid crimson parallel lines on his palms and fingers when he jumped away. His cry of agony became a frothy gurgle when Blue slashed the sharp edge of his armoured forearm across the exposed skin of his neck.

As the guard twitched and spasmed, slumped against the wall, bloody hands pressing against the fatal cut in his throat, Jimmy Blue looked for, and found, the camera in the anteroom.

He made sure it got a good look at him. *Kabuto* helmets didn't just provide protection during the battles of feudal Japan. They inspired fear, with facial armour often designed to make the wearer appear to be a demon. Jimmy Blue had embraced this feature. His *zunari*-style *kabuto*, made of the latest lightweight anti-ballistic materials, boasted all the defensive aspects of the ancient samurai design, including overlapping plates to protect the neck. The *mengu*, or facial armour, covered his features from nose to chin. He was a grinning demon. Which was as it should be. Because, at that moment, every available synapse in Jimmy Blue's brain focused on his immediate plans: to rain down bloody, savage, terrifying revenge on the men who had butchered his family. Anyone who stood between him and them would die.

Blue had smeared ash around his cheekbones and forehead, and his dark green eyes burned like embers of a supernatural fire. This ash had been decanted into a small tin box from a vase in the Soho lock-up, brought to the dungeon when he'd dug out his secret compartment. The vase had belonged to his mother, the ashes inside all that was left of her.

He stared into the camera, letting any watchers drink in the sight of what they had brought into their home.

"I'm coming for you."

He holstered the handgun, took out the hunting knife, and, kneeling next to the dying guard, sawed off his thumb.

Jimmy Blue walked out of the anteroom, ignored the stairs leading to the main house, instead entering the underground garage next door. Nine of the twelve parking spaces were occupied. The dirty white van that had brought him waited next to a dark grey SUV. A row of anonymous German saloons lined the opposite wall.

Only one camera. A burst from the submachine gun destroyed it.

He looked for Winter's midnight blue Mercedes, finding it parked nearest the doors, away from the others. Blue sprinted across and tucked a magnetic tracker under the rear bumper. Winter might run, in which case it was best to have a contingency.

Blue pressed the button to raise the garage door. As it rolled upwards, clanking, he pressed Christopher's severed thumb against a security pad. Jimmy Blue helped build this house, memorising the blueprints. And he was about to give himself another advantage. The door next to the security pad clicked open, and he stepped inside. The cramped room contained the junction boxes for the house's power supply.

It was too small a space to risk firing a weapon. Blue took a grenade from the rucksack, removed the pin, shoved the heavy metal egg among the cables and left.

Three seconds before detonation.

Cautious footsteps approached from the house.

He ducked behind the van as the door from the house opened, putting his hands over his ears. The explosion blew the door off the small room, and the van rocked on its axles, creaking.

Silence and darkness arrived together. He breathed it in. His rage was so concentrated it burned away every imperfection, leaving behind a pure warrior engineered to kill.

Blue took his hands away, listening for the voices behind the door to the house. Two men. Which meant others would approach from outside, in case their prisoner made a break through the garage. He had planned for that. He'd even opened the door for them.

The voices from the house debated whether to go back for torches. Voice one promised to cover the other if he entered the garage. Voice two wondered if they might swap roles. Voice one pointed out the lack of light. If he moved fast he'd be fine, as the cretin wouldn't be able to see him.

The cretin. Nice.

Voice two demurred, but after voice one made a specific threat involving testicles and a hammer, he changed his mind.

The garage doorway was visible only as a grey rectangle. Outside, it was cloudy, the darkness almost as absolute as inside the garage. An orange tinge came from the myriad London streetlights beyond the lake and the woods.

Jimmy Blue had no supernatural powers, no demonic ability to see in the dark. Nevertheless, darkness was his element, his home. His sanctuary.

Blue listened, hearing the truth of things. Born in nothingness, in utter blackness, he had learned to listen, at first, like a baby does, hearing every sound, unable to separate one from another. He began to differentiate noises, separating voices from a dog barking or a car engine starting. Soon he parsed the sounds further, discerning first the difference in pitch between male and female, then more subtle differences of cadence, rhythm, and texture separating one speaker from the next. For much of his early existence, all sounds were equal, the *thwick* of an opening refrigerator as important as an angry shout outside.

But Jimmy Blue knew how Tom Lewis experienced the world. When Tom heard the hundreds of sounds that surrounded him, he screened most of them out. If someone spoke to him, he ignored the music from a radio next door. Blue could choose another way of hearing. It began with perceiving the entire soundscape. If one sound became more important than another, he focused on it, but not at the expense of everything else in the audible spectrum. He did it now, allowing his awareness to open to his surroundings.

Voice two rushed through the door, rolling on the dusty concrete. No scuff of palms on the floor meant he was likely holding his gun with both hands. Simultaneously, footsteps approached from outside, soft wet grass giving way to coarse-grained gravel.

Jimmy Blue's most recent check of Winter's household security, three weeks earlier, revealed no change in the routine. Winter had a female assistant who lived in the house. The guards worked twelve-hour shifts. Four outside the house, two inside. David and Christopher, his daytime jailers; both dead, along with a third, unknown, guard.

Torch beams played across the garage entrance, coming from both directions. A classic pincer movement. Two beams from each side. One guard already in the garage, another behind the door to the house.

Six in total. And the amount of cars suggested visitors. Which meant Jimmy Blue was confronting more enemies than he had anticipated. Which, in its turn, meant more violence, more bloodshed.

More fun.

CHAPTER THIRTY-SEVEN

WINTER AND STRICKLAND were pragmatic men. Those who rose to the top in organised crime did so with a finely balanced mix of leadership and management ability, an unwavering focus, and, when necessary, an excellent set of practical skills. Winter was a good shot. In his youth, he'd been a brutal hand-to-hand fighter. He fought dirty, not that he would have labelled his approach so judgementally. In the early empire-building years, he had been put to the test twice. Both fights left him bloody and injured. His opponents weren't as lucky, and the manner of their deaths contributed to his legend.

Winter knew Strickland's sole trader business model required him to keep his physical skills honed. As he'd grown older, the executioner had adapted his methods. These days, his hits were clean, methodically planned, and undramatic. His reputation remained unmatched.

When Winter and Strickland watched Scott, David, and Christopher die at the hands of the creature that emerged from the maw of the dungeon, they didn't waste time on speculation. Incredible as it seemed, Tom Lewis was now armed, and—judging by the speed and efficiency with which he'd killed three men—well-trained and ruthless. They focused on facts. Explanations would come later, after they'd put this lunatic in the ground.

Winter opened the general channel on the intercom. "Everyone to the house. Armed intruder in the lower level. Shoot on sight. Gatehouse, you're group one. Enter the garage from the north. Patrol team, you're group two. Enter the garage from the south. Drive him back into the house."

He pictured the six remaining men left in the building. Capable, but not exceptional. Scott had been the golden boy. But all the talent and training in the world means nothing when your opponent puts half a dozen bullets in you.

"Penny, give everyone in the house a handgun and two clips each. Split into three more groups. Group three to the garage. Group four, secure the hall. Group five, take the kitchen and back door. All radios on channel two. Only use them to report a sighting. Penny, with me."

Winter opened his gun cabinet. No one entered his house armed. Not even Strickland, his Beretta left in the glove compartment of his car. Winter handed him a Glock and took one for himself. They both checked the weapons, sliding full clips into place.

The various groups headed for their positions.

The explosion in the garage registered as a muffled thud. The lights died as Winter and Strickland reached the study door.

"Smart," said Winter.

Strickland answered without turning. Both men kept their voices low and their sentences short. "Generator?"

"Not anymore, if that explosion was the control room."

Explosives. Surely Lewis wasn't working alone. But there'd been no security breach, no alarm from the invisible perimeter.

If he was alone, then the village idiot was not only not an idiot, but dangerously intelligent. Lewis had blown up the generator. He was following a plan. Meaning Tom Lewis deliberately let himself be captured. Winter became aware of a strange sensation in the pit of his stomach, a kind of lazy flutter. Excitement. Or fear. It had been so long since he'd experienced either emotion, he didn't know which. At some level, he welcomed the novelty. A worthy opponent. It had been too long.

Penny's voice. "Winter?" He hadn't been born with that name. He had chosen a new surname when he left home, enjoying the association with a cold, dark season during which everything died.

"Here," he said.

If the first explosion registered as a thump, the next was more like a giant hand punching the house. The entire building shuddered once, then settled.

Winter and Strickland exited the study, their eyes adjusting to the gloom. As they stepped onto the landing and joined Penny, the situation downstairs worsened.

Below them in the hall, group four waited; one man crouching three feet from the front door, the other eighteen feet away, his head and shoulders a dark blot obscuring the pale tiled floor. Both pointed guns at the open door and the stairs to the anteroom, dungeon, and garage.

A few seconds after the explosion, a cloud of dust billowed up from the basement, filling the hall. The front door opened, and a metal object rolled onto the tiles.

The object hissed, releasing more smoke and an acrid stench. The men downstairs coughed uncontrollably.

One cough turned into a wheezing scream and a liquid gurgle.

A single shot rang out.

CHAPTER THIRTY-EIGHT

Three minutes earlier

IT WAS A GOOD PLACE, a comfortable place. The home of his enemy, but dark now, and full of the dead. Some of the dead still breathed, still moved, still whispered into radios, and pointed guns. The knowledge of their deaths had yet to reach their central nervous systems, but it wouldn't be long. Jimmy Blue would share that knowledge and they would fall before him like harvested wheat.

The torch beams didn't reach his hiding place as he crouched behind the van, but he resented the light all the same. It ruined the darkness, like someone shouting in the middle of a cello recital.

He took a slim black box the size of a cigarette packet from a pouch on his ammunition belt. It had two buttons and a small antenna, which he slid out.

Blue watched the torch beams in the van's wing mirror. The man who'd rolled through the door from the house gestured angrily when a torch picked him out. He crawled back to the door, gun held ready.

The rest of the men searched the garage, shining torches under each car. Blue estimated they'd reach his position in twenty seconds.

After ten seconds, Blue pressed the first button.

Back in the dungeon, an mp3 device began playing through the battery-powered speaker placed beside it on the shelf.

Jimmy Blue smiled at the sound of his own voice.

"Still I sing bonnie boys, bonnie mad boys,
Bedlam boys are bonnie
For they all go bare and they live by the air,
And they want no drink nor money"

"He's doubled back. He's in the dungeon."

At a hissed command, the light-wavers left the garage, handguns braced against their torches, heading for the singer.

Blue squeezed out from behind the van and ran for the garage door, his bare feet whispering on the concrete.

Timing was important now, but it didn't have to be perfect. He pictured the men flanking the dungeon door. Cautious, especially when their torches picked out the three corpses in the anteroom. No one wanting to go in first. They'd take turns waving their lights, getting a glimpse of the room beyond. They wouldn't see the loudspeaker because he'd propped a piece of plastered wood in front of it.

Any time now, someone would get brave. Probably counting down from three on their fingers, going in shooting, aiming into each corner.

As he left the garage and sprinted to the front of the house, Jimmy Blue heard the shots. Soundproof walls made gunshots as dramatic as twisted bubble wrap.

He pressed the first button on the device again, turning the mp3 player off. Timing the next interval relied on guesswork. There would be a moment's confusion as the shooter wondered if one of his bullets had found its target. When no one returned fire, others might enter the room. The shooter, or one of his colleagues, would shine their torch around the room. They wouldn't find a body. But they would find a pile of pale objects stacked up on either side of the door like miniature sandbags. They might wonder what they were looking at, confused, perhaps, by the thin metal rods sticking out of the putty, looking like a child's sculpture of a giant hedgehog.

Then someone would recognise the rods as detonators, or the putty as plastic explosives, shout a warning, and they'd try to run.

No one could run that fast.

Jimmy Blue pressed the second button. The resulting *whomp* made him stumble as he rounded the corner to the front door.

He slowed as he approached the house. Smoke from the explosion drifted into the hallway. He shrugged off the rucksack and removed two canisters. When he replaced the rucksack, he pushed a tube through a hole in its side, feeding it through to his face.

Inside the demon-shaped *mengu* covering his nose and mouth, he flicked a switch. He was now breathing his own air supply. He completed the precautions with a pair of goggles.

Time for stage two.

Jimmy Blue opened the front door and threw in the first canister, springing back. The smoke had already disorientated the guards. The gas disabled them completely. He found the first guard spluttering, struggling to breathe. Blue remedied the situation by cutting his throat.

He looked up, seeing three figures at the top of the stairs. Invisible in the smoke, he pulled out his handgun, aimed, and fired.

CHAPTER THIRTY-NINE

STRICKLAND SAW the flash of the muzzle through the rising smoke. He was aware of movement to his left, where Winter and Penny stood on the landing alongside him, but his attention remained on the danger below.

He returned fire. The Glock 19 Winter favoured held three more bullets in the clip than Strickland's usual Beretta, but its trigger guard was uncomfortable. He emptied fifteen rounds in a tight circle around the area of the muzzle flash, re-accustoming himself to its recoil.

He swapped out the empty magazine and listened. Nothing. Impossible for anyone to breathe quietly in that smoke. Which meant no one was breathing.

Tear gas. Strickland thought of the outfit Lewis wore when he burst out of the dungeon. The lower part covered his mouth and nose. The lack of coughing below signified nothing if he had his own oxygen supply. When this clown was dead, Strickland would be very interested to learn how someone locked inside a soundproof concrete dungeon scored a ninja suit, weapons, explosives, and an oxygen tank.

Strickland checked his colleagues. Winter held a handkerchief to his face, looking as unruffled as ever. He nodded at the wall behind them. Penny slumped there, unmoving. There was a difference between the way a person lay when unconscious and when they were beyond help. Strickland didn't need the ragged hole above Penny's left eye, and the smear of blood on the wall to tell him which this was. Her hair, the brown now streaked dark with red, smeared the white wall like a paintbrush.

Winter used hand gestures to direct him towards the office while he went the other way. Strickland nodded. The back stairs meant Winter would have a second exit available, should he decide the situation warranted a retreat. Strickland had known his old boss a long time. If retreating meant survival, he would do it, regroup, and come back fighting on his own terms. There was a reason Winter still thrived, when most of his rivals were long dead.

Strickland searched Penny's body, taking her Glock and a spare magazine. Winter watched him do it before backing towards the west wing of the house.

Strickland wasn't a team player, or a leader. He wasn't a psychopath like Winter. He was a serial killer who'd got lucky. And he'd kept his secret for thirty years.

Before joining Winter, he'd killed four men and three women. His compulsion was all-consuming. From his early teens, he'd fantasised about murder, knowing he'd never be happy if he didn't act on his desires. But, like most desires, the satisfaction that followed after the first victim faded quickly. Within three months, he could think of nothing else. He re-lived every moment from that first time. The crackling of cartilage in her neck, the change in her eyes when death came.

But with his addiction came danger. Serial killers got caught. If he got caught, he wouldn't be able to kill. Life held no meaning without the opportunity to bring death. So he got smart. He asked around. Slit the throat of one of Winter's enemies as a calling card. Found himself in gainful employment.

After that, his hobby became his business. Strickland learned to hide the pleasure he took in each murder, and he flourished. He had an aptitude, and a talent, for killing. Even in his early twenties, he did it well. These days, no one could touch him.

Strickland didn't plan on leaving Winter's house until Lewis was dead. This couldn't end any other way. His neck flushed with excitement at the prospect.

He backed into the study and opened the windows. The tear gas thinned as it rose. Strickland moved across to the bedroom opposite and opened its window to create a through-draught.

Tom Lewis had fooled them, but that didn't matter now. What mattered was out-manoeuvring this clever, ruthless, combat-ready enemy. Lewis might be outnumbered, but an individual familiar with the territory could evade detection in a dark, smoke-filled house. And Lewis had been familiar enough to go straight to the control room.

The second explosion had been larger than the first. Much larger. There may be survivors on the lower level, but Strickland assumed the worst. The gate guards, the two on patrol, and the two at dinner had all been downstairs. Now presumed dead. The guard by the front door had choked on his own blood, and his colleague's silence suggested a similar fate. Penny was dead. Twelve down in the space of what, ten minutes?

Strickland hunkered down and checked his weapons. He dropped Penny's gun into his left jacket pocket, leaving the spare magazines in his trouser pocket. He reached behind his back with both hands, his fingers automatically finding two heavy brass knuckledusters tucked into his belt. Old school, but useful at close quarters. Even a jab would break skin or bones. The one on his right hand covered the middle, ring, and little fingers, leaving his trigger finger free. It would prevent the infamous Glock trigger guard from causing a blister, too.

The explosion had compromised Strickland's hearing, but not enough to provoke tinnitus. He ran a mental check. Two men in the kitchen at the time of the explosion. They would have heard shots, seen the gas, their eyes prickling. Strickland knew what he would have done. Open the back door and get out. Take cover and watch the open door. London was never pitch black. If Lewis came out, there was enough light to bring him down.

It had been five weeks since his last fix, asphyxiating an investigative journalist. His heart rate rose with anticipation.

Still listening, Strickland left the bedroom and crossed back to the study. Behind the desk, he stood next to the window before leaning out for a count of three. One guard waited behind a box hedge ten yards from the back door. He'd cleared a hole through the branches, aiming at the doorway. The second guard had turned left on exiting and taken cover behind a potted fern.

The guards' strategy was both good and bad. Good, because they'd made the best tactical decision under the circumstances. Bad, because if Strickland correctly predicted their actions, then the guy leaving the trail of bodies behind him could do the same. Strickland put himself in his enemy's position. Lewis would be loath to pursue Winter and Strickland until neutralising the men downstairs. But with enemies outside, hidden, and ready, what was Lewis's next move?

What did Lewis call himself? Jimmy Blue. Weird. Deranged, possibly. His kills were dramatic, showy. None of the clinical tidiness of Strickland's murders. Strickland had never taken the life of another multiple murderer before. Would Lewis die any differently to the others?

A noise from outside drew him back to the window. Something lay on the grass. A metal canister. He frowned. More tear gas? Ineffective outside. The wind shaking the evergreens would disperse it, blowing the gas away from the house. And, unlike tear gas, this canister was puckered with holes like Emmental cheese.

Strickland's instincts kicked in, and he shut his eyes, screwing them up and pulling his head back from the window. When the garden, house, study, and the inside of his skull, flooded with blinding light, his tightly shut eyelids prevented temporary blindness. Nothing to be done about the hundred and seventy decibel bang that followed. Sledgehammers wrapped in blankets hit each side of his head, and he reeled back until he leaned against the desk, stunned.

The first shot, barely audible after the bang, came so quickly Strickland thought it was an echo. A barrage of shots followed, and he returned to the window. The guard behind the hedge sprayed bullets at the house. Strickland tried to blink away the afterimages. He was only certain of the guard's position because of the flash of the man's weapon.

The ornamental fern had a corpse behind it now. Strickland saw movement; a dark figure running towards the end of the box hedge. Strickland raised his gun, but his balance was off. If he fired, he would likely miss and give away his position. He lowered the Glock. Another three shots broke the stillness and the last guard's body spun sideways, coming to rest facedown in a spreading pool of blood.

When Strickland moved to close the window, the fourth shot tore through his jacket and entered his shoulder, an inch to the right of the base of his neck. Strickland dropped his gun and stumbled backwards.

"Fuck!" His voice a dull, muffled bell ringing in his head. "Fuck!"

Strickland pulled back his jacket. A neat entry, the bullet exiting at the top of his shoulder. Just a nick. It had chipped his collarbone on the way through. The wound was bleeding, but not heavily.

He'd been shot before. Once. That one had bled like a bastard. And it had taught him a lesson which he'd apparently forgotten. Find out where the shooters are. If you can't shoot them first, stay out of range or out of sight.

The overambitious pimp who shot Strickland seventeen years ago got lucky. Lewis didn't need luck. This Jimmy Blue wasn't just well-prepared, he was good. Better than good. After taking out the two remaining guards, he'd seen movement in the upstairs window and fired. Someone good enough to find a target, aim, and fire so accurately could have squeezed off more than one shot. Which led Strickland to the alarming conclusion that Lewis had chosen not to. That single shot sent a message. Strickland saw it as arrogance, overconfidence. The pain in his shoulder poured fuel onto his desire. He licked his lips.

Downstairs, an engine roared into life, followed by the squeal of tyres. Winter leaving. The police would find nothing linking him to this house. The computer network would wipe clean every hard drive, corrupting them beyond recovery. But Winter was no longer invincible. Strickland knew he would want to correct that perception as soon as possible.

As for Strickland, he didn't intend to leave anything for Winter to correct. Either he walked away, or Lewis did. And he had no doubt which way it would go.

Strickland's motive was purer than Winter's. He didn't care about his reputation. No one in London, no one in the country, perhaps even in Europe, was better at killing people than John Strickland. Fact. Tom Lewis, with all his skill and preparation, might think he could take him, but it was an error. Strickland was a killer. Strip away the veneer and Strickland was pure predator.

He headed for the back stairs, his thoughts fading to nothing but the hunt, the wound in his shoulder forgotten, his senses alive, his muscles and sinews flexing, nostrils flaring as he brought more oxygen into his body, controlled the adrenaline flooding his brain, every sense ready for the coming fight.

Tom Lewis died tonight.

CHAPTER FORTY

THE CAR LEFT the underground garage and, with a throaty grunt from its V8, bolted for the gate in a spray of gravel. Blue watched it go. Winter's escape had been accounted for in his plans. It wasn't over yet. He had shown Winter he wasn't safe, not even with his enemy locked inside his private dungeon. He would never be safe. Winter's name came last on Jimmy Blue's list. He would die last. The Executioner was all that stood between them.

He re-entered the house through the garage, climbed the stairs, and rolled another tear gas canister into the hall. He'd seen the Executioner on the first floor. Strickland would find somewhere to defend, somewhere he thought he might have an advantage. He would only relinquish the higher ground if the situation changed in his favour.

Blue stepped over the bodies of the fallen as he padded back through the house. The nearest corpse blocked the kitchen door. Jimmy dragged the body into the kitchen. He looked down at a bland face, slack in death. One of the foot soldiers in an organisation that treated some lives as if they had no value. This foot soldier now knew the truth of it.

Blue took off the samurai helmet, leaving the grinning, demonic *mengu* mask in place. He stripped down to his briefs. Before putting the rucksack back on and reconnecting the oxygen, he placed the last stun grenade on the kitchen counter.

For a few precious seconds, Jimmy Blue closed his eyes and allowed himself to return to his childhood home, struggling against Marty's grip as the Executioner pointed a gun at Michael Lewis's forehead. Tom Lewis didn't look away as the blood and gore splattered the wallpaper, his father's face destroyed, because he didn't believe it at first. People got shot in films, not in nice detached Victorian homes in Richmond. But as the twelve-year-old Tom struggled to get free, while Winter poured petrol onto his mother and the Executioner raised the gun, he knew it was real. A cold splash of shame and horror told him why the burglar alarm remained silent, and why Rhoda wasn't there. The memory pounded at him: Rhoda drinking coffee with the man who now doused his mother from a petrol can as if watering a plant. Tom had known something wasn't right, something about the way Rhoda looked, how pale she was. He hadn't told his parents. Now his father was dead, and his mother was next. He freed himself and ran, because cowards ran, and he didn't save his mother, and when Marty Nicholson shot him in the head, part of him was glad, because he deserved it.

Jimmy opened his eyes. He didn't blame Tom, whose damaged brain kept him a frightened twelve-year-old forever. His body entered puberty, his voice changing, his chest expanding as he grew taller and heavier. But Tom Lewis never reached adolescence. Jimmy Blue did it for him. The bullet that hit Tom's skull was the million-to-one sperm, fertilising his brain. The embryonic seed became Jimmy Blue, and Blue did what Tom couldn't.

It was time. He visualised the next few minutes. The Executioner remained a very dangerous opponent. No one who ever tried to kill Strickland survived. Blue wanted to look into the Executioner's eyes. He wanted Strickland to see who had killed him.

Blue caught sight of his reflection in the kitchen window. Too dark to pick out every detail. A pale smudge looked back. An indistinct, nightmarish face, a painted smile under ash-streaked eyes.

He picked up the armoured forearm and shin guards from the pile of clothes on the floor, putting them back on. Then he crouched next to the bloodied corpse of the guard and started unbuttoning the dead man's shirt.

CHAPTER FORTY-ONE

STRICKLAND WELCOMED the icy calm that settled over him. His shoulder was a distraction. He could still use his right hand to shoot, which was stronger than his left. His hearing had returned to normal, and the open windows had dispersed most of the gas upstairs.

The main guest bedroom was at the north-east corner of the house. Strickland dragged Penny's body there. The wound on his shoulder pumped out fresh blood, though not in enough quantities to worry him.

He manoeuvred Penny's corpse into position on the far side of the bed, a pillow under her chin making it appear as if she were watching the doorway. After returning Penny's Glock to her cold hand, wrapping her fingers around the grip, he retreated into the en suite bathroom. In the semi-darkness, Strickland adjusted the shaving mirror until it gave him a view of the doorway while he crouched on the floor.

The plan stood a reasonable chance of success. Lewis would see Penny when he reached the doorway. Strickland's shoulder testified to the speed of his enemy's reactions. As soon as he opened fire, Strickland would have him. With Lewis firing from the doorway, all

Strickland had to do was duck out of the bathroom and pull the trigger.

He waited with the zen-like patience of a hunter. The house was silent, easy to pick out the smallest sound. Something moved downstairs. Not footsteps. Nothing more for a few minutes, then the same sound. Maybe one guard had survived. Strickland breathed as gently as he could. It sounded like someone dragging themselves along the tiles in the hallway. In which case, where was Lewis? Gone? Strickland didn't believe it. Marty and Rhoda had died, and they hadn't killed anyone on that night twenty years ago. It had been Strickland who'd murdered the parents while their son looked on.

No. Lewis wasn't going anywhere. Not with Strickland still alive.

He stretched his legs, then his arms. With every minute, his hearing recovered a little more. An owl hooted. Cars passed the gates at the end of the drive. A jet began its descent to Heathrow, the engine noise dropping to a low rumble.

When the shots came, Strickland brought the gun up, finger tightening.

Two shots downstairs. A gasp of pain. Ragged breathing. A third shot. Silence.

Bollocks to it.

Strickland retrieved the second gun from Penny and darted out of the bedroom onto the landing, checking every angle, every dark doorway. At the staircase, he hung back for a moment, then risked a glance over the bannister. The dead guard by the doorway, his throat open like a sick smile, was still there. Another body blocked the kitchen door, the angle too acute to see it fully.

Strickland crossed to the opposite wall, moving alongside the stain marking Penny's death. He stepped forward, standing above the kitchen door, and leaned out.

The face-down body underneath him wore a matt black outfit and a samurai helmet.

The journey down the fourteen stairs to the tiled hallway took Strickland forty seconds, a gun in each hand. If anyone moved, they died.

In the hallway, he continued his near-silent progress. Close enough to see holes in the back of the black outfit. Shot from behind, meaning the body fell forward into the hall. Who shot him? And where were they now?

When he reached the body, Strickland inched past it, squatting to enter the kitchen concealed by the counter. Holding his breath, he leaned out, looking both ways. No one.

He stood over the corpse. If this was a trap, the most dangerous moment would come when he turned the body over.

Strickland tucked his shoe under the body's shoulder. The corpse had fallen onto one arm, forcing the right shoulder higher than the left. One good push, using the arm underneath as a pivot, should do the job.

He scooped his foot underneath and shoved. He didn't look straight away, instead pointing both guns towards the front and back doors, waiting for the attack. When it didn't come, he looked down. The dead eyes staring back at him from inside the helmet didn't belong to Tom Lewis. But that wasn't his biggest problem.

His biggest problem was the stun grenade, the trigger of which had only been held in place by the weight of the body lying on top of it. At the moment Strickland looked down, it exploded.

The world went white as every photo-receptor in Strickland's eyes were triggered. Both eardrums burst with the bang that followed.

Which meant that Strickland didn't hear the singing.

CHAPTER FORTY-TWO

THE MOMENT after firing the third shot into the back of the dead guard, Jimmy Blue ran. He grinned as he flew through the back door into the night, turned left, and—staying close to the wall—followed the exterior of the building.

The front door stood open. Blue waited there, his back pressed against the smooth architrave. He leaned down and scooped two handfuls of earth from the flower beds, holding them ready.

Strickland was good, Blue admitted. The older man moved so quietly, he probably believed he made no sound at all. If it had been anyone else listening, they may have agreed. But it wasn't anyone else listening. It was Jimmy Blue. And he could hear the first drops of water hit the kitchen floor as the freezer defrosted, or a spider wrapping a bug in sticky silk in the corner of the window. The mouse scurrying for cover as the owl dropped from above, the crackling yawn of underfloor heating pipes adjusting to the drop in temperature, the rustle of Strickland's trousers as he inched downstairs, the hushed, soft creak of shoe leather. Blue didn't need to see Strickland at all.

His grin returned when the toe of Strickland's shoe scuffed the tiles under the guard's body.

Then the louder thump of the corpse being turned over.

One. Two. Three.

Even with a wall between him and the stun grenade, Jimmy Blue screwed his eyes shut, pushed his hands over his ears, the cold, hard soil in his fists blotting out all sound. The grenade registered as a punch to his skull and sternum.

He shook his head and scraped away the dirt, then danced into the hallway.

"Well what is this that I can't see
With icy hands takin' hold of me
Well I am Death, none can excel
I'll open the door to Heaven and Hell"

Strickland's eyes were open, but he saw nothing. He held a gun in each hand and, as Blue skipped across the tiles to meet him, he started firing. Even blind, deaf, and—surely—in fear for his life, his actions remained logical. This was no wild reaction of a cornered animal. Strickland, despite the evidence to the contrary, still thought he was in control. His shooting pattern covered three hundred and sixty degrees. Anyone coming close stood a good chance of taking a bullet or two.

Blue ducked and rolled as the gun in Strickland's right hand swung in his direction, standing up after the bullets passed overhead. One of them embedded itself in the door frame, the other continued towards the gate at the end of the drive, stopped by a tree on the far side of the road.

In the facility where Tom Lewis had learned to walk, and—to a fashion—talk again, he spent hours slumped in front of a television. There was a recurring trope in certain movies and series. A moment when a hero faced the villain, but gave away any advantage they held. If the villain was unarmed, the hero would throw away their knife or gun. Mano-a-mano. The villain might have killed innocent people, set off a bomb that maimed children. Tortured kittens. It didn't prevent a kind of twisted nobility in certain heroes from levelling the playing field for their final confrontation. On TV, the good guy always won.

Good guys are idiots.

Jimmy Blue headbutted Strickland, his hard, broad forehead finding the bridge of the Executioner's nose, decimating the cartilage behind. Blood ran down the man's face as he staggered back a single pace. This was Strickland's only concession to the injury. He processed the information and acted on it with incredible speed. Jimmy wasn't expecting an immediate response from his deaf, blind opponent, and didn't move fast enough to avoid the right hook that came back at him. He leaned away as the fist hit his jaw, riding the punch.

Blue stopped singing for a moment, dancing back and touching his face. The punch rattled his teeth. His cheek went numb, and he tasted blood. When he looked at Strickland's knuckles and saw the gleam of brass, he smiled. At close quarters, with a dangerous opponent, you gave yourself every advantage. Well. He had an answer to that, and it was quite an upgrade on knuckledusters.

Strickland came after him hard and fast, pressing the advantage he thought his punch had granted him. Blue danced back, watching the Executioner blink the after-effects of the stun grenade away. He would be able to make out shapes by now, but he was disorientated. It would be a few minutes before he regained his sight. He'd be dead by then.

Both of the Executioner's guns clicked on empty chambers. He dropped one into his jacket pocket, jerked back his left hand, and threw the other gun. Another smart move; unexpected, and, considering his semi-blindness, accurate. Blue twisted sideways to avoid it, turned the twist into a pirouette, and slashed with the blade on his wrist guard, aiming for Strickland's jugular. The older man had been in enough life-or-death confrontations to have developed reactions so fine they looked like a sixth sense. He flinched, and the razor-sharp steel caught his cheek, opening up a gash before slicing away the top half-inch of his left ear. He didn't acknowledge the pain, dropping to a crouch and sweeping his legs into the space where his enemy stood.

Jimmy Blue jumped Strickland's legs and unleashed a kick of his own. There was no avoiding this one. All the Executioner's experi-ence didn't prevent the sole of a size twelve foot connecting with his chin hard enough to send his head snapping back, his skull hitting the tiles with a smack.

In half a second, Blue landed on his chest, knees pinning Strick-land's arms to the floor. He held the blade on his left arm against his enemy's throat, and the man became still, knowing any move might be his last.

Blue spoke, despite knowing Strickland was deaf. A touch dramatic, but he didn't care. He had waited a long time to say this.

"You murdered my father. You shot my mother in the stomach and left her for Winter to burn alive."

Strickland didn't need to understand the words. He guessed what Blue would say. "You want revenge, Tom? Is that it?"

Jimmy couldn't help but be impressed by Strickland. The man showed no fear. It was over, and he knew it. Even defeated, he wanted to talk. Perhaps he thought he would talk long enough to regain some vision. Or, perhaps, he wanted to ask for forgiveness. Blue was intrigued enough to let him speak.

"Revenge is childish. Pathetic. Irene understood the risks. She played the game, Tom. She played it better than most."

Hearing his mother's name on the Executioner's lips made Blue press down harder. A crimson line appeared on Strickland's throat, but he kept talking.

"Your mum would be disappointed in you, Tom. Revenge is stupid. Unproductive. When she killed someone, it was just business. Although I suspect she enjoyed it more than most. I know how that feels."

Jimmy Blue stared down at the man who'd butchered his family two decades ago. His words made no sense. Why try to desecrate his memory of his mother?

He leaned close enough that the Executioner felt the breath on his face.

"No more lies."

Blue sat up and stared at the Executioner. Every time the man tried to speak, he dissuaded him by pushing down, allowing the steel's edge to deepen the cut. Strickland blinked away the water produced by his eyes as his sight returned.

They stayed like that for a few minutes. Sirens screamed in the distance. Jimmy Blue wondered if the explosion had been powerful enough to rouse a neighbour, or if Winter had called it in, hoping the police would catch his enemy for him. He waited. The sirens came closer, and the first faint, regular strobes of blue light played on the walls. Strickland's eyes strayed towards it, then back to the ceiling. Again, Blue had underestimated the man. The Executioner could see. His blank stare was feigned.

Blue smiled down at Strickland.

"You don't understand. There is *only* revenge. Nothing else exists. I *am* revenge."

He leaned forward and drew the blade briskly across Strickland's throat. Blood arced out of the gaping wound, but Blue didn't move away. He squatted on the dying man and watched the arterial spray spatter the wall.

This had been no epic battle, no heroic confrontation between foes. The man dying underneath him had killed men, women, and children for decades. Tom Lewis's parents had been tied to chairs when he'd shot them. Jimmy's only regret was allowing Strickland to land even one punch. He wasn't interested in torturing him, making him suffer. No punishment matched the Executioner's crimes. He just had to die.

Back in the kitchen, Blue washed the ash from his face, then scrubbed Strickland's blood from his hands and neck. He opened the rucksack and tossed out the oxygen tank, removing the rolled-up jogging bottoms, sweatshirt, and wool hat, putting them on. He had left fingerprints and physical evidence everywhere, but it didn't matter. Tom Lewis, or Tom Brown, had no criminal record, so his fingerprints weren't in any police database. Any investigation by the authorities might eventually include him as a possible, if unlikely, suspect. By then, it would be too late. Winter would be dead, and it would be over.

The question of what came afterwards, what happened when all four names on the list were crossed out, was not something Jimmy Blue had considered. When Winter died, everything ended. Perhaps that meant returning to the darkness that spawned him. A concept of the future relied on the concept of a past, and, with Winter gone, there would be no past.

The final piece of clothing in the rucksack was a high-vis vest. Blue left it in there, along with a GPS device, shouldered the bag, and jogged out into the garden. He ran alongside the lake, following Winter's earlier route, before diverting into the woods.

It took him two minutes to locate the tree he'd identified months earlier, climbing it, then crawling out along the branch that crested the ten-foot, barbed wire topped fence. The tree wouldn't help anyone trying to get into the grounds, but no one had considered its usefulness to someone trying to get out.

A helicopter approached from the south as Blue dropped to the ground and rolled. A spotlight from the chopper swept across Winter's house, the noise of its rotors covering the sound of car engines as the police approached from the north.

When he reached the road, Jimmy Blue put on the high-vis vest and started jogging. They wouldn't be looking for anyone in particular yet, but the nearby roads might attract a patrol car or two. Sure enough, as he jogged along the pavement, a police car slowed as it got close, headlamps picking him out. Although a little late to be out jogging, a man on the run was hardly likely to be wearing luminous clothing.

Blue gave them a polite nod and a smile as he passed. It was Christmas Day, after all.

CHAPTER FORTY-THREE

TWENTY YEARS after Winter gave the order to kill Tom's family, Jimmy Blue's task was nearly complete. One name remained.

Blue ran away from the main road and into a side street planted with mature plane trees. He dropped his high-vis vest into a wheelie bin and walked along the quiet street.

He knew what to look for. The third house in had what he needed. A wide driveway, set back from the road, five cars. All new, all expensive, all pointlessly fast considering they spent most of their time inching round the North Circular.

Lights inside the house, loud music playing, and peals of drunken laughter suggested the occupants would be oblivious to his approach. A motion-sensitive security light flooded the driveway when he jogged up to the garage door, but the flashing fairy lights hanging on the windows meant no one noticed.

Six cigarette butts on the paving by the front door meant two or three smokers popping out at intervals during the evening. One butt still smouldered. Not long since the last smoke break. The door was on the latch.

Blue listened for ten seconds, during which no one entered the hallway. He pushed open the door. Inside, it was enough to make him believe in Father Christmas. Or in fate. On a small table just inside the door, next to a vintage Bakelite telephone, a BMW key.

He grinned.

A 540i M-class. Jimmy Blue's interest in cars was practical. He knew this model was fast, and he needed fast, because Winter had a decent start on him.

He slid behind the wheel, started it up, leaving the lights off as he crept down the drive and into the road, putting them on when he reached the junction. Two minutes later, he pulled into a lay-by and took the GPS device out of his rucksack, plugging it into the cigarette lighter. Winter's car showed up as a red dot on the A1, thirty miles away, heading north. Winter owned a house just outside Manchester, and his organisation had representatives in most major cities. He could go to ground in any of them while he planned his next move.

Jimmy Blue didn't intend to allow him that luxury. It was Christmas Day. Empty roads and a car with 340bhp. He pushed his right foot down hard. The engine sang along with him, and the car's electronic brain prevented a skid as the six-cylinders grunted, sending two tons skittering across the tarmac.

———

The unnatural quiet of the motorway on Christmas night made a surreal contrast to the violence of the previous hour. Winter fought against the calming influence of the Mercedes' hushed leather interior.

He didn't want to be calm. Winter wanted fury and outrage to permeate his entire being. He wanted to be soaked in righteous rage, ready to channel it into an orgy of blood and horror, his enemy's head impaled on a spike as a warning to anyone considering insurrection.

The problem was, he'd outgrown that brand of crazed anger. It was useful in the early years, when personally hacking a rival's family into pieces served a purpose. In those days, Robert Winter was unknown. With no family name to trade off, and few resources, he wasn't the only would-be crime boss jostling for position in London. Reputation ruled everything, so he worked hard to build his.

Back then, he lived by a principle he'd found in an interview with a billionaire entrepreneur: the opposite of success wasn't failure, but complacency. Winter found similar quotes in interviews, books, and recordings. Others named the opposite of success as inaction, or coasting. Winter's least favourite: *decay*, although the wrong-headedness of the idea amused him. An unsuccessful crime organisation didn't decay, it was destroyed, torn apart, its leaders killed.

It happened to Irene Lewis. She didn't see Winter coming, because she took her eye off the ball. She and her husband controlled London's human trafficking industry from their Victorian house in Richmond, cheek by jowl with the bankers, judges, and CEOs whose children attended the same private schools as young Tom. Hidden in plain sight, while Irene deterred potential rivals by disembowelling them.

Irene grew her business by improving the supply chain, developing a fresh stream of income through an innovative programme of high-class sex trafficking. She trained her protégé—Rhoda—to identify unhappy, disenfranchised runaways to be groomed and sold at auction. Irene Lewis built a profitable organisation. She didn't deal drugs; she wasn't involved in fraud, robbery, or extortion. Other crime bosses left her alone, as the few who challenged her position, or impinged on any aspect of her business, ended up in abandoned warehouses, cold, stiff, their dead hands often frozen in the act of stuffing glistening ropes of internal organs back into their bodies.

Her mistake had been slowing down when she ran out of people to disembowel.

No one dared touch Irene Lewis. Which was why Winter killed her. His hostile takeover of the Lewis business fast-tracked him to the top. Not only did he control the London slave trade, he established himself as the most dangerous man in the city.

It took over a year of planning. Rhoda was the key. She still had family in Serbia and sent money home to her mother every month. Threatening the family might have provided the leverage, but at the risk of Rhoda going to her boss for help. If that happened, Winter was dead. He was an upstart compared to Irene Lewis. Instead, he looked for psychological leverage, and applied pressure when he found the weak point: Tom Lewis. Rhoda treated the boy like he was her own son. Winter promised her Tom would never follow in his mother's footsteps. It wasn't a lie.

With the Lewis family removed, he used Rhoda to continue what Irene started. He showed Rhoda recent photographs of her mother and sister, explaining what would happen should she ever betray him the way she had her previous boss.

Nothing in the following twenty years came close to giving him the satisfaction of that night in Richmond.

Winter gripped the wheel, shaking his head. Marty Nicholson. One incompetent coward led to this. One bad shot by a would-be gangster.

The anger felt good, but it wasn't enough. Winter was tired. His decision to retire meant his subconscious was already detaching itself from the mindset and routines of a boss. But he couldn't let that happen. Not now. Not when one man came into his home, his castle, and destroyed everything. And not when that man had Rhoda's email confession and a recording of Winter ordering someone's murder.

He called Strickland's number. It rang and rang. He tried it twice more. Neither of them used voicemail. Strickland was probably dead. Winter took a few minutes to absorb this. He never thought John Strickland would die in his sleep, but he'd always pictured him falling in battle while fighting a dozen men. Not like this. Where did Tom Lewis learn the skills to best a man like Strickland?

Winter would strike back from Manchester. He'd have to lie to his subordinates. If they suspected Tom Lewis achieved this alone, Winter was finished.

With Strickland dead, Winter controlled the narrative. What happened in Elstree tonight became whatever he said happened. His priority: find Lewis and kill him. Forget the recording. If Winter disappeared, it wouldn't matter. Kill Lewis, then live out the rest of his life in paradise, funded by the blackmailed bidders from his auctions. Whichever way you looked at it, Winter remained in control.

How to find Tom Lewis? He had his description, and he knew the stuttering idiot act for just that—a fabrication. Winter needed everyone on the street, every set of eyes. The crazy bastard wouldn't last a day. He'd find him.

He called Manchester. The phone rang three times. "Sir?"

"I'm coming up, Jürgen. Set up a conference call for one a.m."

"Yes, sir."

Good. Success demanded action.

He set the cruise control at sixty-eight miles an hour. No point risking getting pulled over by whichever miserable bastard spent Christmas on traffic patrol. He checked his mirror. Some idiot making the most of the empty motorway was closing fast, doing well over a ton.

Winter pulled into the left-hand lane and waited for the faster car to overtake. As it pulled alongside, its engine note dropped, and the vehicle slowed. With a sick sensation of inevitability, Winter looked across, unsurprised to see the bald head turned towards him, the dark green eyes fixed on his. Lewis's mouth moved, his body swayed. He was singing.

Winter stamped on the brakes a fraction of a second too late. Lewis spun the steering wheel, and the BMW slewed across the carriageway, clipping the front of the Mercedes with sufficient force to send it into the hard shoulder, smacking into the barrier. The Mercedes was already slowing, and the sideways swipe scrubbed off another twenty miles per hour, but the airbag exploded with enough force to stun him as the car hit the barrier and jerked to a halt.

When he opened his eyes, Winter patted his jacket pocket. He still had the Glock. Winter reached for the seat belt release, then stopped. His brain didn't process its relevance fast enough, but he recognised the sound. A car, reversing. It stopped. When the sound of the engine came again, it was accelerating. Louder. Closer.

"Shit!" Gravity shoved Winter back in his seat as the BMW hit the Mercedes a second time. There was a metal barrier on the hard shoulder along this stretch of the motorway where it followed a line of hills, a steep decline through trees on the far side. The second impact sent Winter's vehicle through the barrier. Suspension rods snapped and springs shrieked as it bounced forward, spinning anti-clockwise when the passenger side smashed against something solid.

An oak tree stopped the car's progress and the right side of Winter's head smacked against the glass, hard enough to disorientate him. He forgot where he was. His head throbbed, and he dreamed he wore a crown, a solid silver and gold monstrosity with rubies and diamonds flashing from its ornate peaks. He didn't want it, didn't want to be king anymore.

Strong arms pulled him to one side, big hands slid under his armpits and pulled him away. The crown rolled off, but his head hurt. His feet dragged along an uneven surface, bouncing off stones and tree roots. Despite the discomfort and his sore head, he slept again. Penny tried to tell him something important, but the sound was muted. She slapped him across the face, and he flushed with anger. He was still the king. No one should touch him. She slapped him again. He heard her now, her voice muffled and wrong. He couldn't make out any words. Penny had a mark on her forehead, like a Hindu. What do they call it? A tilaka. He looked closer at the mark. It was a deep red. Not a mark at all, he realised, but a hole. Penny came closer, and the hole got bigger, stretching as she bent over him. He saw her brain, glistening with blood, then the hole opened like a cave mouth and he was falling inside...

The slap came again, and Penny vanished.

Winter opened his eyes. He was propped against a tree, staring at his feet. He moved both arms, flexed his fingers, then did the same with his legs and toes. Pain, but he didn't think anything was broken. He brought his hand up to his face next and carefully placed his fingertips on the right side of his skull. Blood, warm and matted. He pressed. The pain made him wince, but the bone below was solid. He'd have a headache for a while, but he'd live. Then he remembered who had dragged him out of the car and slapped him awake. He'd live, certainly. Just not for very long.

Looking up from his shoes—which caused a hot lance of agony across his right eye and down into his jaw—Winter saw bare feet, tracksuit bottoms, a sweatshirt. Big hands, skin broken on knuckles. A Glock in the right hand. Winter patted his empty pocket, confirming it was his. A muscled neck on wide shoulders. The moonlight put Tom Lewis's dark green eyes in shadow under his brows, but Winter knew they were staring down at him. The raised scarring on his head was extensive, intricate, a braille transcription of what had happened twenty years ago. Winter didn't need to read it to know. Or to work out what came next. He wasn't afraid. At least he didn't think so. He was cold, uncomfortable, and he felt his age. Die here, or lying in the sun on a Caribbean island. Were they really so different?

"Hello, Tom. Haven't you turned out to be full of surprises?"

CHAPTER FORTY-FOUR

JIMMY BLUE STARED down at Winter. Everything led to this moment. From the first awareness of his own separate existence, a new creation, unique, intelligent, and deadly, everything brought him here. Only Winter remained of those who murdered Tom Lewis's family. Tom might never have woken up again, but a pool of darkness grew inside him as he slept, and in that pool Blue was born.

The man on the forest floor, the right side of his face streaked with blood, offered no threat. Not like the Executioner. Strickland's skills were formidable and practical. Winter was something else. A leader. A thinker, a planner. The man who ordered the Executioner to pull the trigger. Rational, but not reasonable. Colder than his surname. He looked in decent condition for a man his age. If not already in his sixties, they couldn't be more than a year or two away. Jimmy Blue could break him over his knee like rotten wood. Should he kill him that way? As with Strickland, he had no interest in torture, no desire that Winter should suffer a long, drawn-out death. The man just needed to die. Nothing would ever be right while he lived. Justice. Simple justice.

Blue guessed the injured man had been unconscious for no more than a minute. Mild concussion. Nothing serious. He wanted Winter to see him, really see him, before the end.

Blue had followed the Mercedes through the hole in the barrier, jumping out of his own vehicle as it rolled down into the trees. A pair of headlights rounded the long curve of the carriageway while he stared at the wreckage, but he dodged out of sight. Best-case scenario, he had all night. Worst case, a witness had called 999, and he had ten minutes. Best get on. He lifted the Glock, pointing the muzzle at the top of Winter's nose. Right between the eyes, partner. T-box, like he'd told the Forger. Bam.

Winter wanted to talk. "You remind me of her."

Blue thought of another movie cliché. Two ways this could go. One: the bad guy stalled for time while help arrived. Good guys did the same. Semi-catatonic Tom had watched it play out a hundred times. Two: the bad guy revealed something momentous to the good guy. This rarely ended well for either of them. The good guy, instead of delivering the villain to the authorities, was driven crazy by the last-minute revelation and killed the bad guy on the spot. Or, worse, he spared him, let him go.

Jimmy Blue had no intention of handing him over to the police, so option two was a really poor choice for Winter. What was he going to do—say something to hurt his feelings? Blue had no feelings. Revenge was the black flame at the heart of his existence. It smouldered for years, but never went out, always ready to flare up into a dark conflagration.

"Your mother, Tom. You have her eyes. But it's more than that. You're good at this, Tom. Killing, I mean. You find joy in it. It's only business for me, no more. But your mum, she enjoyed killing. I think she got off on it."

Blue should pull the trigger now. Why was Winter resorting to this nonsense, goading him? Pointless.

Winter nodded, as if hearing his thoughts. "Don't let me stop you, Tom. I'm ready to die. I just wonder if anyone ever told you the truth. Rhoda said you never knew. That's why she did what she did. She loved you like her own."

Enough. Time to put things right. Jimmy Blue aimed the Glock. His finger tightened on the trigger and stopped.

He hummed tunelessly.

No.

He willed strength into his hands. Jimmy's own body conspired against him.

Winter carried on talking. Blue concentrated on letting the darkness flow through him, but somehow, Tom was there. Not awake exactly, but stirring. Blue held him back, but he couldn't pull the trigger. Not yet.

"Rhoda said your mother planned to bring you into the family business. Irene saw your potential, and she wanted you to take over when you were old enough. I watched her work once. I was working for Grant Beesley. Before your time. He used to run guns. He got greedy, stiffed Irene on a deal, and she came calling.

"The writing was on the wall for Beesley. When an armed crew raided his warehouse, I made sure to be there. I knew it would be Irene. Partly because my instincts are good. Mostly because I tipped her off. I watched from behind a crate on the mezzanine.

"She did it herself once they tied Beesley to a chair. Me, I delegate most wet work to others. Your mum, though, she was hands-on. I watched her slice Beesley with a butcher's knife. She didn't want information, she wanted him to bleed and scream. After ten minutes, she slid the blade deep, both hands on the handle to saw across his belly. She stuck her hand in and showed Beesley his own innards. Then she left him to die.

"You are your mother's son, Tom. You're smart, resourceful. Best of all, you have no conscience, nothing to hold you back. The apple didn't fall far from the tree.

"Your mother would be proud of you."

Jimmy Blue stayed still, the gun pointing at his enemy's face. But everything else faded.

Tom lay in bed, a Batman comic open beside him, scribbling story ideas in a spiral-bound pad. Dad's music provided the soundtrack as he wrote.

He hadn't told anyone yet, but he wanted to write comics when he grew up. Batman was cool, sure, because he did everything without special powers. Unless being mega-rich counted as a special power. Tom's hero was different. He had no costume, no special car. He lived like a vampire, only coming out at night. His training covered multiple methods of fighting, with or without weapons. Disguises stopped anyone identifying him. He was cleaning up London, taking out the criminals. Without mercy.

The whole of the first page was covered with Tom's ideas for the character he had created. Mostly ideas for his name. Names were important. Really important. He'd started with traditional superhero monikers. Ratman, Owlboy, Foxman. The Shade, The Void, The Dark Wolf. Then he'd tried plays on words. Dead Lee Nightshade. Cameron Obscura. None of them worked. Finally, he'd gone back to the very first name he'd written, almost a joke. A name from a song on the radio. Not one of Dad's folk songs, but a story about someone escaping, with a chorus he couldn't get out of his head. He'd drawn a circle around it. It worked, although he couldn't say why.

Jimmy Blue.

Tom pushed his notes away when his mother's voice broke the spell. She was saying something to Dad, who snapped something back, his tone harsh. Defiant. Her voice stayed low, unwavering. They'd argued before. All parents argued. It meant nothing. This one went on, though, and Tom opened his door, creeping along the landing towards the stairs, staying away from the bannisters.

"He's in his room," said his dad. "Reading comics, or doing Lego, even though he says he's too old for it now. He's just a kid, Irene."

"The same age as when I stole my first car, Michael. And I don't want to keep lying to him. He deserves better."

Tom's eyes widened. His crawl along the landing had seemed like a game, Jimmy Blue creeping up on the bad guys. Not anymore. He didn't want to listen, but they kept talking.

"He's not like you, Irene. When are you going to realise that? He's getting on great at school, his teachers say he's Oxbridge material."

"So? What's your point? You think he has to choose? That he can't get a good education and learn to run the business? You're wrong, Michael. And that's not all you're wrong about. What about the kid he beat up?"

Tom wanted to swallow. His mouth dried. He couldn't move. How did she know about that? Steve Conway had pushed him over in the last week of term. Tom waited for him after school, and Conway ended up in hospital, Tom kicking and punching even when the other boy stopped moving. He was suspended the next day. During the holidays, Conway changed his story, said a boy from a rival school jumped him, that Tom wasn't involved. Conway never came back to school. Tom hated himself for what he'd done. He took Conway's change of heart as a second chance and swore never to hurt anyone again. He imagined hurting a bully would feel good, but he'd thrown up after the fight, run home, and, before exhaustion claimed him, cried with shame and guilt. For days, he kept to his room. He dreamed about the fight. In his dreams, he experienced no guilt. Only when he woke up did the horror descend again.

"What he did isn't important, Irene. It's the way he reacted afterwards. Jesus, the kid puked for a week. He hated himself. He doesn't want to be like..."

"Like what? Like me? Fuck you, Michael. What, you're ashamed now? Ashamed of me, you coward? Ashamed of the money, the houses, the Caribbean villa, the cars, you ungrateful bastard? If I hadn't visited that little shit's father, Tom would have been expelled. No exams. No Oxbridge. You didn't complain then."

His father crossed the front room, and Tom tensed, ready to crawl backwards at the first footstep on the stairs. But Dad stopped in front of the record player. He turned the volume up high, and Tom scurried back to his room, picked up his comic and pretended to read, while the song pursued him down the hall and through his closed door.

> "My staff has murdered giants,
> my bag a long knife carries
> For to cut mince pies from children's thighs,
> with which to feed the fairies"

Winter blinked blood out of his eye. "Rhoda tried to save you. It's how I convinced her to betray your folks. Did she tell you about her own kid?"

Blue should never have let Winter speak. He tried to pull the trigger again, with fingers made of stone.

"N-no," he stammered. Winter smiled. He actually smiled.

"Stillborn. Rhoda was fourteen. She ended up on the streets afterwards. That's where Irene found her. She saw something in her. Or maybe there was some compassion in your old mum after all, eh? Probably she just wanted a free nanny. Either way, she took Rhoda in. You were a toddler. She fell in love with you, didn't she? Of course she did. And you loved her back, right?"

Jimmy fought to regain control. He wrestled with a cloud, Tom's presence a fine, misty rain that seeped through his skin.

The gun barrel dipped, moving away from Winter's face.

"Mm. Rhoda, mm, Rhoda helped you."

Tom had borrowed enough vocabulary to assemble a sentence. Blue weakened, his rage diminishing. But he had to finish this. He had to.

The gun now pointed at the floor. Winter looked at it, then back up to the man holding the weapon.

"When I told Rhoda your mum expected you to run the trafficking business one day, she already knew. She wept for you, Tom. She was heartbroken. Helpless. I told her she didn't have to be. She could stop it happening."

"You, mm, lied. Lied to, mm, Rhoda."

"I didn't lie, Tom. Not that it matters. Lying's a tool, like everything else. I'm sure you appreciate that. Your whole life's a lie, right? But I did stop you taking over the business. And if Marty had been a better shot, my promise not to hurt you wouldn't have been a lie either. A good, clean head shot. No pain. Like your dad."

Tom's presence faded as a fresh wave of rage brought Jimmy Blue back to the fore. Strength returned to his arms and shoulders; the familiar joy coursed through his veins. The words from Dad's old folksongs danced around his brain, and a smile twitched at his lips.

His fingers became flesh again, the metal of the Glock's trigger cold against his index finger.

Winter had one last thing to say. "You've become what your mum wanted you to be, Tom. But Rhoda didn't want this. She wanted to save you. It broke her, thinking you were dead. I wonder what she thought when she found out. I wonder what she thought just before you killed her. What did she think of what you've become?"

Blue raised the gun and pulled the trigger.

CHAPTER FORTY-FIVE

"DEBBIE CAPELLI."

"Happy Christmas! Are you well, my love? Celebrating? At a party?"

Debbie frowned at her mobile phone in its dashboard cradle, as if blaming it for letting the call through. Beyond the windscreen, the empty motorway glistened with frost. A gritting lorry's yellow lights pulsed across the opposite carriageway.

"Fabio. How drunk are you?"

"Debbie. Come on. Do I have to be drunk to speak to my wife?"

"Ex-wife. And yes, experience suggests you do. What do you want?"

"Want? Why should I want anything? It's Christmas. A man's thoughts turn to his life. The wrong turns, the bad decisions. And he wonders if anything is ever irreversible, if something so beautiful as our relationship is ever truly broken."

"Two things, Fabio."

"Call me Fab."

"I don't think so. First, why do you always start talking about your-self in the third person when you're bullshitting me?"

"I do not! I mean, I am not. It's just, well, a man's thoughts turn to—"

"Yes. Exactly. And you already said that bit. That was my second point. You've written this down, haven't you?"

During the pause that followed, Debbie passed a sign. *Next Services 12 miles*. Not far now. She had left in a hurry, pulling on a pair of jeans and the footwear closest to the door, which turned out to be wellies. Underneath her puffa jacket, she wore a pyjama top.

"Si. I wrote it down. Only because English is my second language, and I wanted to get it right. Italian is the language of love."

"Really. And where was I on the list of calls tonight?"

"Scusa? When a man—"

"Of your three ex-wives, where was I on the list? I imagine you called Maria first, but I'm curious to see where I rank in the sad, lonely, drunk, desperate Christmas list of calls. Are you currently between slappers?"

"There is only room in my heart for you. A man must declare his feelings. Think about what you are saying, my only love. There is no list. Do not throw our future away, Charlotte."

"Debbie."

"Shit."

"Goodbye, Fabio."

The satnav claimed she would reach her destination in eight minutes. Debbie didn't want to spend the time in silence. She found an eighties radio station and sang along to *Human League*. Single, a few years away from possible early retirement, and she was spending the holiday alone. At eleven thirty-two p.m. on Christmas Day, she was driving up the M1 in her pyjamas.

She turned up the radio and sang louder.

———

Tom Lewis wasn't difficult to spot. Other than three generations of an Asian family and two truck drivers, the food court in the services was deserted. The truckers and the family sat at one end, as far from Tom as possible, eyeing him warily between sips of overpriced drinks. The staff members of the only fast food outlet still open kept looking over at the solitary figure, and Debbie noticed that Tom occupied the centre of an invisible twenty-foot circle, where no tables were cleared, or floors mopped.

He didn't look up as she approached. His hands stayed on the table's plastic surface and he stared at the floor.

Her police-trained brain ran its own report. *Male, Caucasian, early thirties, bald. Heavy scarring on head. The scars are old, but there are fresh injuries. The right cheekbone is grazed and bruised. Both hands are cut, and the knuckles are scraped, suggesting a recent fight. He is wearing soft black cotton jogging bottoms and a sweatshirt. No shoes. Both feet filthy, cut and grazed, soil and grass between the toes. Suspect shows no sign of aggression.*

"Tom?"

The big, bald head didn't move. He blinked, but his eyes remained unfocused.

Debbie slid into the seat opposite. The staff members and other customers shifted to get a clearer view. She supposed if you spent Christmas Day in a motorway service station, you'd make the most of any free entertainment.

Tom looked bad. His demeanour reminded her of the weeks after he came out of his coma, when he showed no interest in anything. The doctors thought it unlikely he would speak again. Tom's progress over the next few years surprised everyone. Not Debbie, though. The kid witnessed his parents' murder, was shot in the head, and crawled out of a first-floor bedroom window, dragging himself thirty feet away from a burning house. Tom was the strongest person she'd ever met.

He didn't look strong today. He looked lost, beaten, confused. A little boy again. Debbie reached across and slid her hands under his, thumb on top. He had the biggest hands of anyone Debbie knew. They were builder's hands, thick and tough, like the hard skin Debbie pumiced away from her heels in the bath. His knuckles were swollen and cracked. She stroked them with her thumb.

"Tom? It's Debbie. You called me."

The first tear dropped onto the table. Tom didn't seem to notice.

"I'm here now. And I'm not going anywhere."

Three more tears fell. The room was so quiet, the sound they made as they hit the table was audible, like a dripping tap in an empty house. Debbie watched the tiny puddles they made. Then Tom squeezed her hands. He looked at her. The contrast with his demeanour of a few minutes earlier was so marked that she gasped. He was *present*. Tom Lewis was here, not wandering the labyrinth of his damaged mind.

"Tom?"

"Mm." His eyes flicked away, then back to hers. A common gesture for most people when they tried to remember something. She'd never seen Tom do it before. "Mm. Tell me. My, mm, my ... "

She waited. No point pushing him. Tom understood questions, and responded to them, usually in monosyllables. He never asked one of his own. Never initiated a conversation.

"Mother."

Oh crap. Not a subject she wanted to discuss with him.

In all her meetings with Tom, his past had never come up unless she raised it, and when she did, he had been unresponsive. The psychiatrist assigned to his case believed the shooting provoked a mental break more permanent than the physical damage. For Tom Lewis, little existed before the coma. The boy who opened his eyes when he emerged was a newborn, remembering little more than dreamlike fragments from his first twelve years of life. Debbie had asked for a second, then a third opinion, but only one of the three suggested Tom might ever recover enough memory to testify. That slim possibility was enough for Debbie. Tom had surprised the doctors already. He could do it again. Connections in his brain were still active, even if he couldn't yet consciously access them.

Debbie's hope had always been that Tom might remember enough to point the finger at Winter. John Strickland, too, the probable shooter. She hadn't considered that Tom, if he ever remembered, might have questions of his own. Questions about why an organised crime boss targeted his family. Questions about Irene 'the Butcher' Lewis.

"Tell me, mm, ab-, about, mm, my mother."

Tom trusted her. Debbie didn't want to lose that trust. She told him about the Butcher. Not all of it. Telling the truth was one thing. Cataloguing that woman's horrors was another. DNA evidence found at the scene of the Richmond fire linked Irene Lewis to a murder in East London the month before. An eyewitness picked out her photograph a week after she died. They'd identified the mastermind of London's flourishing slave trade. Too late to bring her down. Too late to stop Robert Winter taking over, and Winter hadn't made his move until confident he had enough politicians and police in his pocket.

Tom listened. She suspected she was confirming what he already knew. He seemed to understand every word.

When it was finished, they sat in silence. Debbie didn't look at her watch. When a skittish staff member with a name badge and a set of keys told them he was closing up, she showed him her police ID and waved the man away.

Finally, Tom said the words she'd waited twenty years to hear.

"I, I, mm, remember, Debbie. I remember."

———

The scared-looking manager waited by the doors, keys in hand, while Tom went to the toilet.

Debbie called the office. She recognised the desk sergeant's voice.

"Hi Julie, it's DI Capelli. I know the boss won't be there until next week, but I need to bring someone in—"

"Have you heard, Debbie?"

Debbie let the use of her first name slide. In interviews with a suspect, she always played good cop. People at work liked her. They took her for granted, too, but she chose to be herself over being a dick, so she could live with that.

"Heard what?"

"Winter's place. His gaff at Elstree."

Debbie knew it. They all did. On paper, Robert Winter had nothing to do with that house, and his name didn't appear on any records. But they all knew he lived there when in London, in his modern palace.

"What about it?

"Blown up. Well, not the whole thing, but a lot of it. It was an organised hit. Military style. Lots of bodies. Ooh, you'll never guess who's dead. Go on, have a guess."

"Julie, people have died. It's not a game."

"Oh, come on, Debbie. It's Christmas."

"Fair enough." Debbie ran a list of names through her mind. Then she thought of the photos on the corkboard next to her desk. Marty Nicholson. Rhoda Ilích. Both involved with Winter at the time of the Lewis murders.

"John Strickland."

"Oh, bollocks, someone told you. There are loads of journos buzzing around. We haven't released a statement yet. It's a bloody war zone, I tell you. Before you ask, no sign of Winter's rotting corpse, more's the pity."

Tom came out of the toilet. Debbie managed a weak smile, holding up a finger. Julie's voice cut into her thoughts.

"Did you say you wanted to bring someone in?"

Strickland. Of the people CID thought they could place at the scene twenty years ago, only Robert Winter and Tom Lewis were now still alive. She looked over at Tom, at his bruised face. His cut knuckles. She shook her head. She'd known Tom since he was a child. And a thirty-two-year-old man barely capable of tying his own shoelaces would hardly take on the most dangerous crime organisation in the city. So what was going on?

"Debbie? Are you still there?"

Winter had police officers on the payroll. If she brought Tom in, he'd be in the system, logged onto the database. And the more people who found out Tom was a credible witness, the more danger he'd be in.

"Hi, Julie. Sorry. Got my wires crossed. Forget it. Thanks for telling me about Winter. Have a good Christmas."

"Yeah, I've got a mince pie and a bottle of sherry for breakfast when my shift's over. Whoop de do."

Debbie thought fast as she and Tom walked out to the car park. The only other vehicle was a Jeep, which the relieved manager headed towards. How the hell had Tom got here? Hitched a lift? Who would pick up a barefooted, bruised, bald giant on Christmas night?

"In you get." Debbie held open the passenger door, and Tom sat down. The Fiat sagged. He looked like he was wearing the car. She got in the other side and started the engine. Tom had to lean away to allow her to reach the gear lever. Good job it was an automatic.

She let the car move forward a few feet, then braked. If she was going to be paranoid about protecting him, she should do it properly.

"Tom?" She looked across at him. Tom Lewis, the lost boy. And maybe the only chance she had of ever securing a conviction for Winter.

"Do you like the seaside?"

CHAPTER FORTY-SIX

COLD. Not cold enough to bring on hypothermia, but too cold to spend the night under a tree. He'd better get moving. Particularly with a cut that needed stitches. Quickly, too, considering the gaping hole in the motorway barrier, two damaged cars a dozen yards away, and the fact his name topped the UK police wish list of unconvicted criminals.

Dark. Still dark. It might have been minutes, or hours, since his confrontation with Lewis.

Injured. Winter stood up and leaned against a tree to stop himself falling over. He was light-headed. He allowed himself a few minutes to collect his thoughts and wait for the pinpricks of light dancing at the edge of his vision to subside.

After a while—he couldn't have said how long—he blinked and shook his head, prompting a brief return of the dancing lights. For the first time in his life, Winter understood the expression *thick-headed*. Skull heavy, neck weak. His thoughts refused to be collected. Every time he tried to focus on events since dinner in Elstree, his head throbbed. His mind, trained over decades with the same daily dedication as a concert pianist, let him down. A rare image from his childhood provided an apt metaphor for his scattered thoughts:

apple bobbing with his father, his face wetter and wetter with every attempt to sink his teeth into the elusive pieces of fruit. He remembered his fury, pushing his father's hand away when he tried to help. How old had he been—four? Five? The fierce satisfaction when he worked out how to win, pinning an apple to the side, his teeth breaking the skin and sinking into the flesh beneath.

The tree he now leaned against was a silver birch. Winter celebrated a coherent thought, even one so useless. In a small hole in the bark, something gleamed in the moonlight. A bullet.

Lewis could have killed him. Winter would have done it in his place. But Lewis fired into the tree instead, then threw the gun away, sending it sailing into the bushes. Before leaving, he leaned down to punch Winter. That explained the pinpricks of light. Well, that and the car crash.

Good. He'd pinned an apple or two to the side of the barrel. His brain wasn't anywhere near optimal, but he could make basic decisions. Take things one step at a time.

The first order of business involved getting out of here. He was injured and hardly dressed for the weather. He kept an overcoat on the back seat of the Mercedes.

The car had come to rest side-on, the driver's door against a big oak. Three trees stood between him and the Mercedes. He paused at each, checking for dizziness. He stumbled once, but didn't fall. Falling, he imagined, would be bad. If he smacked his head again, he might never get up. His right eye blinked slower than his left, its lashes sticky with dried blood. When he covered his left eye with his hand, everything swam out of focus.

Near the open passenger door, Winter traced the parallel lines on the hard soil where he'd been dragged away by Lewis. He found a bottle of water in the cup holder and gulped it down. The BMW Lewis had used to ram Winter off the motorway was parked—wrong word, but he couldn't think of anything better—four feet back from his own car. His enemy left on foot. Unless he had an accomplice. Winter didn't trust his brain enough yet to make a solid deduction, but instinct told him Tom Lewis worked alone. Alone, on foot, and unarmed. Winter looked around. Plenty of shadows to hide in. He listened. Just the occasional passing lorry.

He knelt on the door sill, reached under the driver's seat and slid the handgun from its holster. His phone was in the footwell.

After putting on the thick overcoat and the gloves he found in its pockets, Winter felt stronger. He thought back to the few minutes before the crash. Where was he, exactly? How long since he passed a junction?

His phone. Winter took it out. Phones had maps. He reminded himself not to make big decisions until the concussion had passed, then took off his glove and tapped the phone.

The next services were four miles north.

Winter put the phone in his left pocket and the gun in his right.

He started walking.

————

At first, Winter thought the service station was closed. A single motorcyclist filled up at the pumps before paying a cashier in a Santa hat. The food court sign was dark.

Winter walked parallel to the fence, sticking to the shadows, until the main building came into view, a bridge across the carriageways linking it with its twin on the southbound M1. Two cars outside. Inside, a man stood near the main doors while, further back, a woman talked on a phone. No sign of Lewis.

After the woman put her phone away, a door opened and a third figure joined them. If his size and bald head weren't enough of a clue, the twenty-year-old bullet scars were visible even at this distance.

Winter pulled out the gun, his forefinger clicking off the safety lever inside the trigger guard. He waited while the first man—the manager, judging by the bunch of keys—opened the doors, locking up behind them.

Lewis and the woman headed for a white Fiat 500. Winter estimated the distance from his position behind the fence at a hundred and fifty yards, give or take. He was no novice with a handgun. On a good day, at that distance, he reckoned his chances of hitting Lewis in the torso were about fifty-fifty. But this wasn't a good day.

He left the cover of the trees and knelt in front of the fence, resting his gun hand on the second rail, bracing it with his left, sighting along the barrel. He closed his left eye. The Fiat became a white smudge. He spat on his sleeve, wiped away dried blood, tried again. The end of the barrel wobbled like a kite in a storm. He held his breath. No better. If he fired, only a miracle would see him hitting Lewis, and it would take more than one shot to put him down. He risked his quarry getting away. With shots fired, a police chopper would be here in ten minutes, an armed response unit not far behind. He might as well call them himself.

"Screw it," he said, with no particular animosity. His equilibrium was returning. Not only that. His luck, too. When he put the gun down, he turned his attention to the woman with Lewis. Maybe Lewis had been working with someone on the outside all along.

When he got a clear view, he realised he knew her. Police. Carlotto? Carlotti? Capelli. Wearing wellington boots, of all things. No uniform. No back up, either. Alone, in the early hours of Boxing Day, meeting a man who'd walked into the services barefoot and bloody. Winter thought it unlikely she was acting in an official capacity.

The Fiat passed him as it headed for the motorway. Lewis's head was bowed, Capelli's hand on his shoulder. A very maternal gesture.

Winter pressed redial on his phone. "Jürgen. Change of plan. I need you to come and pick me up. Just you. I'll send a postcode. Leave now."

His head cleared minute by minute. As he returned to something closer to his usual intellectual capacity, Winter felt a chill, imagining being mentally compromised. To stumble through life in a fog of half-grasped concepts, never understanding the way the world worked, not being able to manipulate others through the greed and fear that drove them. He would rather die.

Winter spent the next hour celebrating his renewed sense of clarity by making big decisions. A brush with death simplified things.

His house in ruins, his team killed. Strickland and Penny dead. His organisation compromised. Winter couldn't rule by fear once proved vulnerable. As soon as the news got out, it would be plain to all ambitious men and women, inside and outside his crew, that a vacuum had opened at the top. Power abhors a vacuum. And the people ready to fill that vacuum would put a bullet through his head before taking over.

A true leader is adaptable. His plans are elastic, and he always has a contingency. Time for Winter to put his into action.

Jürgen's was the only car to ignore the slip road for the petrol station, instead heading for the darkened services building. Winter waited for him to park and turn off his lights before phoning.

"I'm behind the fence, in the trees. About ten yards to the left of the litter bin."

The car engine started. "No," hissed Winter. "Turn it off."

He waited for Jürgen to comply. "There are cameras. Get out of the car, look at the building, then come towards the fence. It'll look like you need a piss, but the toilets are closed. Quickly."

Jürgen did as he was told, heading his way. He wore a similar overcoat to Winter's, a wool cap pulled down over his thinning blonde hair. Winter's luck was holding. He retreated behind the trees.

"Winter? Winter? It's Jürgen."

"I know it's you, you idiot. I'm over here."

Jürgen vaulted the fence. He wasn't bright, but he was loyal and vicious, a useful combination. Winter sat with his back against a tree, wrapping his arms around his side as if his injuries were more serious. The dried blood on his face helped.

"Boss?"

Winter slid the Glock from under his coat and shot Jürgen in his left eye. He fell backwards without a sound. A dozen birds, woken by the crack of the shot, rose from their perches with an explosive riffling of wings, seeking quieter lodgings.

Winter counted to thirty. No shouts, no lights, no alarms. He retrieved Jürgen's car keys, pulled off his hat, put it on his own head, and climbed the fence. Jürgen was an inch taller than Winter, and broader, but the overcoat hid most of the discrepancies. The cap was a nice convincer. When the police checked the CCTV footage, after finding two wrecked cars and a bullet in a tree four miles away, they'd watch a man get out of his car, walk out of shot to piss in the woods, returning a few minutes later. The body couldn't be seen from the carpark. It would all buy him some time.

And time was all he needed. Not much time, either. Enough to put the contingency plan into operation, with one small addition. Tom Lewis was persistent. Under other circumstances, Winter might have admired that. Not now. If he didn't want to spend the rest of his life looking over his shoulder, Winter needed Lewis dead. And DI Capelli's involvement made things much easier.

CHAPTER FORTY-SEVEN

Nine days later

THEY STAYED AT DEBBIE'S PARENTS' house in Pakefield, a village on the Suffolk coast south of Lowestoft. The larger settlement to the north had absorbed it as it expanded in the nineteen-thirties. Too close to the struggling town to appeal to second-home buyers, property prices had stayed low for decades. When Reg and Doreen Smith retired, they moved out of Walthamstow into a detached three-bed house on a generous plot overlooking the sea. To them, it was a palace. They called the house The Oaks, despite there only being one tree. Debbie hadn't wanted to be the pedant who pointed it out.

Debbie had already booked Christmas off. Calling into the office with a fake bout of flu enabled her to add an extra week.

It was her first visit to The Oaks since clearing and tidying it after her mother died in June. Doreen, always an organised woman, left Debbie her house and savings, plus a letter identifying the town's best estate agents, and warning which to avoid. The letter ended with the secret family recipe for fruitcake. Debbie had read it weeping at the kitchen table.

When she and Tom arrived before dawn on Boxing Day, they found tinned goods in the pantry and saw in the new morning with a breakfast of black tea and sardines.

The house backed onto low cliffs at the end of a road, its neighbours angled to prevent any property being overlooked. The oak tree, decades older than the house, dominated a windowless north gable. An east-facing rear looked out towards the rising sun over the North Sea.

They established a routine during the first few days. Tom rose with the dawn, sitting in the backyard, looking across the cliff to the shingle beach beyond. Debbie got up an hour later, bringing him a hot drink. On dry days, they used the stone steps to get down to the sea. At this time of year, they only met a couple of fishermen and a handful of dog walkers.

Debbie had always loved the sea, and this was her favourite kind of beach. Working boats, faded blues and yellows, dragged by chains through the stones, waiting for the tide. No shops, no amusements, no fish and chips or ice cream sellers. Sea, sky, and the same long, gentle curve of shore the first fish to grow legs had crawled onto.

Tom liked it too, and Debbie noticed the healing effect it had on him. Over the first week, his demeanour changed. He became more relaxed, more confident. Even his posture altered. He stood taller. Debbie watched him jog back from the beach one evening and didn't recognise him. The shambling awkwardness was barely present.

Most afternoons, Tom dozed for an hour on the settee. More evidence of inner healing, Debbie hoped.

This afternoon, while Tom slept, Debbie took her phone to the en suite off the master bedroom. She couldn't bring herself to sleep in their bed, staying instead in the guest room next to Tom's. She stood on the avocado toilet and propped her phone on the shelf until it bleeped with incoming messages. It was the only place in the house with a decent signal.

No urgent work emails to worry about, and logging into the

intranet confirmed that, while progress had been made identifying the Elstree bodies, Robert Winter was not among them. And Winter had gone very quiet. No confirmed sightings, nothing from the usual sources. For now, he had disappeared. But he wouldn't stay hidden forever, and—when he emerged—Debbie wanted to be waiting with a warrant.

She just had to get Tom talking on the record. Debbie had put in a request for unpaid leave on top of the annual holiday and the sick days, but she was running out of time.

Later, after Debbie's signature prawn risotto—cooked, as always, while listening to an eighties radio station—she read to Tom while finishing the white wine she'd cooked with. Mum's complete works of Dickens shared a shelf with a block of encyclopaedias and an inch of dust.

"*After tea, when the door was shut and all was made snug (the nights being cold and misty now), it seemed to me the most delicious retreat that the imagination of man could conceive. To hear the wind getting up at sea, to know that the fog was creeping over the desolate flat outside, and to look at the fire, and think that there was no house near but this one, and this one a boat, was like enchantment.*"

Debbie shut the book, replacing it on the coffee table.

"Do you want a cup of tea?"

Tom Lewis shook his head. "Is the, mm, b-boat real? The one, mm, David s-stays in?"

"I don't think so. But if it was, it would be about twelve miles up the coast from here. Great Yarmouth, I mean. Blundeston is even closer, where David Copperfield was born."

"Debbie?"

"Yes?"

"Mm. Can we, c-can we, mm, go there?"

"Maybe."

He smiled. Tom looked like a twelve-year-old when he smiled. He didn't do it often.

"Once your witness statement is done, we'll go, okay?"

The smile disappeared, and the scarred head dropped. Debbie

didn't enjoy pushing him, but the information needed to nail Winter waited inside this traumatised man's head.

"Tom. You said you remembered. I know you want to stop Winter hurting anyone else. Once I get your statement, we can do that. We can take him to court, Tom. He belongs in prison. He's a very bad person."

The head rose a fraction, but he didn't look at her. "Mm. L-like, mm, like my, my, mm, mother."

Debbie had answered his questions about Irene Lewis. He didn't deserve to be lied to. Sometimes, in the afternoons, he cried in his sleep.

"Your mother did some bad things too, Tom. But no one deserves to die the way she did. And we can make those responsible pay."

"Blue makes them pay," mumbled Tom.

"Pardon? Tom? What did you say?"

"Mm. Tired. Mm, bed."

It was six-thirty. Tom shuffled off without another word.

With no TV, Debbie put aside time in the mornings to help Tom with his reading. He was a willing student, and keen, but—after four or five minutes—Tom always developed a headache painful enough to stop him. Debbie suspected psychological reasons behind his inability to learn, but she had neither the time nor expertise to help. Once she had his witness statement, she would get him all the support he needed.

Since arriving in Pakefield, despite the emotional pain around his parents, Tom was a changed man. He'd started to speak in complete sentences and even asked questions of his own. Every day he became more engaged, more present. And, when she read to him, Debbie often looked across to see Tom enraptured by the pictures in his mind, caught up in the story's spell.

She admonished herself for being impatient. Tom told her he remembered, but she couldn't predict the trauma it might cause to return to that night. He would do it when ready. DCI Barber, her boss since Stevens retired, was a steady, methodical woman who liked things done by the book. She granted Debbie's holiday request, but she'd been suspicious. Debbie hardly blamed her. She knew it must look odd to Barber. Bringing down Winter had been Debbie's ambition for most of her career, and now—with her quarry attacked in his own home and on the run—she had extended her holiday. Barber asked if Debbie wanted to tell her anything. She didn't like lying to her boss, but it would be worth it in the end.

A few more days. That was all she needed.

A few more days.

CHAPTER FORTY-EIGHT

AT FIRST, she was dreaming. A male voice sang nearby.

"Still I sing bonnie boys, bonnie mad boys,
Bedlam boys are bonnie
For they all go bare and they live by the air,
And they want no drink nor money"

In the dream, Debbie watched Tom sing and dance on television, then look straight at her, a horrible, mad intelligence in his eyes. His hand reached out, came right through the screen, and strong fingers closed around her neck.

She woke up coughing. The red figures of her clock supplied enough light to find her glass and take a sip of water. 03:42. The only noise was the wind rising and falling, and the long shush of waves dragging tiny stones up and down the shore. Normally, Debbie would take comfort in those familiar sounds; tonight they reminded her of how isolated she was inside this house, only a garden and a footpath away from the cliff edge. The nearest neighbour had gone away for Christmas. The other house was an Airbnb, and the last occupants had departed on January first, taking their hangovers and leaving a bin full of bottles.

She and Tom were alone. Tom Lewis, who, even now, struggled to get through a sentence without two or three pauses and his habitual humming. Tom, the damaged, traumatised man she brought back from the MI services, where he'd waited barefoot, bloody, his hands covered in bruises.

Tom, in the bedroom next to hers.

Tom, singing. It hadn't been a dream.

She turned on her bedside lamp.

The heating turned off at night, and the sweat that prickled on Debbie's skin became cold immediately. She shivered, pushed back the heavy eiderdown, and walked to her door, putting on her mother's towelling dressing gown. It still smelled of her face cream.

She stood by her door for a minute, listening. It was Tom's voice —who else could it be?—but it wasn't. The confidence, the lack of any stumbling, the lilting phrasing, it all sounded like someone else.

> "They hired men with the crab-tree sticks
> To cut him skin from bone,
> And the miller he served him worse than that,
> For he ground him between two stones"

Debbie had taken all the right courses at work, stayed up to date with sensitivity issues around mental illness. But the relish in which the unseen singer rolled the words around his mouth, the glee, the occasional giggle between lines about cutting skin from bone, all of this made Debbie shake, her entire body prickling with goosebumps.

She crossed the landing, putting her hand on Tom's bedroom door. She remembered the famous description of Lord Byron. Mad, bad, and dangerous to know. She had a feeling the singer was all three.

Debbie took a long breath, held it for a count of five, then released it. She twisted the handle and stepped inside.

The light from her room spilled through the open door. Tom had his back to her. He danced as he sang, swaying from side to side.

When he stopped singing, he did it in the middle of a line. Debbie put her hands over her mouth to stop herself from gasping.

241

There was a palpable presence in the room, unlike anything she had ever experienced. Her mind stuttered between unease—something was terribly wrong here—and the kind of primal fear the first humans felt when they came face to face with a sabre-toothed tiger.

This creature was a predator. Did that make her the prey?

He spoke without turning.

"You should think carefully about what you're doing, Debbie. Very carefully indeed."

His speaking voice was unfamiliar. If she had been listening on tape, she would have never attributed it to Tom. There was intelligence, an easy eloquence free of the limitations Tom Lewis struggled with. The words weren't overtly threatening, but the room was full of poison, redolent with menace. She had never felt in such danger in all her life. Never.

"He needs me, Debbie. Without me, there is no Tom. I am his alpha and omega, his sun and rain, his daily bread."

The head of the silhouetted figure tilted to the side, and—for a couple of panic-stricken seconds—Debbie thought he would turn and look at her. *Don't turn around. Please don't turn around.* A voice in her head said she needed to be rational about this. He wasn't some monster, he was Tom Lewis. But that voice spoke in a whisper, and any power it might have was sucked away by the creature itself.

Please don't turn around.

"I know you think you're helping, but you're not. He can't survive on his own, with his half-life half-lived. Poor, mad Tom. Poor, poor, mad Tom. You can't save him, Debbie. He needs me too much."

He turned then, just a little. Enough for one eye to be visible, and the curl of a smile on his lips. Debbie made a noise she didn't know she was capable of making—an awful, low, trembling moan of terror.

He laughed again. There wasn't much sanity in the sound.

"Don't worry, Debbie Capelli, I won't hurt you. Blue could never hurt you. You've been good to Tom. The only one. But you need to leave him alone now. Can you do that for me, Debbie?"

The silence was only broken by her own rapid gasps of breath.

To her amazement, Debbie found she could speak. "Who are you?"

"I'm Jimmy Blue."

He faced her. Debbie screwed her eyes shut like a child watching a scary film, turned her back, and blundered out of the room.

She put a chair against her bedroom door and stared at it until she heard Tom go downstairs at dawn. Half-an-hour later, his footsteps returned, and she listened to him get closer, stopping outside her door.

"Mm, Debbie? Are you aw- w- wake? I, mm, I made tea for you."

"Thank you, Tom. Can you leave it outside the door? I'll be down in a minute." Her voice sounded shrill to her own ears, but Tom didn't notice, and she heard him clump away.

After five minutes, she stood up, limbs aching, removed the chair, and opened the door. A mug of tea on a tray, a snowdrop from the garden in a saucer. She took them both into the bathroom, sat on the toilet, and cried.

———

Tom didn't show any sign of remembering the night before, and, as the day went on, it faded like a vivid dream. But it had happened. Debbie only had to look at the marks on her palms where her nails had dug into them.

She wondered if she should call a psychologist, discuss what she had witnessed. Debbie had dealt with schizophrenic people, either as the perpetrators or, more often, victims of crime. But she had never heard of anything like this. The man in Tom's bedroom last night (and she had to force herself to think of it as a man) was utterly unlike Tom. Not just his voice, level of intelligence, and manner. Even his body. Tom moved like a small, frightened child trapped in an ungainly frame. The thing... Jimmy Blue... filled that frame and, impossibly, expanded it. Debbie swore the creature she had seen was taller and broader than Tom.

No. She wouldn't consult a professional yet. Anyone she spoke to would want to meet Tom. Once Tom had given his statement, she'd get him some help. If, that was, she could fight the urge to get as far away from Tom Lewis as possible.

There was only one hint during the day that Tom knew what had happened. He fell asleep on the sofa while she read to him. Debbie stayed where she was, sitting by the three-bar fire, wondering if she'd done the right thing bringing him here. Exhaustion caught up with her, and she slumped into an uneasy sleep. When she woke up, sticky-mouthed and disorientated, Tom was kneeling in front of her, his eyes wet with tears.

"Debbie? Are you, mm, are you okay?" He spoke with such child-like sincerity that Debbie found herself crying too. Tom held her hand. She didn't recoil. She wasn't afraid of Tom.

"Tonight," he said. "Mm, after d-dinner. I'll, mm, tell you. About that, that, mm, night. I'll, mm, tell you."

She squeezed his hand. "Are you sure, Tom?"

"Sure."

———

Ten minutes after Tom left for his run along the beach, someone knocked on the back door.

It was the first time anyone had knocked since she'd arrived, and Debbie jumped at the sound. She looked out of the back window, but the angle was too acute. She couldn't make out who was there.

No one knew she was in Pakefield. She ignored the knock. Then it came again, followed by a male voice.

"Hello? Is there anyone there? I need to use a phone. I don't have any signal."

Debbie said nothing.

"I saw a light on. Please. A man has collapsed on the beach. I need to call an ambulance. He was out running. He might have had a heart attack. Is there anyone in? It's an emergency."

Debbie ran to the back door, threw back the bolt, and opened it.

"What does he look like?" she said, then stopped. The man on her doorstep might have been a policeman. Tall, well-built, fit, and he carried himself with a focused, heightened readiness. But police officers in Britain didn't carry guns. Only the armed response units. And ARU didn't use silenced sub-machine guns.

The man shot her in the leg, pushed her backwards, and walked into the house, closing the door behind him.

CHAPTER FORTY-NINE

WINTER WASN'T a man to celebrate early, but he'd brought a bottle of champagne up to his hotel room after lunch, pouring himself a glass while waiting for updates from Phillips. He plugged the laptop into the ethernet, the sixty-five inch television acting as a second monitor. He would enjoy the show in high definition on the big screen.

The island of St Thomas was four hours behind the UK. When Winter's phone buzzed, he pictured the east coast of England, dark and cold.

Arrived at the beach, weather fine. The B&B is perfect. Will call you after the show. P.

Communications relying on riddles and code words was a habit Phillips evidently found impossible to break. Winter wasn't sure whether to be amused or annoyed by it. Under the circumstances, and with the afternoon's entertainment in store, he opted for the former.

Phillips was one of Strickland's contacts. Winter had used him once before, when a Russian oligarch made noises about taking over certain UK criminal organisations in the same way his peers scooped up Premier League football clubs. When the Russian started muscling in on his patch, Winter called Phillips. He and his team parachuted into a country club thirty miles out of St Petersburg, killed the businessman, his bodyguards, his entourage, and his family, and left on a container ship out of Primorsk before the bodies were cold.

If you needed untraceable mercenaries to do your dirty work, Phillips was your man. Strickland had spoken highly of him, and Strickland never praised anyone. Winter contacted the mercenary through a convoluted series of emails, texts, and phone calls full of code words, setting up the operation for this afternoon.

The B&B meant the house in Pakefield. DI Capelli's file had been in Winter's hands fourteen hours after leaving Jürgen dead in the trees by the M1 services. Her parents were listed as next of kin, although the sergeant who provided the file confirmed they were dead. By the time confirmation of a white Fiat 500 parked outside the Pakefield address arrived, Winter was in the Caribbean.

A few hours trawling online realtors and he'd made an offer on a Caribbean property available in a month. Beachfront, private land, secluded. He planned to lie low for a few years, catch up on some reading. Then, perhaps, some light plastic surgery, and a change of scene. He'd put aside enough ready money for this contingency, and the rich, powerful individuals he was blackmailing had received details of where to send their reasonable quarterly payments. The amounts he demanded wouldn't hurt them financially, although he imagined it would sting their pride.

His sponsors had much to lose. Money, reputation, political power. They couldn't afford the exposure.

Tom Lewis, in his seaside hideaway with DI Capelli, thought Rhoda's confession and recording gave him leverage over Winter. But Winter no longer existed. A new identity, a new country, and a new life. If Lewis felt safe, he was wrong. He would soon find out just *how* wrong.

While lawyers tackled the paperwork for his beach property, Winter checked in at the best of the St Thomas hotels aimed at the super-rich, where discretion was assured for those who could afford it. The concierge knew Winter expected a female guest later, and a hundred-dollar tip meant he would escort her to his room.

The sex trafficking trade was basic in the Virgin Islands. Winter smiled at the inherent pun. He sniffed a business opportunity, but the old hunger had gone. He'd got out at the right time. A shame about the circumstances.

Winter's guest wasn't a local. She was flying in from the US mainland. Although his sexual tastes were fairly vanilla, he considered himself somewhat of a connoisseur of paid companions. Twenty-four hours of this young lady's time cost twenty-thousand dollars, but why drink cheap beer out of a dirty glass when you can afford the finest wine?

Winter owed himself a release. His emergency retirement plan had gone off without a hitch, but a swift exit brought its own stresses. He'd been out of Britain before the police forensic team finished their first sweep of the Elstree house. It felt like running away. A remnant of pride didn't want him to be perceived as beaten, leaving with his tail between his legs. Watching Lewis die would help give Winter closure. Afterwards, he would take his time beating up a prostitute who looked like a super model. He intended to get his money's worth before screwing her.

Winter drew the curtains against the Caribbean sun, sipped the champagne, and sat back on the emperor-size bed. The buzz had little to do with drinking in the afternoon. This was personal, he admitted. Robert Winter wanted Tom Lewis dead, for his own satisfaction. A great leader made decisions unencumbered by likes or dislikes, and rarely kept a grudge. It was bad for business. But Winter had retired. And weren't retired people supposed to pursue their hobbies and have fun?

The television flickered into life. Phillips and his team, broadcasting live via a satellite phone. It had cost Winter extra to watch. Half a million extra. He hoped it would be worth it.

The screen divided into four squares showing jerky black and white images from the cameras on each team member's shoulder.

He topped up his glass and settled down to watch.

CHAPTER FIFTY

TOM HAD RUN to get fit before, but he didn't remember when, or where. He had a memory of running uphill in the rain, scrambling over rocks, his body alive with pain, muscles burning. Falling, getting up, falling again, his sleeve torn, and his arm slick with blood. No matter how many times he fell, he always got up. Always.

Now, his body craved the exercise, and he loved the openness and wildness of the beach. Tom had holidayed at the seaside as a small child. Buckets and spades, rock pools, greasy sun cream, and the satisfaction of peeling dead skin from burned shoulders. This was different. The pebbles grated and crunched underfoot as he jogged parallel to the perpetual sea.

The water shone through dark, metallic greys to burnished bronze as the sun dipped itself in other seas on other horizons. Darkness fell. Seabirds wheeled and shrieked, wings spread, making constant adjustments to pin themselves unnaturally against the sky. Others settled on rocks and watched him pass.

His breaths found a natural rhythm with his long, easy strides. He looked into the distance, seeing nothing in particular.

As he followed the line between sea and land, he was neither Tom nor Blue. He wouldn't describe himself as happy, exactly. More that certain constants were absent. No fear, worries, nerves, embarrassment, or shyness. No plans. Not haunted by blood and fire. The darkness wasn't drawing around him. No anger. If happiness meant the absence of all these things, then, yes, he supposed he was happy.

He ran south towards Kessingland, turning after twenty-five minutes. It got dark fast here. He slowed to a walk for the last half-mile before Pakefield.

Tom stopped before the house came into view. He looked out at the sea, respectful of its unimaginable power. It waited there whether he was asleep or awake. Always moving, throwing itself against the land, withdrawing, then throwing itself back. For hours. For days, weeks, months, years. For ever.

The cliffs were eroding here. Debbie pointed them out the first day, told him to stay clear. In places, he saw tubing, pipes sticking out of gouges in the cliffs, laid bare by sea and storm.

Nothing could resist the sea.

Tom stared out. He stared as it got darker. He stared until a noise made him stagger forward on the stones, blinking, wondering who was screaming, finding out it was him.

"Come on! Come onnnnnnnn! Come onnnnnnnn! Coward, mm, cowaaaaard!"

With the onset of darkness, his dream of the night before washed over him with the tide, and he knew it was no dream. Jimmy Blue had scared Debbie. Terrified her. She had believed he would hurt her.

He screamed at the waves, as if they might stop splashing the shingle, and leave forever.

Drained, he headed back up the beach, feet slipping on the shifting stones. Whatever his mother had been, whatever his parents concealed from him, all the truths he only half-understood, none of it had to shape him. He could be like David Copperfield. He mouthed the first words of that book. When Debbie read them to him, he had felt, for the first time in his life, that someone he had never met, someone long dead—a man called Charles Dickens—saw him, understood him. He'd asked her to read them again.

Whether I shall turn out to be the hero of my own life, or whether that station will be held by anybody else, these pages must show.

Was it too late for Tom to be the hero of his own life?

Near the top of the worn stone steps leading to the cliff path, Tom stopped. He sat on the concrete and listened. Other than the beat of waves on shore, there was no sound. Nothing at all.

Debbie cooked dinner at the same time every day, and the radio always played while she prepared their food. She liked music from the eighties. She said it was the best music ever. Tom didn't want to be rude, so he said nothing.

No radio this evening. No *Duran Duran, Nik Kershaw, Prince,* or *Grandmaster Flash.*

Tom took his phone from his pocket, checked for the usual message. Debbie texted when dinner was nearly ready. *Spag Bol in ten. Stew tonight, putting the dumplings in now. I feel lazy, fancy a takeaway?*

Tom hoped that, one day, he might learn to read the words on the tiny screen. For now though, he pressed a button and listened as his phone read any messages to him in a voice like a robot.

No messages, and no missed calls. The wind was coming from the north-west. Tom breathed in. No cooking smells.

Something was wrong.

He crawled up the last few steps and, instead of coming out onto the cliff path, edged up behind the low wall. Inch by inch, he leaned out. When he could see the rear of the house, the gate, the hedge, and the back door beyond, he stopped moving.

Tom stayed still for three minutes. Then a figure in the shadows moved.

At first, he thought it was Blue, and he was filled with a dull anger. Then he made out a stranger, bearded, in dark clothes, carrying a gun.

Where was Debbie?

A voice whispered in his ear, a voice only Tom heard.

"What's up? Changed your mind about me, have you? Poor, mad Tom. Do you, mm, do you, mm, want, mm, my help, Tom? Do you?"

Tom blinked away a tear.

"You gonna cry, Tom? Is that what you're going to do, poor baby? Cry while they torture your friend? Maybe kill her?"

No. No. I can, mm, help her. I will h-help her.

"You will? You, Tom? You're going to find the nasty men and beat them all up, are you? Going to rescue Debbie?"

Yes. I, mm, I am.

"Okay. Before you try, just answer some basic questions, so I know you're ready. How many of them are there?"

Tom didn't reply.

"From the shape of that gunstock, it's most likely a Heckler and Koch MP5SD, am I right? Not a weapon you see often in the UK. I imagine you worked that out, eh, Tom? Suppressed, too. So the neighbours won't hear the shots. That narrows the field. I'm guessing mercenaries, sent by our friend Winter."

No, mm, not a friend.

"Really? Are you sure? Because you stopped me putting a bullet in his head, remember? The man who killed Mum and Dad. After twenty years, after everything I've been through, after all that planning and preparation, you suddenly turn into Jiminy Cricket and ruin everything. Well, here's the result, champ."

Jimmy Blue giggled. "Come on, T-T-Tom. Come on. I'll give you some help before you start. I'd put money on there being four of them. A bigger team might draw attention, and they don't want anyone spoiling their fun before they're finished. A lookout at the back, another at the front. Two in the house with the hostage. If she's still alive."

No. No. They, mm, mustn't hurt her.

"Whatever. While she's alive, it gives them power over you, so I doubt they've killed her yet. They will, though, once you go blundering in and get yourself shot."

Blue started singing inside his head. Tom hadn't understood everything. Jimmy spoke too fast, and Tom couldn't keep up. But Tom knew he had to decide. It was up to him. But if he answered Blue's call this time, allowed him to take over, he'd lose what ground he'd gained since sparing Winter. For the past few days, he'd dreamed he might not need Jimmy Blue. Not anymore.

Okay. Mm, mm, you do it. S-s-save her.

"What's that, Tom? Didn't quite catch it. Did you say something?"

S-s-save her.

"And what's the magic word, mad Tom?"

Mm. P-please.

As the tears dried on Tom's cheeks, he forgot why he was crying. He turned back towards the sea. Shadows thickened and massed around the top of the stone steps, drawing themselves into the shape of a man. A man who looked like Tom, but confident, moving with the ease of someone sure of their place in the world. Someone with focus so sharp he bends reality to his will.

The sea roared, but Tom no longer heard it. He breathed in and inhaled the shadow man, becoming empty as the darkness filled him.

Jimmy Blue watched the mercenary scan the horizon. When the man looked towards the lights of Lowestoft's piers, Blue moved silently away from the bin and scooped up a handful of loose stones, crouching behind the low wall at the end of the small yard.

His body shook for a second with silent laughter, wondering what Winter had told the mercenaries to expect.

He hoped they liked surprises.

CHAPTER FIFTY-ONE

TIMING WAS EVERYTHING NOW.

When Jimmy Blue attacked Winter's crew on his home turf, he had engaged the enemy from a position of strength. The element of surprise was considerable. No one considered an unarmed man in a concrete dungeon behind a steel door to be a credible threat. By the time they appreciated their mistake, he had gained the advantage, following a plan made years before, every move mentally rehearsed for weeks.

This was different. Very different. Jimmy held no advantage tonight. Winter had seen Blue work, so the mercenary team would be briefed and ready. Blue knew what he would do in their place. Lookouts front and back. The hostage upstairs, so anyone coming had only one route available. One mercenary with the hostage, another watching the stairs.

The mercenary team needed to communicate with each other, but they were maintaining radio silence. So how did they do it? Jimmy reviewed Tom's memories for the answer. Tom had seen—without understanding—the left hand of the lookout resting on something clipped to his belt.

Blue watched closely. Once a minute, the mercenary pressed

something with his thumb—four rapid pushes. If each member of the team had the same device, they could check in that way. The pattern was clear: the man waited until the others checked in: one buzz, then two, then three. That was the rear lookout's cue: four pushes from him.

A clever system, new to Jimmy. But with an exploitable weakness.

Blue grinned in the darkness. He looked up at Debbie's bedroom window, the middle window, not expecting to see anything. Seasoned professionals didn't stand in front of windows, inviting any enemy to take a shot. He thought of Strickland and stifled a giggle. Blue heard a muffled sob. Debbie was still alive, then. In pain from the sound of it. And in her bedroom with at least one mercenary.

Jimmy Blue waited for number four's turn to check in, listening for the quiet *tuk tuk tuk tuk* as the mercenary pressed the button on his device. When he heard it, Blue threw the handful of stones, lobbing them to land at the foot of the house's gable end. He vaulted the low wall a split second after they hit the ground, the mercenary turning towards the unexpected noise. An old trick, and the man's training meant his next reaction was to return his attention to the yard. He was fast. Just not as fast as Blue.

A straight-fingered jab to the throat is a brutal, sometimes fatal, move, but it's risky. A fraction too high or too low, and all Blue would achieve would be making an armed man angry. But Blue never doubted his aim for a second. This wasn't one man trying to kill another man. He was Death, coming from the darkness. Jimmy Blue flowed out of the night, fingers crushing cartilage. The lookout wheezed once and crumpled, twitching as he died.

Taking the man's gun, knife, and the vibrating device, which looked like a tiny, old-fashioned pager, Blue listened for any sounds upstairs. His kill had been almost silent, but he needed to be sure. After a minute, the pager vibrated as everyone checked in. Jimmy Blue added his own four pushes to the tally before climbing over the wall to the north and, once out of earshot, sprinting down the next set of steps to the beach.

There were no more vibrations after his four-push confirmation, confirming his guess. Four enemies. Three, now.

The upturned fishing boats slept like giant beetles, the starlight that fell across them as the clouds passed overhead lending them the illusion of movement. Blue knelt beside the nearest boat, hooking his fingers underneath, lifting. He rested the gunwale on his shoulder while he reached inside, exploring the wooden hull. Nothing. The pager vibrated, and he checked in again.

He dropped the boat back onto the pebbles; the sound lost in the sea's crash and boom.

The third vessel yielded a length of coiled rope. Blue looped it over his head and shoulder, then ran back.

He took a moment to review what he expected to find at the front of the house. The lookout would have to stay out of sight. It might be a quiet dead end, but that didn't mean no one would walk, cycle, or drive by. An armed man in sleepy Pakefield would provoke an immediate 999 call. The mercenary would be concealed somewhere that commanded a view of anyone approaching the house.

The bike store. It was by the hedge, and someone sitting inside would be hidden in the shadows. There were no bikes in it now, if there ever had been.

Blue stood at the edge of the wall, his back pressed against it. Lampposts out front meant he would be visible the moment he came around the corner.

He waited for the next round of pulses from the pager, checked the safety was off on the Heckler and Koch, put his weight on his left arm and pivoted around the corner of the wall. The bike store was empty. He swept the gun barrel left to right. No one in the garden either. Which meant...

Blue dropped to his knees as the bullet zipped through the air above him. If the shooter hadn't gone for a head shot, he would have been hit. He rolled to his right, braced his arms against the hard ground, and started firing, five muffled *phuts* as the bullets left the chamber. One metallic *ping,* but the other four shots found their target, and the next sound was a heavy *thump.* His enemy got one more shot in, the bullet digging a channel into the grass to his left.

The reactions that saved him were so fast, his escape must have seemed supernatural to the sniper who squeezed the trigger. The truth was less esoteric, but possibly as rare. Jimmy Blue acted on the information his senses provided, but did so without hesitation. In a combat situation, every synapse he could spare operated in accord. When he swept the gun barrel across the open space, he registered the van parked side on a hundred yards from the house, the open sliding door, the darkness within. A perfect spot for a sniper. When he rolled into position, he fired blind through the hedge, the van's open door almost as clear to him as if looking right at it.

If he moved forward now, he risked being seen by anyone upstairs. Instead, he crawled to his left until he saw the van through the open front gate. The vehicle still rocked on its axles. His first shot had hit the side of the van. The next four pumped into its dark interior. The *thump* had been the sniper's body falling. Blue waited until the van settled, and everything became quiet.

Nothing stirred in the street, the suppressed weapon's shots not loud enough to draw attention.

Shit. The pager. It was overdue. Which meant the sniper was number one, and because his body was full of bullets, he missed his cue. The two remaining mercenaries now knew Jimmy Blue wouldn't walk right into their trap. Couldn't be helped.

They'd expect number four—the rear lookout—to investigate. Blue toyed with the idea of continuing to pretend to be number four, then discarded it. No; better to let them believe he killed two of their colleagues within the same minute without them hearing a thing. Let them wonder if they still had the upper hand.

He tossed the buzzer into the bushes and turned back to the old oak. The young Tom Lewis would have found the gnarled tree impossible to resist climbing, and Jimmy Blue was no different. He took a running jump, caught the lowest branch and, as it sagged under his weight, pulled himself up. He wondered if the remaining two mercenaries were discussing whether sticking together or splitting up was the smarter play. Blue didn't mind which they chose. It ended the same way. He pressed his lips together to stop himself singing.

He climbed quickly, reaching the fourth limb up, which stretched out towards the roof. After pulling himself along the branch, he lowered his feet to the tiles beneath. The roof had the steep pitch of a nineteen-thirties house, with concrete tiles instead of the original clay. Blue's experienced eye guessed at a late seventies job—nicely done, solid. Easy to walk across without dislodging anything.

When he got to the red brick chimney, he looped the rope around and knotted it. He fed the rope out as he walked down the steep roof to the back of the house, stopping just above Debbie's bedroom window. Once in place, he leaned out, the rope tight across his shoulder.

He looked down at the first lookout's body in the backyard, thirty feet below. No one came to check when number four and number one stopped broadcasting. More evidence of the team's experience. The leader would be inside. It wouldn't do to underestimate him, or her. Then again, Jimmy Blue considered, as he played out an extra five feet of rope between his hands, they expected him to arrive from below.

At the exact moment he jumped, before his mind returned to the dark, silent stillness he embraced in combat, Blue remembered a moment from his years of training. The tawny owl. He was travelling through a dense Bavarian forest, learning to leave as few signs of his passage as possible. This meant choosing each footstep, aiming for silence, but never quite achieving it. It meant taking a route through the tree branches when necessary. It meant a long wait when no cover was available, crouching in absolute silence until a muntjac, fox, or badger provided an audible distraction, then sprinting through the open landscape, exposed for a few intense seconds. During such a sprint, a shape drew his attention to the left, passing about five yards away. A tawny owl, swift, deadly, and utterly silent. Until that moment, Jimmy Blue thought he was intimate with the silence of a predator stalking its prey. But the owl moved soundlessly. Beautiful, lethal, and impossible to defend against.

Blue faced the chimney, leaned out, bent his knees, and jumped, the rope spooling out in front of him. Just before it snapped taut, he fell into the darkness, and the scene inside the bedroom came into focus. It was as close as he'd ever get to that owl. Those inside had no idea what was coming.

CHAPTER FIFTY-TWO

THE LANDING LIGHT gave Jimmy Blue a freeze-frame of the dark bedroom in the half-second before his entrance.

Debbie, pale, sweating, ankles lashed together, left hand cable-tied to the bedpost. Her right hand pushing down on her upper leg. White sheets stained dark with blood. By the door, a mercenary with a spider tattooed on his neck, looking away from him. Lucky.

Debbie looked towards the window as Blue dropped into view. She may have made an involuntary sound, because the man at the door turned.

Jimmy's arms flexed, muscles knotting as the rope—wrapped twice around his hand—went taut. He knew he would get cut. Sugar glass in movies exploded without injuring anyone. Actual glass wasn't so amenable. To minimise the damage, he turned his head away, his left shoulder taking the brunt of the impact.

He hit the window at speed. This helped him avoid deep lacerations as the glass imploded, driven by the weight and velocity of his body. The force of the impact sent glass flying towards the door. The mercenary threw an arm over his face to avoid being hit.

Blue rolled and came up fast. Spider didn't try for a shot. At the speed his opponent was coming, he would never get the Heckler and

Koch angled towards him in time. Instead, he jabbed the stock at Jimmy's sternum. The mercenary was fast and strong. When Blue moved to block him, he reacted, pulling the gun back, jabbing again at his stomach, expecting him to retreat. Instead, two huge hands closed around the weapon, stopping its forward motion. Then a clockwise twist forced Spider's left hand from the barrel, and the butt was under the man's chin. Two snaps upwards and he spat blood, jolted, unbalanced. He stumbled backwards onto the landing.

Ready to finish him, Blue took a step, then stopped. His enemy's dazed retreat was a ruse intended to signal Jimmy's position. Which meant the final enemy was positioned close enough for a shot at Blue, if he followed Spider onto the landing. Better not to, then.

Spider darted back into the room, unleashing a flurry of punches. Jimmy Blue knew the attack was a diversion. He blocked the blows, but stood his ground. Blood sprayed onto his face as his opponent hissed rapid breaths through crimson teeth.

When the mercenary dropped to a squat, he dropped with him, rewarded with the adrenaline-spiked illusion of time slowing during a life-or-death moment. Time to see shock and dismay in the man's eyes. Time to see Debbie twist her arm on the bedpost, trying to free herself. Time to register the shadow of a man in the doorway preparing to fire. Time to ensure he never got the chance.

Jimmy put the flat of both hands on Spider's chest and grabbed two fistfuls of jacket. He was already pushing him ahead when the barrel of the gun came into view. The final mercenary stepped into the doorway and his comrade barrelled into him, Spider's shoulders knocking the sub-machine gun to one side with enough momentum to send both men into the wooden handrail across the landing.

It was a beech handrail; solid enough, but not designed to withstand a quarter of a ton of battle-hardened muscle and bone hitting it at speed. It gave way with a sharp, splintering crack, and the final mercenary fell twelve feet to the bottom of the staircase. Something snapped in the man's shoulder, the back of his head smacking hard against the worn carpet. His eyelids fluttered, his pupils rolled up, and he sagged.

Spider hung in space, held by Blue's grip on his jacket. Before he could act, Jimmy Blue unleashed a series of moves so fast it was a shame the only witness would be unable to applaud, on account of his being dead.

A headbutt first, pulling the man forwards as Blue whipped his forehead into the centre of his face. Blue let go of his jacket and the man fell backwards. When his fall was arrested by Blue's left hand grabbing him, the mercenary looked almost relieved, until he saw the other hand contained a knife.

Blue plunged the knife between the ribs into the mercenary's heart, removed it, then repeated the same action twice more. The mercenary's vital functions were already shutting down when Jimmy Blue spotted the camera on his shoulder. Larger than the cameras he'd concealed in London beneath streaks of fake bird shit. Fixed focal length. Why wear a camera unless he was filming? And if he was filming, who was the audience? One man came to mind.

Blue looked into the lens. He smiled, blew a kiss, winked, and dropped the dead man.

The noise the body made when it hit the stairs was wrong. Too hard. Not cushioned by the first body. The last man had gone.

Blue reviewed the incomplete information available. There was Debbie to consider. The mercenaries hadn't killed her, which meant they thought she had value as a hostage. They were wrong. Blue didn't care if she lived or died. The window and the rope gave him a route to the yard. The fourth man was injured. If Blue pressed his advantage, he would prevail, as the mercenary would expect him to protect Debbie.

He crossed the bedroom and stopped. His plan was sound. But it left Debbie in danger. He found, to his consternation, that he did care after all. Or Tom did. Putting aside this revelation to process later, he cut the cable ties that held her.

Jimmy sat on the edge of the bed. "Get on my back."

"What?" Debbie was in shock.

"Put your arms around my neck and hang on. Don't make a sound."

She did it, and he stood up. Her body knocked against his, and he felt her tense with the pain of the bullet wound. She didn't cry out. He climbed out of the broken window, grabbed the rope, took two quick steps along the sill, facing the house, then jumped to the side. When his feet hit the bricks, he climbed quickly, panting with the extra weight.

Once on the roof, he walked up the tiles to the chimney where Debbie slid off. He tossed the bloody stolen knife down into the yard.

Debbie pressed her back against the chimney. Blue examined her wound.

"It's too dark," she said. "You can't see anything."

He peeled back some shredded material and pushed gently. Her eyes were full of tears, but she didn't say a word. He took a bandana from his pocket, folded it and put it over the wound. "Bullet's lodged in there. Keep pressure on it. I'll be back in five minutes."

Jimmy Blue stood up. Debbie's voice shook.

"And if you're not?"

"Then you'll be dead in ten."

Blue jogged across the roof and leaped for the tree, sacrificing a near-silent descent for speed. He had an idea.

CHAPTER FIFTY-THREE

PHILLIPS REELED from the enormity of the clusterfuck this operation had turned into. It should have been simple. Winter had warned them the target was trained, both with weapons and in hand-to-hand combat. But he also said Tom Lewis was mad. In Phillips's experience as a soldier—first for his country, then for money—the berserker insanity that turned competent fighters into killing machines was worse than useless. Berserkers not only disobeyed orders, they disregarded everything they'd learned. Yes, he witnessed men and women draw on incredible reserves to slaughter multiple opponents with crazed, illogical attacks. But berserkers rarely survived long enough for anyone to learn anything of use from their methods. It didn't matter how fast, or how powerful, a blood-crazed fighter became. They were made of meat and blood, and that was how they ended up. They also often forgot whose side they fought on. If Tom Lewis was mad, it gave his team an advantage.

Not, Phillips thought, as he gritted his teeth, grabbed his left arm with his right hand, and yanked his dislocated shoulder back into its socket, that they should have needed an advantage. Four against one, a hostage, and the element of surprise. Still. Spilled milk and all that. He sat in the kitchen, letting his head clear. He had only been unconscious for a few seconds at most, but he knew it would compromise his reactions. Markison's corpse lay on the stairs. Grey and Coulter had stopped signalling five minutes ago.

Outside, something dropped past the window. A shadow flickered. Phillips raised the gun, counted silently to three, stood up. An empty yard. No, not quite. A knife lay in the moonlight, dark with wet blood. He edged closer, saw the rope swaying.

Phillips stared at the knife for ten seconds, then punched his injured shoulder, welcoming the clarity accompanying the pain. He wasn't operating anywhere near his optimum capacity. Time to end this. Either Lewis and Capelli had run, or the dropped knife was supposed to make him believe that. In which case they'd stayed in the bedroom, waiting for him to enter the yard, an easy target.

Either way, he decided, screw Winter. Screw all of this. His team was down. He could live without the other half of Winter's payment, especially now he didn't have to split it four ways.

Time to cut his losses.

His belt vibrated. One long buzz. He put his hand onto the pager and waited. After ten seconds, it buzzed again. One long buzz. Number one. Coulter. The sniper. Still alive. Must be injured, as he hadn't signalled for ten minutes.

One last chance to salvage this. If Phillips left through the front door, and Lewis tried for a shot from an upstairs window, Coulter would put a bullet through his eye the second after he appeared. Coulter wouldn't have signalled unless back at his post, and the man never missed.

Decision made, Phillips limped through the house to the front door. His right foot ached, but it supported his weight. Torn ligaments. It didn't hurt as much as his back.

He pushed the door open and looked out towards the van, giving Coulter time to spot him. He wondered how many physio sessions it would take to sort out the damage to his back. When he saw the first muzzle flash from the van, he smiled in triumph. Then three bullets hit his chest and he fell.

Phillips landed face-first, his blood flowing into the crazy paving beneath him. He lived long enough to watch the man they failed to kill emerge from the van and jog back to the house.

CHAPTER FIFTY-FOUR

It was cold on the roof, but Debbie suspected that wasn't the chief reason for her shivering. She was going into shock. Her mind kept slipping away from the situation, away from the concrete tiles digging into her hip, the rough bricks against her back, and the throbbing wound in her leg.

Going into shock would be bad. And she couldn't rely on Tom. No, she corrected herself, not Tom. The creature who terrified her the previous night. She wasn't the focus of his anger tonight, but she'd witnessed what happened to those that were. And he'd slung her over his shoulder like a summer jacket, clambering up to the roof with the confidence and grace of a circus performer.

He promised to come back for her. She wasn't sure how to feel about that promise.

Her lower back ached. She shifted position, and pain lanced through her leg as if someone had upended a kettle full of boiling water into the wound. Debbie dug her nails into her palms, banging her head back against the chimney to stop herself screaming.

For a while she looked out to sea. She talked to her dead mother about the illegal campfires teenagers lit on the beach during the summer.

—They're just kids, Mum

—Yes, Mum, I know, but that's not how policing works. We have to prioritise. Five kids having a barbecue isn't...

—When did he get so ill? I would have come earlier, Mum. Please don't cry...

—Look, Mummy, I drewed you a picture of a flower

The pain didn't seem important now. She had been warm with her mum in the kitchen just then. Not the Pakefield house, but back in North London, windows rattling every time a train passed. The warm kitchen with pale yellow walls. Debbie's favourite room. Always summer in there, Dad at work, Mum letting her lick cake mix off the beaters.

Debbie snapped back to the cold roof and the throbbing pain in her leg. Definitely shock. And, with no jacket or coat, the risk of hypothermia. How long had she been up here? She didn't think Tom was coming back.

She shuffled towards the tree at the edge of the roof, putting her weight on both hands to lift her body away from the tiles. As soon as she moved sideways, a fresh stab of pain caused her to gasp and drop back. Fresh tides of agony followed the impact, receding like the waves she saw reflecting the blurred stars.

That option was out, then. She lifted the folded bandana away from her leg. Soaked red, stiff with blood. The bullet might have nicked an artery. If she didn't get to hospital soon, she could die. Her phone was on the table downstairs. No use screaming for help with armed men out there. The thing running around in Tom Lewis's body—Jimmy Blue—was her only hope. God help her.

When her mind began the subtle drift into memory and fantasy again, she bit the inside of her cheek hard enough to draw blood. She mustn't pass out. Think about something. Stay awake.

She concentrated on the last few books she'd read. Debbie got through her fair share of thrillers. Police procedurals mostly, because she liked to laugh at the errors when fictional characters investigated crimes. Her personal favourite was a clichéd detective with an alcohol problem. In reality, he would be off the case, off the force, and looking for a job as a security guard within a day of a colleague smelling his breath. Police work was hard and dangerous enough. You relied on your fellow officers. Your life might depend on it. No good trusting a maudlin piss artist, however stunning his left-field, case-solving deductions.

Despite this, her bookshelf heaved with flawed, depressed detectives. She couldn't get enough of them. Despite trying other literary genres, her ideal escapist read was an unrealistic police procedural with a deeply flawed central character. What that said about her, she didn't know.

On the roof, a bullet in her leg, her life in the care of something she considered half-demon, she kept herself alive by picking apart the plot of the last potboiler she'd read.

You can't wander around a crime scene like that, leaving DNA all over the corpse. And in the real world, no one would have let you near this case in the first place. If they had, you would have crashed your pretentious sports car, been breathalysed, and spent the night in a cell while someone sober caught the serial killer you've been unwittingly banging for thirty-seven chapters.

When Jimmy Blue climbed back up the tree and joined her by the chimney, she giggled. He said something to her, but she didn't respond. He reached down, put his huge hands under her armpits, and hoisted her onto his back. Debbie passed out.

When Debbie opened her eyes, she was back in bed. Not her own bed, the sheets soaked with her blood. Tom's room. He was there, packing clothes into a rucksack. Tom now, or his alter ego?

She lifted her head from the pillow. Her vision blurred, and her skull buzzed. When she dropped her head back, the buzzing faded.

Tom faced her. One look at the face showed her it wasn't Tom Lewis.

"I dressed your wound. You lost a lot of blood. You might need a transfusion. I called an ambulance. Three of the bodies are in the backyard. The fourth is in a van outside."

"Did Winter send them?"

"It's not important." He zipped up the rucksack. "I'm leaving."

He opened the door.

"No. Wait."

He didn't turn, but he stopped moving.

"Winter's house. I emailed the lead officer. They think a small team took out all of his people, including John Strickland. The evidence suggests only one perpetrator, although that's implausible. Was it you?"

No answer. The first distant siren became audible.

"All of them? Did you kill Marty Nicholson? Tay Harper? Rhoda Ilích?"

No denial from the silent figure.

"How is that possible? What happened to you? Who are you?"

His voice was soft when he answered. "Jimmy Blue."

Debbie shivered. "What does that mean? What about Tom?"

He became unresponsive. The sirens got closer.

"I've known you most of your life," continued Debbie. "You're gentle. You're kind. If you can hear me, Tom, you don't need to live like this. You can choose a different life."

His dark green eyes, when he looked at her, were implacable, unreadable. "Who protects the Tom Lewises of this world, DI Capelli? You? The police? And what can you do with people like Winter, or Strickland? You lock them up if you catch them. But that doesn't happen often, does it? They pay good money to make sure it doesn't. But you'd put me away in a heartbeat, wouldn't you?"

Her turn to say nothing.

Blue put a hand on the door. "No one protected Tom back then. But he's protected now. Who's going to cry about the people I killed? Will you?"

A chorus of sirens now. Ambulance and police. Debbie wondered what they would make of what they found. And what she would tell them.

Jimmy Blue waved her car keys at her and laughed. There was blood on his fingers.

"Don't come looking, Debbie. It's over. Oh, and I'm stealing your car. Sorry."

CHAPTER FIFTY-FIVE

BY THE TIME the ice in the champagne bucket melted, Winter had yet to finish his first glass.

He was angry. But his anger was understandable, and under control.

The other emotion battling for supremacy was disbelief. No point in rejecting the evidence of his senses. But he wanted to. Tom Lewis had butchered four seasoned mercenaries, led by a man who'd never lost a single team member on previous missions. Winter watched each man fall. The worst was the third, when Lewis blew a kiss at the camera. Winter experienced an almost supernatural dread when that maniac winked at him before dropping the corpse. The wink said, *still think you're safe? Think I won't come after you and finish this?*

At least, Winter reassured himself after turning off the screen and shutting down the laptop, that last unspoken threat meant nothing. His long-planned departure from Britain ensured his safety. Robert Winter no longer existed.

As the afternoon turned into evening, he focused his powerful, logical mind on this last loose end: Tom Lewis. As shocking, and as unpleasant, as it was, Lewis had won. Winter needed to accept that.

In time, he would learn to do so. Living out his remaining years in luxury would make the process easier.

In the short term, a night's worth of stress relief arrived in half an hour, and he intended to squeeze every drop of value out of the twenty grand.

Winter took a long shower, letting the hot jets of water pummel his scalp and shoulders. Whenever he closed his eyes, he saw Tom Lewis wink.

He waited on his balcony, wearing the hotel's silk robe, looking out across the clear turquoise waters as they lapped at the white sand.

When the door chimed to announce his visitor, he was halfway to accepting his failure. He had a new life now. The old Winter needed to die so this one could enjoy a long, luxurious retirement.

He pulled a fresh, cold bottle of champagne from the fridge and placed it on the table with two glasses. Once sitting on the bed, he buzzed her in.

Blonde, as specified, but with hair shorter than Winter's taste. Tall. Her dress ended mid-thigh in a strip of gauze the colour of a summer sky. She wore a linen jacket. Her eyes were blue ice.

"Good afternoon, sir. My name is Amy." A well-educated European accent, hard to place. Swedish, perhaps. Her name didn't fit. He didn't want to use it, anyway. It made it harder to objectify her.

Winter didn't smile. "Come in and open the champagne."

If his abrupt manner disturbed her, she didn't show it. She moved with a confidence earned by those who understand their value. He would dismantle that confidence piece by piece. He felt better already.

'Amy' put her white leather bag on the chair. It looked heavy. As well as passing through the hotel's metal detectors, Winter had instructed the concierge to search his guest. Underwear and exotic toys, probably. Unnecessary for what he planned.

She hung her jacket on the back of the chair. Her arms were more muscled than Winter liked. He overcame his irritation. He would be more specific about his requirements with the next agency. She smiled as she twisted the cork from the bottle and poured a single glass. A non-drinker? Some party girl. And her smile needed a lot of work. Demure would be better. Subservient, eager to please. A little scared. Not so confident. He noticed something else in her manner. It took Winter a moment to identify it. Anticipation. Dilated pupils and parted lips. Unfeigned excitement. Ah. That explained the price. She wasn't acting. She wanted this.

Winter smiled back this time, the afternoon's disappointment fading. He admired the whore's perfect teeth. He would leave knocking them out until near the end.

She picked up the glass and took a sip. Was she teasing him now? Time to take control. He was about to get up when something in the way she held her head stopped him.

"Do I know you?" he said. Something about the shape of her face. He tried picturing her with darker hair, longer hair, glasses, maybe... he almost had it.

"No. You don't know me, Mr Winter." Did she just call him Winter? His stomach lurched, but he didn't allow his expression to change. "You don't know any of us, do you? My real name is Marit. You referred to me as Lot Six."

Shit. He slid his hand under his pillow. Another illegal service provided by the hotel. He pulled the gun out and waved it towards the woman. Infuriatingly, she smiled.

"Fine. Amy, Lot Six, whoever you are. Step away from the table. Sit down over there. Don't try anything. In this establishment, I could kill you and all it would cost me would be a surcharge for cleaning the rug."

Lot Six ignored his instructions. She took another sip of champagne. With her right hand, she reached into her bag.

Winter didn't believe in warning people before killing them. What was the point? He pulled the trigger. The hammer fell with a quiet *click*.

"It's a fake," said Lot Six. "Like the Rolexes they sell on the beach. Not fit for purpose. This one, however,"—and she pulled a handgun with a long silencer from her bag—"is the real deal. Keep nice and still for me, Mr Winter."

Winter processed the new situation. Too many variables to get a clear picture of how this had happened and what she wanted. But he was still breathing. An encouraging sign. Hired killers didn't waste time talking.

"Tell me what you want," he said, "and I'll see what I can do for you. You're obviously a very resourceful woman. I'm impressed you found me. Very impressed." That last comment was no exaggeration. How could anyone have found him, let alone this trafficked piece of shit?

"Don't speak, Mr Winter. Listen."

The hand holding the gun didn't waver. Winter looked her in the eye and nodded. Fine. He would listen. Then they would negotiate.

"You sell human beings as though they are objects. I imagine most of us at your auctions end up in sexual slavery. But not all of your buyers have the same outcome in mind for their purchase."

Winter mentally reviewed his auction regulars, wondering who she was referring to. Then she told him, and he had the first intimation this might not be a negotiation.

"Herr Blüthner, for example, offered me a choice. I can never be free again, that much is obvious. Not with what I know. But he offered me the chance to train as a troubleshooter for his business."

"A troubleshooter?"

She raised a finger to her lips. "Yes. A troubleshooter. Let me make it clearer. You have antagonised many people, including my employer. You, Mr Winter, are the trouble."

Lot Six pointed at him, then angled a thumb back at herself. "And I am the shooter."

She pulled a chair to the end of the bed and sat down, keeping the gun aimed at the centre of Winter's chest.

"I accepted Herr Blüthner's offer. And here I am. Now then. Just one or two things you should understand before we get to business. This hotel. A luxury resort that caters to the ultra-rich. Owned by Herr Blüthner. He bought it three years ago. Hence your toy gun, and the fact I can walk in with a real one."

Winter's options narrowed every second. She might be younger and fitter than him, but, by her own admission, she lacked experience. He maintained eye contact, looking for the moment of hesitation. He still had the useless gun. He'd throw it, then rush her.

"Herr Blüthner owns five hotels worldwide, including this one."

She kept talking, and Winter's skin went cold under the silk robe. His emergency retirement plan, locked behind a chain of fake IP addresses in a dozen fake names, gave him five bolt-holes. Lot Six named all of them.

"Herr Blüthner wants me to tell you why he bought the hotels. It's a remarkable story. He was travelling between New York and London on a commercial airline one night. His private jet had developed a last-minute fault, although subsequent events led him to believe it was sabotaged. He took his seat in first class with one other passenger. When they reached cruising altitude, the passenger approached him. A young man, polite, well-spoken. Huge, like a wrestler, Herr Blüthner said. For a moment, he wondered if one of his enemies had arranged this meeting.

"He was wrong. The young man wanted to discuss you, Mr Winter. He told Herr Blüthner about your retirement plans, and how you intended to fund them. He hacked your computers years ago. Herr Blüthner was impressed enough with his skills and patience to offer him a job. He declined. He preferred to work alone.

"This young man expressed..." Lot Six tutted. "Ah, English words. Sometimes, the right one escapes me. Wait... animosity. The young man in first class expressed a long-held animosity towards you. He passed on the information necessary to arrange today's troubleshooting, should it become necessary. He suggested Herr Blüthner keep bidding at your auctions so as not to arouse suspicion. As a show of good faith, he gave Herr Blüthner access to the information you'd intended to blackmail him with. Among others. And here we are."

She stood up. Winter prepared himself to act. He looked into her eyes, watching.

"Oh!" she said suddenly. "I nearly forgot. First time nerves. Sorry. The young man's payment. He only wanted one thing."

"Which was?"

"A message. For you."

Winter suddenly knew he had been wrong about her. She wouldn't hesitate. He braced himself to move, but found he couldn't. He wondered if this was how fear felt.

"Jimmy Blue is here."

Lot Six shot Winter in the stomach first. She took a step closer and shot him in the shoulder. The pain was shocking, and Winter gasped and retched. The next bullet tore into his neck, and, as he wheezed, air and blood escaping through the fingers he pressed against his throat, she shot him a further five times, the last three in his head.

CHAPTER FIFTY-SIX

THE LAST TIME Debbie Capelli had been in hospital, she'd had her tonsils removed. At eleven years old, hospitals were glamorous, mysterious, exciting places. The staff treated kids like royalty. She remembered lying back in bed with everything done for her. Her parents brought gifts, and the daily ice creams continued long after her sore throat had gone.

Everything was different now. The yellow-walled room they wheeled her into after surgery wasn't glamorous. The nurses who came in to see her every hour weren't the breezy, funny, angelic presences she remembered, but tired and harassed. Every time she opened her eyes during the first twelve hours after they removed the bullet, she saw a different face checking her charts, adjusting the IV bag, taking her temperature or blood pressure.

By lunchtime on the second day, she'd regained her appreciation for the National Health Service. Easy to be complacent until a pair of paramedics stops you bleeding out in your spare bedroom.

One cliché that turned out to have a basis in fact was the hospital food. Either the stew Debbie ate at lunchtime was tasteless, or her medication prevented her from identifying the meat. The dessert that followed was much too sweet. She ate it anyway. As she spooned it into her mouth, she remembered the paramedic who'd squeezed her hand in the ambulance as they roared away from the house.

When the doctor came to see her, she was still crying into the remnants of her blancmange.

"Are you in pain? I'm Mrs Gopal, the surgeon who removed the bullet in your leg. Does it trouble you?" Debbie sobbed louder. Gopal patted her on the shoulder while scanning her charts. Perhaps the medical students with the worst bedside manner gravitated towards surgery. Debbie took the tissue Gopal proffered and blew her nose.

"I'm fine. Just glad to be alive."

"Oh. Good. Yes. You lost rather a lot of blood. We gave you a transfusion." Debbie wondered if some of Gopal's brusque manner could be attributed to her gender. The police force still dragged its heels regarding equality. Debbie got called 'love' by the occasional commissioner, and few promotions had come her way compared to male colleagues.

"No sign of internal bleeding. You'll need a crutch for a couple of weeks. Do you have any questions for me?"

Gopal looked at her watch as she said this. Debbie decided against playing the sisterhood card.

"No. Thank you. For saving my life."

"You're welcome. Try not to get shot again."

This last may have been an attempt at humour, but it fell flat, as if someone who had never found anything funny was imitating a comedian. The momentary grimace as Gopal acknowledged her failure suggested that might not be far from the truth.

The surgeon said, "Hm," and left.

Debbie must have dozed off, because it was dusk when she next opened her eyes and looked through the window at the bare, wet branches of the tree tapping at the glass.

Someone had brought her bag. The local police, perhaps. It was on the chair next to the bed. She should check her messages. Part of her didn't want to find out what had changed since she'd arrived. There was a strange comfort in staying inside this odd bubble, the pain relief making everything soft focus, a smear of Vaseline on a camera lens.

Debbie didn't listen to that part of her, being the practical, stolid, reliable daughter of Reg and Doreen Smith. When she pulled off a plaster, she did it with one quick tug. When she ended a marriage, she did it with a bonfire of Italian suits in the garden and a note saying *Up yours*.

She reached in and pulled out the phone, then frowned at it for a few seconds. It wasn't her phone.

It powered on without a code. It was a decent smartphone. Better than hers. Unusual in one regard, though. The home screen contained the bare minimum of apps. Debbie pressed the call button and checked the history. Empty. No messages, either. There was, however, a folder named Debbie. She clicked on it. It contained two files. One named Winter—audio only—and another named Rhoda.

Debbie went back to her bag and found her earbuds. She listened to the audio first. Poor sound quality. When she recognised one of the voices, and realised what they were discussing, Debbie knew the muffled recording was because the device had been hidden. Three voices spoke: one female, two male. When the female referred to one of the males as Winter, Debbie held her breath. Twenty-seven seconds later she released it, her fingers tight around the phone. She had just heard Robert Winter order Elliot Ling's execution. Ling, an independent London mayoral candidate, had gone missing shortly after announcing his candidacy.

She had him. Finally, she had him.

The short video made for compelling viewing. It played like a cheap horror film. Debbie had studied the information around Rhoda Ilích's extraordinary murder. It was one thing to read the report, but quite another to see Tom Lewis look into the camera before picking Ilích up and tossing her from the top of a Parisian landmark like an unwanted doll.

"Christ on a bike."

Debbie turned the phone off and put it back in her bag, finding her own. Three messages. One from her dentist. The other two from DI Matt Drummond, recently promoted and keen to please.

Did you hear? Winter's dead. Bet you feel better already!

His second message ended with a thumbs-up emoji. *Glad you're not dead!!*

While she processed the news about Winter, a nurse put his head around the door. "Visitor for you. Are you up for it? Police. A Detective Chief Inspector Barber."

Debbie took a ragged breath. For the first time since regaining consciousness, she wondered how she looked. Like shit, presumably. Oh well.

She'd expected a visitor from her own station, but not this soon, and not DCI Barber. Yes, she'd been shot, four armed men found dead at—or near—the Pakefield house. Villages in north Suffolk didn't see many multiple homicides. She expected to give an initial statement to the senior officer of the local Major Investigations Team. Barber making the trip surprised her.

Her boss looked her up and down, the expression on her face not exactly sympathetic.

"Hello, Guv." A weak smile in response.

Detective Chief Inspector Barber sat down in the only chair. Ten years younger than Debbie, a high-flyer on her way to greater things. Barber made lists and set targets. With a reputation for shrewdness and efficiency, she didn't have a single friend in the department. Debbie liked her.

Barber produced a paper bag full of grapes and ate them while staring at Debbie. The silence got awkward.

"Guv, I—" Barber held up a finger. "Shh. Hope you didn't think these were for you."

She carried on eating. "I'm starving. Took forever to get here. Why do some people retire to the arse end of nowhere?"

She reached further into the paper bag and produced a peeled boiled egg, taking three bites to consume it. She looked for something to wash it down with, finding only Debbie's glass of water.

Barber raised her eyebrows. Debbie shrugged, and the DCI took three big swallows, emptying it.

"That's better. Right. Not dead then?"

"Apparently not."

"Doctor says you lost a lot of blood. If the bullet had been a millimetre to the side, blah, blah." Barber picked at a piece of grape skin which had lodged itself between two of her front teeth.

"Yes. A close thing. Good job the ambulance got to me in time."

"Wasn't it just? We'll come back to that. You can give your official statement later. Tell me what happened."

Debbie looked up at the ceiling. "Winter's dead."

Barber said nothing. Debbie looked back at her. "Were you going to tell me?"

"Probably." The younger woman didn't look surprised that Debbie knew. Police officers gossiped. "Winter will still be dead after you tell me what happened."

"How did he die?"

Barber tutted, but answered. "Multiple gunshot injuries. They found his body on the beach. Naked."

At the word *beach*, Debbie's pulse rose.

"Not Pakefield beach," clarified her boss. "Now that would have been interesting. Virgin Islands. St Thomas. He entered the country on December twenty-seventh under a false name. Between then and his corpse being washed up yesterday morning, there's no trail at all. Nothing. He vanished."

"Not completely. Someone found him," said Debbie.

"Yes, they did. Now, then, DI Capelli." Down to business. "One ambulance and three police cars attended the house in Pakefield. The front door was open, and paramedics found you slipping in and out of consciousness in a bedroom with a bullet in your thigh. The police discovered four male bodies. Two shot, one knifed. A crushed windpipe did for the last chap. Four Heckler and Koch sub-machine guns recovered, plus one Chukavin sniper rifle with a night scope. Would you like to tell me what happened?"

Barber had another go at a stubborn strip of grape peel, sliding it out of her teeth. She flicked it at the wall where it stuck. She did all of this without taking her eye off her subordinate officer.

Debbie thought of the video on the phone in her bag, showing Tom Lewis murdering Rhoda Ilích. She looked at her boss, who held up a warning finger.

"Answer carefully. You took annual leave at short notice, you haven't been hassling us daily asking about the investigation at Winter's house... your behaviour has been unusual. Very unusual. Make this statement good, Capelli."

Debbie reached for her water before remembering the glass was empty. Barber didn't offer to top it up. She thought of the twelve-year-old Tom Lewis facedown in his murdered parents' garden, leaking blood and bone from the bullet hole in his head. Tom, who stumbled through life afterwards, unable to settle, his life choices narrowed by that bullet.

"I don't know, Guv. I remember making a cup of tea. There was a knock at the door. When I opened it, someone shot me. After that..."

Debbie shook her head to convey confusion and memory loss. Barber's expression suggested she wasn't having any of it. "After that, what, exactly?"

"Nothing, Guv. I passed out."

"You passed out."

"Yes, Guv."

"Right. Well, while you napped, here's what the initial physical evidence suggests. Your blood was found downstairs by the front door. Which is where you said you were shot. There's more of your blood—a lot more—in one bedroom. Not the one they found you in. There's blood there too, of course. The first bedroom had a smashed window. A rope was hanging from the chimney into the back yard. Your blood was on the rope. And on the chimney. The chimney, DI Capelli. Ringing any bells?"

"No. Sorry."

"Are you? So, these armed men—mercenaries, judging by the equipment, the Russian sniper rifle, and tattoos suggesting they were ex-military—dragged you around the house, including a trip to the roof. Then they were set upon by assailants unknown. In the ensuing contretemps, they were all killed. Does that sound about right?"

Only Barber would say *contretemps*. Debbie shrugged. "Or they turned on each other for some reason."

There was a very long silence after this. When Barber spoke again, her tone was calm, deliberate, and frostier than a frozen Siberian lake during a particularly cold winter.

"You're not a stupid woman, Capelli. If you tell me nothing, there's a good chance we'll never know what really happened up there. You know that's not the way I operate. I expect honesty and transparency from my officers, if they wish to continue their police careers. Am I making myself clear?"

"Perfectly."

"So what really happened?"

Debbie sighed.

Barber stood up. "Last chance. The 999 call was made by an unidentified male. The mercenaries were dead by then. Want to change your story?"

Debbie closed her eyes. "I was unconscious. I have no idea who they were or why they were there."

She didn't open her eyes again until she was sure Barber had left.

———

The taxi driver helped her with her few belongings when Debbie left hospital four days later. She gave him the address of a Lowestoft hotel. Forensics were still busy at the Pakefield house, but she should be able to pick up her belongings tomorrow and head back to London. She stared out of the window as they drove. An unfamiliar world slid past the glass. A parallel universe, maybe, where Winter was dead and a thirty-two-year-old brain-damaged man could, some-how, be two people, one of whom was, well, what exactly? Even thinking about Jimmy Blue made her afraid all over again, but she kept returning to the memory like a tongue unable to avoid probing a painful cavity.

No official word from Barber yet, but Debbie knew it would come. Her career was over. Unless she gave Barber Tom Lewis. She took the phone out of her bag as the cab followed the road south, past holiday resorts, pubs, caravan parks, and a golf course. Jimmy Blue was a multiple murderer. She'd watched him kill. He did it with the lethal efficiency of a carnivore. No compunction. No remorse.

She turned the phone over and over in her hands as the taxi drove through Lowestoft. A huge wind turbine dominated the skyline.

"Excuse me? Can you stop for a minute?"

The taxi driver pulled over and she got out, her crutch in one hand, the phone in the other. "Back in a sec."

She limped to the end of the street, following the flashing orange lights reflected in the shop windows. Rounding the corner, she saw it: a bin lorry, chewing up trade refuse as it inched up the street. She walked around to the rear and lobbed the phone between the metal-crushing jaws.

She was fifty-four years old. And her pension pot was healthy enough. She'd survive leaving the force. With Winter dead, the idea of going back held little appeal.

She limped back to the waiting cab.

CHAPTER FIFTY-SEVEN

THE LORRY DRIVER had a nervous laugh. He couldn't help it. Under stress, he found it hard to stop himself laughing. And the adrenaline was pumping tonight, because he'd never made this trip before.

When he pulled his truck into the vast concrete lorry park at Calais, the darkening sky meant most vehicles had turned on their headlights.

The X-ray and CO_2 checks were automatic. He drove the forty-footer through the narrow lane where cameras and sensors scanned the vehicles' emissions and contents. His contacts had told him not to worry about it, but he couldn't stop a laugh escaping when he went through without setting off any alarms.

The CMR check came next. Despite being in France, the hut beside the barrier was manned by UK Border officials. The middle-aged man took the CMR document, which detailed the contents of the trailer. The docket claimed his trailer contained tinned anchovies. This made him laugh before he could stop himself.

"What's so bloody funny, pal?"

The driver looked across at the grey-headed man in the booth. Short hair, clean shaven, immaculate white shirt under a blue jumper stretched over a pot belly. The driver wondered how he looked to the official, with his baseball cap, long hair, beard, and Lee Scratch Perry T-shirt. The pot-bellied man checked the papers again. The driver wondered if something had gone wrong. He had followed the lane they'd told him to follow, so this should be the right customs official. Unless this was the wrong lane. Another set of giggles escaped his lips.

"Christ's sake!" The official banged his fist on the door of the cab. The driver stopped laughing. "What's wrong with you? You're new, right?"

"Right. Yes. I'm new. Sorry. I laugh when I'm nervous."

"Jesus. Well, that's just brilliant, isn't it?" The man curled his lip in disgust, then pointed a thick finger at the driver. His voice was low, and he spoke fast. "You'd better get your shit together. If you screw up, you go to prison. Not just you, though. Pull yourself together, all right?"

The driver took a few deep breaths, composed himself. The official was right. There would be no reward if he didn't obey the instructions. He held out his hand for the documents. The official stamped them and handed them over.

"Good. You're nearly there. Don't talk to anyone, okay? And don't screw up. Jesus, where did they find you?"

The traffic light turned green. With a hiss of air brakes, the driver drove on, now officially leaving French territory. He joined a queue of trucks.

After forty minutes of sitting still, driving ten yards, and stopping again, a skinny man in a yellow jacket waved him onto the train. Eurostar freight trains were a series of flatbed trucks with scaffolding. Once his engine was off, he followed the other truckers to a bus which took them to the passenger train, and the 'driver's club car', a fancy name for their carriage. He found a seat near the back and pretended to be texting. Not that many of his fellow drivers were chatty. A few shouted greetings across the carriage, but most kept to themselves.

The trip to Folkestone took thirty-five minutes. The driver was the fifth lorry in line to leave the Eurostar. He checked his watch. He'd kept it on British time. Nearly nine p.m. Dark, cold, wet. Welcome home.

The phone stuck on his dashboard picked up the UK signal almost immediately, and his satnav showed the route as he pulled on to the M20. Twelve miles to the rendezvous point.

Eighteen minutes later, after taking the first Ashford junction, he pulled into a bus stop. Two men climbed up and joined him in the cab. One black, one white, both—the driver suspected—armed. They wore the kind of puffa jackets it was easy to conceal a weapon beneath. The driver selected first gear, and the truck pulled away from the kerb with a throaty rumble.

"I'll direct you," said the nearest man. "Any trouble? Extra checks, anything like that?"

The driver shook his head.

His passengers smelled of cigarette smoke. "Cargo behaving?"

"Haven't heard a peep out of them," the driver replied. For a second, he nearly laughed again, but he caught it this time.

"Good stuff. Go straight on at roundabouts unless I tell you otherwise."

The driver did as instructed, steering the long vehicle through the outskirts of Ashford. He wondered who decided which product appeared on the documents. Were tins of anchovies a common choice?

The two men started talking.

"I still reckon it's bollocks. No way one guy could do that. You ever meet Winter's crew?"

"No."

"They were the nastiest, most brutallest bunch of bastards I ever saw. Wouldn't think twice about killing you if you looked at 'em funny, know what I mean?"

"Brutallest? Don't think that's a word."

"Oh well, I humbly beg your pardon, professor. Now piss off."

"But, T, listen, Georgie said he saw him. For real."

"Georgie? The grass?"

"Yeah. He saw the pictures from Winter's house. Police say it was one guy. One guy."

"Yeah. Right."

"I'm telling you, T. He saw the photo of Strickland's body. This guy slit Strickland's throat. And you wanna know what Georgie said they found on Winter's desk?"

"Now you're talking shite. Winter was a ghost, Jordan. No trace of him, wherever he'd been. He'd never have left anything lying around."

"I know. That's not what I'm saying. So do you want me to tell you what they found on his desk or not?"

"Go on, then, you're dying to tell me."

"A note. It said *Jimmy Blue is coming.*"

The man on the far side—T—started laughing. The driver thought it might be safe to join in, but they both gave him a look, so he shut up.

The nearest one pointed at the road ahead. "Next roundabout, take a right. Third set of lights, go left."

T spoke more quietly after that. The driver was glad of his excellent hearing.

"Don't start on that shit. You read too much, and you watch too many shit films. The Devil's not real, you know. Neither is Batman. And there isn't some tooled-up lunatic picking off people."

"But crews are disappearing. Bodies keep showing up."

"What did you expect with Winter gone? It's a turf war. No need to put the shits up yourself with this vigilante bullshit."

"I'm just saying, some of the Dagenham boys said they heard Jimmy Blue singing the night Westy drowned."

"You what? You don't half talk a load of bollocks considering all them books you read. They heard Jimmy Blue singing? Will you bloody listen to yourself? I suppose he did a little dance, too, did he? He's not real, Jordan. We've got enough on our plate without you going all Scooby Doo on me. Oi! Take a left here."

The driver braked harder than he would have liked and took a side road into an industrial estate.

"Third warehouse. Go round the back."

The rest of the estate was lit by a series of security lights, but the third warehouse and its car park remained dark as the driver pulled up in front of a pair of large sliding doors.

The two men got out. T opened a heavy padlock and removed a chain, then they took a handle each and pulled the doors apart. They waved the driver through, and he drove the lorry into the darkness. When he turned the engine off, the doors closed behind with a deep metallic clank.

Fluorescent tubes hanging from steel girders high above crackled and flickered, revealing an empty concrete floor and not much else. Tyre marks suggested recent use.

The driver got down from the cab. Jordan and T waited at the rear of the lorry.

"C'mon. We need to check the cargo against the manifest."

The driver produced the key to the rear doors. T indicated he should unlock them. Both men unzipped their jackets, revealing holstered handguns.

"Hope there were no mistakes at your end," said T. "We lost a whole cargo once because some dozy twat forgot proper air holes. Last mistake he ever made, you get me?"

"I get you," said the driver. He opened the doors wide, pinning them back against the sides of the arctic. Only then did he look inside. Thirty scared, miserable faces stared back. They sat on packing cases; men, women, and children. Vietnamese or Thai, he guessed. The cases boasted *Premium Anchovy Fillets*. Another laugh threatened to bubble up. He backed away.

T and Jordan took his place at the back of the lorry.

"Anyone speak English?" called Jordan. One of the blank, drawn faces—a woman near the doors—nodded and said something to the others. She had a fresh cut on her leg. The driver remembered the sudden left turn he'd made.

"Good. Tell the rest of 'em this. You made it to Britain, but you're not safe yet. Not unless you do as we say. In about half an hour, a coach will be here to pick you up. It will take you to a hotel where you can clean up and get some sleep, then someone will tell you about your new jobs. Okay?"

"Okay," said the woman, eyeing the butt of the gun nestling in Jordan's shoulder holster.

The speech was bullshit. By the expression on the woman's face, she suspected the same. If she knew what Jordan and T's bosses planned for them, the driver imagined she would probably rather be shot now.

The two armed men conferred as the woman translated what she'd been told. "Half an hour? We're early, aren't we? Reckon we've got forty minutes or so."

"No. Look, you know what happened in November. We keep them here in the lorry. All of them. And we shoot anyone who tries anything."

"Oh, come on. None of these poor bastards are tooled up. They're all shitting their pants. I'm just saying, she's tasty, we've got a bit of time, and I'd just like to show her where the toilet is, in case she needs to go, know what I mean?"

"Yeah, I know what you mean. I'm just saying it's not a great idea. Besides, if you remember, it's my bloody turn."

"I don't think so. Don't forget who's in charge. I get first choice. Maybe, if you're lucky, I'll..."

T stopped talking. Jordan tensed beside him. "What?" said K. "What is it?"

The miserable human cargo inside the lorry, exhausted, hungry, and terrified, weren't looking at the two armed men. They were all staring at something behind their captors.

The two men turned around. The driver had taken off his baseball cap. He'd taken off his long hair and beard. One side of his bald head was a mass of scars. He was holding two sharpened hunting knives, one in each hand, and he was smiling.

"Who fancies a sing-song?"

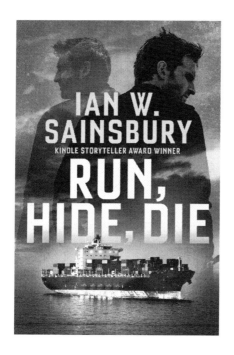

fusebooks.com/runhidedie

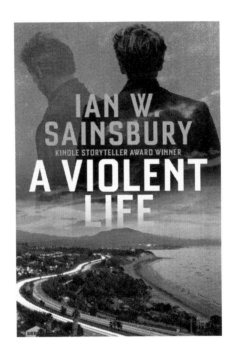

fusebooks.com/aviolentlife

AUTHOR'S NOTE

I've loved telling the story of Tom Lewis's revenge. I've already written the next Jimmy Blue book, and the one after that. And I know there will be more to come.

Please leave a review if you can—it makes a big difference.

If you haven't signed up for your free Jimmy Blue story yet (and the occasional email from me), you can find it here:

fusebooks.com/ian

I have a website imaginatively named after myself, and I can be found in the usual social media places. I don't post photos of my dinner there, I promise.

Thanks for reading,

Ian

Norwich, 2021

Printed in Great Britain
by Amazon

76058613R00180